WHOM THE GOD LOVES BEST,
DOTH HE MOST CHASTISE . . .

Mr. Ram was a small Egyptian statue. Old, ages old. The wisdom of the powdered centuries lay behind his eyes. He was a colorful little figure and quite authentic. Mr. Ram, through the sheer charm of his persuasive personality, had established himself as a household deity from the first days of the Willowses' joint experiment.

From the first, Tim and Sally had been drawn to Mr. Ram. He, on his part, was attached to them both, although of late their constant bickerings had worn a trifle on his fine Egyptian nerves. He was beginning to suspect that perhaps a little something should be done about it . . .

By Thorne Smith
Published by Ballantine Books:

TOPPER

TOPPER TAKES A TRIP

THE NIGHT LIFE OF THE GODS

THE STRAY LAMB

RAIN IN THE DOORWAY

TURNABOUT

THORNE SMITH

Turnabout

A Del Rey Book

BALLANTINE BOOKS • NEW YORK

A Del Rey Book
Published by Ballantine Books

Library of Congress Catalog Card Number: 79-55331

ISBN 0-345-28725-8

Manufactured in the United States of America

First Ballantine Books Edition: October 1980

Cover art by Norman Walker

For My Brother, Skyring,
His Wife Irene, My Nieces, Virginia and Carol
Also for Pal, a Dog
That Served as
a Pillow.

Contents

CHAPTER I

Mr. Willows Removes His Socks

CLAD IN A FRAGILE BUT FROLICSOME NIGHTGOWN which disclosed some rather interesting feminine topography, Sally Willows sat on the edge of her bed and bent a pair of large brown eyes on her husband. This had been going on for some minutes—this cold dispassionate appraisal. At the present moment a growing sense of exasperation was robbing it a little of its chill. Warmth had crept into her eyes, making them even more beautiful and effective, but still they were not pleasant. Far from it.

As yet, however, Mrs. Sally Willows had denied herself the indulgence of speech. For this she is to be commended. It was a piece of self-discipline she seldom if ever inflicted on her tongue. She was waiting, waiting for that sock to come off, hoping against hope that the crisis would pass and the evening remain calm if dull.

Meanwhile she was content to sit there on the edge of her bed and silently consider her husband. At the moment she was considering him as she would have considered a mere thing, or some clumsily animated object that forever kept knocking about her private life and getting in the way. Terribly in the way.

Five years ago everything had been so different. Then she never would have looked at Tim Willows as she was looking at him now. In those early marital days this man creature had never been in her way, could never get in her way too much. Naturally. That had been before he had become a mere thing in her eyes. Also, that had been before her own personal experience, enhanced by the vicarious liaison dished up by the high priests of Hollywood, had given her a true

1

appreciation of men, had shown her how really attractive and devastating men could be and yet retain a quality so charmingly boyish and unspoiled . . . great, silent, passionate men with whimsical eyes and just a shade of helplessness . . . men who could find a taxicab when no taxicabs were to be found and who could purchase first-night tickets or reserve an illimitable vista of rooms on the *Ile de France*—never forgetting the flowers and a trick toy or two—with admirable precision and dispatch and without the slightest display of nerves. Whenever her own husband attempted similar operations on a much smaller scale, of course, he invariably returned unsuccessful, a nervous wreck bitterly complaining about the chicanery of mankind and the complexity of modern existence. Why, the poor beast could hardly make change without becoming so helplessly entangled that he was forced to turn to her with trembling hands. Frequently she feared the man would begin to chatter instead of talk.

As she sat there on the edge of the bed, a trim, sleek, wholly desirable figure with a smartly tailored head of glossy black hair, Sally Willows could think of at least a couple of dozen men more appealing to her than her husband, more worthy of her favors. When she had married Tim Willows she had not sufficiently appreciated her own possibilities or the possibilities of others. Idly she wondered how it would feel to be kept by a gloriously wealthy man who would give her everything she wanted, including unlimited freedom to exercise her charms on other men perhaps a trifle younger. Like most women who permit themselves to think at all she felt at times that she had it in her to become something pretty good in the line of a demiminde, one in a position to pick and choose her votaries, even to command them. Nothing sordid, of course.

And at that moment, sitting on various beds in various parts of the world, innumerable wives were thus considering their wretched husbands and thinking the selfsame thoughts. Who can blame them?

Yes, things were a good deal different now from what they had been five years back. For some time past—ever since she had danced with Carl Bentley, in fact—she had come to regard her husband as being just an animal about the house, an animal of the lower order that had been thoughtlessly endowed with the gift of speech and an annoying ability to reason rather trenchantly. It had to be fed at certain times, kept clean and profitably employed. In a way she was responsible, and it was all so very tiresome. Occasionally she still found this animal useful, extracted from it a certain amount of physical satisfaction. It brought home money and did things to the furnace. Sometimes it even made her laugh and feel unexpectedly tender. But romance—where was romance? Deep, vigorous, headlong passion—what had become of that? Had the cinema screens absorbed that precious commodity as blotting paper absorbs ink? And why did this animal fail to arouse in her that deliciously meretricious feeling that lent such zest to her flirtations with other men ... with Carl Bentley, especially?

All of which goes to show that Sally Willows was in rather a bad way. The girl stood sadly in need of a friendly but invigorating kick in her spiritual step-ins. But who was going to confer this favor upon her? She was worth it. She really was, for fundamentally Sally Willows was a good sort. One of the best. And at twenty-eight even a modern woman still has a lot to live and learn as well as to forget.

Cheerfully unconscious of his wife's protracted scrutiny, entirely ignorant of her state of mind, Mr. Willows, his slender body plunged in a deep armchair, was dreamily engaged in removing his socks. That is not quite accurate. The man was not actually removing his socks, but rather working himself up gradually to such a pitch that he would be forced to take some decisive action about his socks, one way or the other. It was almost as if he entertained the mad hope that the socks, once having ascertained his purpose, would obligingly remove themselves. From the expression in his rather dim, dissipated-looking eyes one would have been led to believe that he was enmeshed in the web of some mystic ritual of transcendent loveliness.

After thirty-five years of hostilities the man was still at war with himself and the world in general. So many men are, and like Tim, not altogether without reason. He had not succeeded in getting himself anywhere in particular, and he rather more than half suspected he never would. Somehow he could not bring himself to care greatly about it. That is bad, the very antithesis of the red-blooded, two-fisted, he-man attitude that invariably leads to success. He was too erratic ever to establish himself securely in the advertising agency that tolerated his presence. Also, he was far too brilliant. Brilliance in business as distinguished from cleverness is a disturbing factor. It is slightly immoral and always subject to change.

Underpaid although frequently patted on the back, he was nevertheless held suspect by the powers that were. An accusing aura of cynical detachment seemed to surround him. He was unable to shake it off, unable to conceal it. From somewhere within his being emanated a spirit of unorthodoxy. At times in his presence his superiors experienced a vague feeling of insecurity and for the moment even suspected the efficacy of their most dependable platitudes. Even while they were showering praises upon him for some brain wave they seemed to realize that in Tim Willows they did not have a willing worker for whom the honor and the glory of the Nationwide Advertising Agency, Inc., trod hot upon the heels of God and country, so hot, in fact, that at times both God and country were left a trifle winded.

From his point of vantage on a nearby bookcase Mr. Ram, in his turn, considered both husband and wife.

Mr. Ram was a small Egyptian statue. Old, ages old. The wisdom of the powdered centuries lay behind his eyes. He was a colorful little figure and quite authentic. Mr. Ram through the sheer charm of his persuasive personality had established himself as a household deity from the first days of the Willowses' joint experiment. He had moved with them from house to house, traveled with them over land and sea and shared in the ebb and flow of their never opulent fortunes. During those five years he had observed much and thought more. Whatever detractors might say about Mr. Ram they could not accuse him of having failed to take seriously his responsibilities to Tim and Sally.

Tim was more fortunate than he realized in possessing the casual affection of a globe-drinking uncle beside whom the blackest of sheep would have appeared pallid. Dick Willows, so far as the family had ever been able to ascertain, had only two aims in life: to keep bartenders on the alert and to ward off the pangs of solitude from as many lonely ladies as time and nature would permit. Upon the occasion of his nephew's wedding this amorous philanthropist had from some corner of Egypt dispatched Mr. Ram to the young couple, together with an indelicate note in which he suggested that the little man be appointed chamberlain of the ceremonies of the nuptial couch, adding that Mr. Ram was that sort of little man and that his presence would banish the last shred of decency as was only right and proper at such a time.

From the first Tim and Sally had been drawn to Mr. Ram. He, on his part, was attached to them both, although of late their constant bickerings had worn a trifle on his fine Egyptian nerves. He was beginning to suspect that perhaps a little something should be done about it.

To-night as he considered the pair there was something inscrutable in his beady, black little eyes. Although time meant absolutely nothing to Mr. Ram he could not figure out for the life of him why Tim was consuming so much of it in the removal of his socks. They were not such remarkable socks. Just the opposite. They were the most infamous-looking socks, an unsightly hole disgracing each crumpled toe. And as he watched and waited on the bookcase a suggestion of gathering purpose touched the usually benign features of the colorful little idol. Most assuredly, something should be done.

Apparently Sally felt somewhat the same way about it. She fixed her bemused husband with an unadoring gaze and gave utterance to a single word which sounded strangely cold and hostile in the silence of the room.

"Well?" she said.

Across vague leagues of nebulous speculations Mr. Willows's eyes sought Sally's.

"Huh?" he inquired inelegantly. "You said what?"

"The sock," she went on in the level tones of one exerting the utmost self-restraint. "Does it come off?"

Slowly and uncomprehandingly, Tim's eyes journeyed down the long reaches of his thin leg until they rested broodingly on his sock. Gradually intelligence dawned.

"Oh," he exclaimed, a pleased expression animating his face. "It's the sock. How stupid of me, Sally. It comes off. In fact, I'm going to take it off myself."

"That's good of you," said Sally Willows. "I would."

And he did.

He took the sock off, then sank back in the chair and regarded his liberated foot with an expression of mild surprise, as if trying to remember where he had last seen the thing. Then he indulged in a display of sheer animalism which his wife found exceedingly trying to bear. With a sigh of almost voluptuous contentment he deliberately wiggled his toes, some of which in the process gave tongue to a crackling sound.

"Don't," was all she said, slightly averting her gaze. "Please."

"What's that?" demanded Tim, who under the fascinating spell of his toes was rapidly receding into a vast expanse of fresh speculation.

"Don't wig——" Mrs. Willows began, then hesitated. "What you are doing," she continued with dignity, "is both revolting and extremely childish. Don't do it."

Tim Willows stilled his agitated toes and thoughtfully considered the surprising request.

"Can't see anything wrong in a man wiggling his toes a bit," he observed at last. "Good thing to do. Good for the toes . . . for the entire foot, for that matter. Why don't you wiggle yours? Exercise 'em."

"There's only one place where I'd like to exercise my toes," replied Sally.

Mr. Willows disregarded this ruthless ambition and pondered a moment more.

"You know," he offered in a confidential voice, "I'll bet that almost everyone wiggles his or her toes at one

time or another. It's not nice to think of Keats or Shel-
ley or Lord Byron doing it, but they must have done it.
Even that sloppy movie hero of yours. I'll lay odds he
wiggles his priceless toes."

"Perhaps he does," conceded Sally, "but he doesn't
explode a bunch of writhing firecrackers virtually in his
wife's face."

A smile slowly arranged itself on Tim's lips and became fixed in a grin.

"I'm different," he declared irritatingly. "Bigger than
he is. I take you into my confidence."

"There are certain little intimacies which even after
five years of married life might just as well remain un-
revealed," replied Mrs. Tim. "I don't like toes and
never have. Can't bear the thought of toes, much less
the sight."

"But I didn't ask you to think of my toes," observed
Tim, in one of those gentle reasonable voices that drive
wives mad. "I can jolly well think of my own ten toes."

"How can I help it when you're waving the horrid
things before my eyes?" A tragic note had crept into
Sally Willows's voice.

"Trouble with you," continued Tim reflectively, "is
that you've got a phobia against toes. You allow them
to dominate your mind. They get the best of you. Now,
take these toes, for instance. Look at 'em."

"I won't take those toes," Sally protested passionately. "You take those toes and get them out of my
sight. Cram them into your slippers. And, furthermore,
I have no desire to get into a long, involved argument
with you about toes or any other part of your miserable anatomy. Is there no fragrance in life? No romance? Must I be compelled to sit here all night with
my thoughts no higher than your crablike toes?"

"Oh, all right. All right," Tim hastily agreed, realizing from past experience that the breaking point was
dangerously close at hand. "We'll say no more about
toes."

He snapped off his other sock, thrust his feet into his
slippers, struggled out of the chair and strayed off na-
kedly about the room.

"I say, Sally, seen anything of that shirt?" he called

out after he had succeeded in methodically disarranging the contents of the closet and knocking down several of his wife's dresses, which he gropingly retrieved and blindly flung back in the general direction of their hangers. "Wonder why women invariably hang up their things in such a hell of a way," he continued irritably. "No brains at all. Now where could that shirt have got itself to? Just where? Tell me that."

"I just saw you taking it off," replied Sally, ice edging her words. "For goodness' sake cover your nakedness. You're unlike anything in heaven above or the earth beneath or the waters under the earth."

Mr. Willows allowed this remark to pass unchallenged, but stuck gamely to his aimless quest.

"I don't mean that shirt," he explained. "I mean that long voluminous garment I bought in Paris."

"When drunk," supplied his wife, then asked in a rather hopeless voice, "Aren't you ever going to use your pajamas, Tim—the bottoms as well as the tops? Is it essential to your happiness that you rig yourself up in these weird costumes and go trailing about the house like some anemic beach comber? Are you so physically different from all other adult males of your species that you must flaunt the lower half of your body in the eyes of the world?"

"I keep telling you," Tim retorted with weary patience, "that I can't stand pajama bottoms. It's like toes with you. And I don't know anything about other men. I don't go around investigating. Anyway, it doesn't matter. If the Lord Himself appeared before me at this very moment clad in a pair of pajama bottoms I could only find it in my heart to feel sorry for him. The damn things get in my way. They roggle up. They—they choke me."

"You needn't trouble yourself to make it any plainer," said Mrs. Willows with some attempt at dignity. "Don't give me a demonstration. Just the same, I'm sure other women's husbands must wear the trousers of their pajamas."

"Sure, a lot of lizzies," proclaimed Mr. Willows derisively. "Real men take their pajama trousers off when they go to bed."

"Don't be vulgar," said Mrs. Tim.

"Well, we won't go into that," he remarked, turning to a bureau drawer and pawing through its contents. "I'm different, as I told you before," he went on. "Much franker. I take you into my confidence—entirely."

"You're altogether too frank for decency."

He dragged several yards of material from the drawer and finally succeeded in draping it over his body. Above this tentlike arrangement his face emerged with a triumphant expression. The remainder of him was far from lovely.

"I imagine the reason the French build their shirts like this," he observed, "is because they're constantly running in and out of doors with husbands and wives and entire hotel staffs running after them. It must be that."

"I'm not interested," returned Sally, "but I do know that that atrocity you're wearing is neither one thing nor the other. There's too much of it for a day shirt and too little for a night. It's simply an unsatisfactory compromise."

"Well, at any rate," replied Tim thriftily, "I'm not letting it go to waste. I'm getting my money's worth out of it like any French gentleman would do."

"I'd even pay good money to have you take it off," said Sally.

"Oh, my dear!" her husband murmured, looking at her archly.

"Shut up," interrupted Sally. "You're not amusing. Is there no romance anywhere in that feeble frame of yours? Must I spend all my nights with a comic-strip character—a clown?"

Tim looked thoughtfully down at his wife.

"Romance, my child," he told her, "does not reside in the tail of a shirt. Its seat is here—in the heart."

He slapped himself so vigorously just below that organ that the front of his shirt gave a startled flip, and Mrs. Willows hastily closed her eyes. The effect of his little speech was somewhat marred.

"If I were you," remarked Mrs. Willows, "I

wouldn't strive for nobility in that costume. It doesn't quite come off."

"Is that so?" he replied unenterprisingly, turning his back on his wife and running his eyes along a row of volumes in the bookcase. "What shall we read to-night?"

"I don't feel like reading anything to-night," Sally Willows replied petulantly. "That's all we do in this beastly place, anyway. It's read, read, read, night after night. No change. Nothing. First thing you know we'll be old. Life will be over. Other wives go places and do things——"

"Right!" shot back Mr. Willows. "They sure do."

"And I don't mean that either," Sally went on. "They are seen—not buried alive. What do I see? Where do I go? Cooped up here in this miserable house all day long. No companionship. No relaxation. Same old thing day in and day out, year after year. Then home you come, his lordship from the office. And what do you do? Do you offer me a couple of tickets to a play? Do you suggest going out to a dance or something? Ha ha! Not you. No. You go prancing round the house in a horrid old shirt like a third-rate comedian in a burlesque show. And then you ask me to read. Of all things, to read. Well, do you know, my darling husband, you haven't even taken me to one honest-to-God night club? Not one. When I married you——"

Tim Willows swung round to confront his wife, and the tails of his shirt flared alarmingly.

"If you made a phonograph record of that set lament of yours," he said nastily, "you could turn the damned thing on whenever you felt like it and save no end of breath. I know it myself by heart. Word for word, sentence for sentence it's graven on my brain. Now go on and tell me what I led you to expect before you married me—how I tricked you to the altar with false promises. Come to an hysterical climax about my unjustifiable jealousy and then we can both rush out into the night and offend the damn neighbors."

He turned bitterly away from the small, furious figure seated on the bed and, going to the window, stood there gazing out into the pinched face of winter. Hardly thirty feet away stood another neat little suburban home—with garden and garage—and in between lay nothing but dirty snow, its flat surface broken by a straggling line of frozen shrubs. Lifting his eyes a little he saw the roofs of other houses. There were thousands of them—too many of them. He felt himself sinking, going down in a sea of neat little suburban homes. In desperation he again elevated his eyes and let them rest on the dark outline of the distant hills. Bright stars were hanging above those hills. The stark limbs of numb trees reached achingly up to their cold beams. And lights studded the hills, the lights of other homes. 'Way off there people were living and carrying on life. Tim wondered idly what they were like, those people who lived over there. Did they, too, commute? Did they go eternally to offices? Did they have to hang up their pride with their hats and coats and swallow rebellious words in the teeth of secure executives? Was economic necessity always goading them on, marshaling them down windy platforms, cramming them into subways that steamed and stank and finally plopping them down in front of dreary-looking desks, nervously baited and physically ruffled even before the long day had begun? Was life just going to be like that all the damn time? He had a dim understanding of his wife's restlessness of spirit. In a way he sympathized with her. Probably their glands were all wrong. They weren't real people. Not properly equipped for life. Maladjusted to the world. Tim did not know. Nor did he give a hang. Something was all wet somewhere. He, too, would like to try a night club, look at a lot of naked girls. It might be entertaining. Damned if he knew. He'd like to vary the monotony of the daily routine and talk with some interesting people—that is, if they would talk with him. Whom had he ever licked? Never done anything much. Only thought and talked . . . complained. But as things stood, what could he do about it? He was in no position to create his own circumstances . . . to pluck friends, funds, and entertainment from thin air. And anyway, what the hell was she grousing about? She was out all the day gallivanting round. She had freedom of action, thought, and speech. What was eating her? God knows, she was not repressed unless she created her own inhibitions through sheer intellectual vacuity. She had her day, her bridge, movies, shopping, teas, lunches, and even men. He was painfully aware of the latter. No, there was little about which she could complain. Perhaps he was wrong at that. What, after all, did he know about this woman? What did she know about herself? They were all in it together. A mess . . . a cul-de-sac.

Tim Willows, standing by the window, experienced a feeling of utter frustration. It was a spiritually debilitating feeling—a miserable thing. More profoundly hopeless than a nauseating hangover after a long-distance spree. More hopeless because now the brain was clear and could look into the future. And what a future it was! Tim realized he had just about reached his highest peak. He wouldn't be earning much more money ever. Less, if anything. And he did not have much faith in breaks. People who waited for breaks, he had found, usually went broke. There she blew, the future, the taunting white whale. Constant bickerings and recriminations paved the way. And the rest—just sour grapes and shabby expedients. Well, it was a good thing they had no spawn, although a baby or two barging about the house might have given them a bit of a kick. At least they'd have something to think about besides themselves.

"There's going to be a change," came coldly from the bed. "I don't intend to stand this life any longer. Other women work. Why shouldn't I? If you won't make a life for me I'll make a life for myself. I deserve a life. I'm still under thirty and not altogether unattractive. All you seem to care about is reading and writing and bad gin."

At that moment she saw herself as the glorified secretary of a huge Wall Street wolf with a boyish smile. She was helping him to ruin thousands of inoffensive lives in one mad and dazzling coup. Then the Riviera and a series of top-notch seductions. Perhaps in the end she would discover that she had always loved her husband. But, of course, she'd have to do considerable experimenting before she found that out.

Tim's mirthless laugh smeared a streak across the pleasant picture.

"You've got a damn poor chance of finding life and romance on a desk top," he said. "And if you're satisfied with what you do find there you're a whole lot dumber than I thought you were, and that would make you a little less than a half-wit." He turned from the window and confronted the charming feminine figure which for him at the moment had lost a great deal of its charm. "What in the name of God are you kicking about, anyway?" he demanded. "You haven't a damn thing to do, no drudgery or monotonous routine. The Twills, such as they are, still take care of the house. You can pound your ear all day long or do what you jolly well please. No cooking, no washing—not even a child. I leave you here in the morning literally drugged with sleep only to find you at night a nervous and physical wreck. Your first words are either a complaint or a criticism. And always in the offing is the threat of a nice, noisy case of hysterics. You hold that in reserve as a last resort because you've found out that it's an infallible weapon. You can win every time no matter how wrong you are, but nothing is ever changed, nothing is ever settled. You don't even drive me down to the station in the morning. At night you habitually arrive there late through some unavoidable delay. Your excuses are so illogical they fairly sicken me to hear them. I wish to several different sets of gods I could change places with you for a while. Believe me, I do. I'd jolly well find something to occupy my time without looking for work. I'd sit down and write myself a book. It might be a rotten book, but at least I'd have the satisfaction of finding it out. I know I could do it, and in your heart, when you use it, you know I could do it, too."

Strange to say, Sally did know he could do it. Even at that heated moment she realized that this husband of hers was a little better than she allowed herself to admit. There was a lot more to him than any of the men she knew. That was just the trouble. There was too much to him. He was not a normal male animal and he wouldn't act like one. He was a sort of artist without an art, which was much like being a man without a country. An unexpected wave of sympathy almost smothered the retort trembling on her lips. That would never do. They were often like this with each other now, their best words remaining unspoken while their worst ones came tumbling out.

"I'd like to take you up on that," she flung at him. "I wish I could change places with you. Oh, how I do! You clear out of it all every morning, go to the city and see something new—eat where you like and what you like—interesting men to talk to—good-looking girls to see—lots of them. And you don't miss one, I'll bet. You've got a rotten pair of eyes. You're like a little old lascivious hermit—a twittering dog."

"Why like a twittering dog?" Tim Willows inquired. "I don't quite get that. Twittering dogs and hermits don't seem to—"

But the course of Sally's words was not to be deflected by irrelevant questions.

"Don't worry, my darling," she continued. "I'd change places with you quick as a wink. At least, you do something, move about, create a little world of your own, travel places and stay overnight. I never stay anywhere overnight. No, here I am—chained down. A prisoner. All I need is a striped suit and a number."

Mr. Willows smiled fleetingly at this, then stood for a moment, looking seriously down at his wife.

"Sally," he said gently, "I think you must be mad or else you get a certain backhand satisfaction in being so consistently wrong-headed. You know damn well I don't enjoy the work I am doing, the mock importance and the hypocrisy of it, the daily drip I have to listen to and the humble pie I have to eat. A week of it would bore you to tears. Don't know how I've hung on so long myself. And I wouldn't have if I hadn't exploded occasionally. But I don't think I'll be able to hang on much longer. I feel a bust-up collecting itself right in the pit of my stomach. It's due almost any day now. Old man Gibber gets dottier all the time. He and his Nationwide——"

"Do all men complain——"

Sally's question was never finished. A knock sounding irritably on the bedroom door put an end to further hostilities. As if overtaxed by this unreasonable formality, Mrs. Twill, as was her wont, opened the door just wide enough to permit the inthrust of her head. More than once Mrs. Twill had told her husband that it always made her feel foolish to knock on Mr. Tim's door, "him being hardly out of the cradle yet."

"You'll feel a whole lot foolisher some night if you don't knock," had been Twill's sage advice.

For as far back as Tim could remember, the Twills had worked in tandem for one or another member of his family.

"Would you like to have the Twills help you out for a while?" his grandmother would ask some visiting relation, and upon receiving an affirmative reply, the Twills would be packed up and bundled off to another household. In this way they gained a more comprehensive knowledge of the Willows family history and private affairs than was possessed by any single member. It had been an old family of old people. Most of them were now beyond the need of servants, but the Twills still went on tenaciously clinging to a world which for them was peopled mostly with memories. It was as if they had been granted a special dispensation by Time to keep on going until the last of the Willowses had stopped. Then their work on earth would be ended and they would be free to follow into another world the family they had so faithfully served, there to begin the whole thing over again under the divine auspices of a chatty, pro-Willows God. Although the Twills were rather more of an obligation than an asset, they were comforting to have about the house. Their chief interest in life centered round Sally and Tim. Sally's girth they constantly studied with patiently hopeful eyes, but so far no embryonic Willowses had rewarded their watchful waiting.

"I can't stop him," Judy Twill announced tragically.

"Whom do you want to stop?" demanded Sally.

"The old fool," continued Mrs. Twill. "I know he'll

break his neck on those basement stairs. Will you call him up, Mr. Tim? The furnace is stone cold."

"The mother of that damned furnace must have been done in by an ice box," complained Tim as he made for the door, uttering loud and discouraging noises as he went.

"Do hurry," called Sally, all other considerations forgotten in her anxiety for the safety of the venerable but pig-headed Mr. Twill.

"Come out of that, Peter," shouted Tim down the back stairs. "Don't you dare put a foot in that basement."

Through the floor, hollowly, came the protesting voice of Twill:

"But I can fix it, Mr. Tim," it said.

"God, Himself, couldn't fix that furnace," replied Tim. "Don't you even breathe on the thing. Snap out of it, Peter, and go to bed. Get yourself a drink if you can find one."

There was no response to this, but certain noises in the kitchen assured Tim that Peter had changed his mind and found warmth for himself instead of the house.

"Yes, Miss Sally," Mrs. Twill was saying as Tim returned to the room. "I certainly agree with you. It's a shame and scandal he doesn't wear pants."

"I can stand to hear very little more of that," announced Tim, looking darkly at the two women. "What I do with the lower half of my anatomy is no one's business."

"Oh, is that so?" put in Sally, slightly elevating her eyebrows. "Well, I like that."

"How do you mean?" asked Mrs. Twill.

"Be still," snapped Tim. "I'm speaking of raiment now. If you mention those pajama trousers again I'll take them out of the drawer and cut them up into little bits. I'll burn the——"

"He was just like that as a baby," interrupted Mrs. Twill as calmly as if he had not been present. "No matter what we put on him at night you'd find him mother-naked in the morning—bare bottom and all."

"You can find him like that almost any time when

he's not at the office," announced Sally. "But who wants to?"

"If you all have thoroughly finished," said Mr. Willows with frigid politeness, "I'll go down to the basement. Good-night, Judy. Tell that ancient wreck of yours that if he ever attempts to go down there again I'll put him on the retired list for good."

When Judy had withdrawn, Tim Willows looked down long and thoughtfully at his young wife.

"You know," he said at last, "my idea of hell is to be chained to a line of smugly secure home owners. Every one of them is stoking a glowing furnace and liking it. Every one but me. I am crouched on my bare knees, eternally doomed to pull cold clinkers from the sneering mouth of that damned thing down in the basement. That would be hell, and I'm already getting a sample of it right here on earth. In fact," he added as he walked to the door, "everything in this house is a little bit of hell."

"Then why not say 'To hell with everything in the house'?" inquired Sally, with one of her most disagreeable smiles.

"I do," replied Tim earnestly. "I most emphatically damn well do."

There was a pained expression in Mr. Ram's eyes as he watched Tim Willows leave the room. High time that steps were taken to show those two mere mortals the error of their ways.

CHAPTER II

Interlude with a Furnace

WEDGED RATHER THAN CRAMMED INTO THE NARROW confines of a packing case the great animal slumbered, sighing deeply in its sleep. It looked terribly uncomfortable, this creature, but was either unaware of the fact or ascetically disregarded it.

"With the entire house at his disposal," Tim wondered as he stood in the kitchen and looked down upon the dog, "why does he insist on pouring himself into that box? It's sheer stupidity—an inability to adapt himself to changing conditions."

Dopey was a large dog—too large, thought Tim Willows. Dopey would have made a better cow or even a small mule. The man's sense of irritation increased. Why, in God's name, why did this dog prefer the slow torture of that box to a pillow-strewn divan, a soft rug, or a comfortable corner in the front room?

Tim failed to realize that what little mind Dopey owned ran on a single track. He had always slept in that box; why should he not continue to sleep in that box? Night after night and even on dull afternoons, on fair days and foul, in sorrow and disgrace that box had been his refuge, his sanctuary. Other dogs no doubt were just waiting for an opportunity to take that box from him. This long had been Dopey's secret fear. But it would never be. That box was the one thing in the world that he actually owned. Growth, either physical or intellectual, meant little or nothing to Dopey. He brushed them aside as trifling considerations. He liked the smell of that box. It was familiar, homelike, and soothing to taut nerves.

When Tim had acquired this dog he had not been in search of a small dog. No. Neither had he wanted a

large dog, a pounding, crashing, monolith of a beast.
What Tim had been looking for was a nice, middle-size
dog, and Dopey had appeared about to fill the bill. As
a pup he had given every indication that in the due
course of time he would evolve into a conservative,
moderately proportioned creature. At that time there
had been no suggestion that the dog secretly entertained ambitions to become if not the largest of all animals at least the largest of all dogs. In short, Dopey
had appeared to be just such a dog as Mr. Willows
most desired, a creature whose size would conform
with the specifications of a modest suburban home. But
in this Mr. Willows had either been deliberately tricked
by the seemingly guileless pup or else had mistaken his
intentions. It is possible that Dopey for some time had
been deliberately curbing his natural tendency to
vastness until he had attained the security of a good
home. Certain it is that immediately upon arriving at
the Willowses' establishment the dog had abandoned
all pretense of self-regulation and had started in
growing dizzily before the alarmed eyes of his master.
It is barely possible, on the other hand, that the
thought of deception had never entered the dog's mind
and that he was merely giving an outward manifesta-
tion of his appreciation of his great good fortune. It is
just conceivable that Dopey said to himself, "This kind
gentleman seems to have his heart set on owning a dog.
Well, just to please him, I'll make as much of a dog of
myself as I can manage. In me he will have more than
just a dog. He'll have half a dozen dogs in one."

This might have been Dopey's attitude of mind, although his subsequent conduct makes it rather dubious.
He speedily developed into a thief, a glutton, and a
hypocrite, a nervous wreck in the face of attack, a
braggart when danger was past. Had he been able to
speak he would have lied steadily from morning to
night, for the sheer sake of lying. He was a dog without
a redeeming trait, without a spark of pride or an ounce
of chivalry. Small dogs were his dish—that is, if they
were small enough. In spite of which this animal had
succeeded in worming his way into the good graces of
Tim and Sally. Even the Twills tolerated him. On his

part Dopey liked almost everybody who did not frighten him and who belonged to what he fondly believed to be the upper classes, but as almost everyone frightened him Dopey had few friends. He was also a snob.

For this attitude there was no justification whatever. He was the lowest of low-bred dogs. It would have taken several commodious closets to accommodate his family skeletons. At first there had been some loose talk about his Airedale ancestry. There was nothing to it. At some time during the love life of his indefatigable mother things must have become terribly involved. The result was Dopey, a creature who could call almost any dog brother with a fair chance of being right nine times out of ten. He was a melting-pot of a dog, carrying in his veins so many different strains of canine blood that he was never able to decide what breed of dog he should try hardest to be, or to develop any consistent course of canine conduct. He had no philosophy, no traditions, no moral standards. Dopey was just dog. His mother might have seen an Airedale once or even made a tentative date with an Airedale, but after one good look at her son it was obvious that the date had never amounted to anything definite.

Dopey now lifted a long, tan, knobby head and gazed meltingly at his master, his moist nose quivering delicately. Heaving his great, angular bulk out of the box he stretched painfully, yawned, shook himself, then suddenly became possessed of the devil. After a crashing, three-lap turn about the kitchen he flung his moplike paws against Mr. Willows's chest in a whirlwind of hospitality.

"God Almighty," protested Tim, ruefully regarding several parallel red welts running down his chest, "What's the meaning of all this? Down, damn you, down."

Now nothing, save perhaps an amorous woman when a man wants to sleep, can be more exasperating, more fiendishly tormenting than a dog that insists on being violently playful and affectionate when one's nerves are about to snap. It is then that one's mind morbidly conceives the idea that an evil spirit has entered into the dog for the purpose of driving one mad. Tim Willows's nerves were at their worst and Dopey was at his. The harassed man turned to the stairs leading down to the basement, cursed them bitterly from the depth of his heart, then slowly descended while Dopey, in close attendance, licked the back of his neck with a tongue that felt like a recently used wash rag. He paused before the furnace and directed the stream of his profanity against its cold, bloated sides. Then he opened the door of the fire box and peered unhopefully into unresponsive blackness. Dopey went him one better and tried to crawl in. This resulted in a struggle between man and beast for the possession of the furnace. It ended in a draw. Tim pulled out the clinkers with one hand and pushed Dopey's inquiring face away with the other. This operation finished, Tim Willows sat down on a box and looked murderously at the dog.

"Blast you," muttered the man. "It's hard enough as it is without you making it harder. Why don't you go away somewhere and find something else to do, you great big ninny?"

He reached out to cuff the dog, but Dopey, his tongue lolling foolishly out, pranced just beyond reach and stood in an attitude of sportive attention. At that moment Tim thoroughly despised this dog with its silly face and ungainly paws. Rising wearily from the box he set about to collect some sticks of kindling wood, an action that sent Dopey into ecstasies of excitement. With wild eyes and teeth bared the dog snapped and lunged at the sticks, several of which he succeeded in snatching from his master's hands. Then strange noises were heard in the basement of that house. They issued from the distorted lips of Mr. Willows. That gentleman was chattering to himself with exasperation. He was in no fit condition to be allowed at large. Finally he picked up the dog bodily, staggered with him to the far end of the basement, dropped the perplexed creature, then rushing back to the furnace, seized some sticks and hurled them into the fire box. It had been an elaborate but successful maneuver. Mr. Willows was breathing heavily both from emotion and fatigue. Sweat ran down his face and cut paths across patches of soot and coal dust. His hands were the hands of a man who has toiled long in grimy places. At last he started a blaze, then once more seated himself on the box and thought up horrible tortures for Dopey. That stout fellow, nuzzle pressed to the floor, rump outrageously elevated, front paws spraddled, was uttering deep-throated growls of mock ferocity.

"Shut up, you," said Mr. Willows, flinging a stick of kindling at the dog.

Dopey dodged adroitly, seized the stick in his powerful jaws and crushed it. Realizing he was entertaining rather than injuring the animal, Tim pretended to ignore it.

The business of putting coal on the fire proved even more trying. Every time the man attempted to swing the shovel the beast flung himslf upon it, thus diverting its aim and spraying the floor with lumps of coal. This, thought Dopey, was the best game they had played so far. Mr. Willows made even more peculiar noises. He experienced a strong desire to break down completely and to abandon himself to waves of maniacal hysteria. Presently he took hold of himself and faced the situation squarely. He realized that nothing short of brutality would be effective in dealing with that dog. But at that moment Tim was too exhausted to employ such methods. Therefore he was forced to resort to subterfuge. It was an example of mind over matter.

Taking up the shovel he filled it with coal and placed it within easy reach. Then, squatting down, he lured the unsuspicious dog over to him. Suddenly he rose, delivered a kick of some force on the astounded rump of Dopey, seized the shovel and hurled its contents into the furnace before the dog had time to recover from his surprise and indignation. Mr. Willows was elated. He hurled insults at the baffled dog.

"Got you that time, you reptile," he grated, and then proceeded to tell the discomfited creature just what he was a son of. The information left Dopey cold. Nor did he appear to be any the worse from the punishment he had received. Not so Mr. Willows. That gentleman's right foot, encased in a soft slipper, was throbbing with acute pain. He hobbled to the box and sat down. Perhaps he had broken a toe, one of those toes against which Sally was so unreasonably prejudiced. Tim Willows felt the return of his former depression, which had been momentarily dispelled by his triumph over the dog. He realized now that it had been a hollow victory, Dopey's mental capacity being what it was. Anyone with the merest suggestion of a brain could outwit that dog. And then there was the toe. Surely it had been one hell of an unpleasant evening. . . . Sally? That dear young thing was probably asleep by now. What a wife. Well, he would go up, grab off a consoling drink, and do a little reading. It was cold as the grave in that basement unless one kept moving. No place for a man clad only in a French shirt. Unconscious of the fact that he was still carrying the shovel, he made his way wearily up the steps, with Dopey panting hotly, but happily, on his heels. At the head of the stairs he stopped and looked down at the dog. In the presence of that great dumb beast words seemed inadequate.

"This is the end," he told the dog. "To-morrow you go. If I wasn't so tired now I'd cut you into tiny little bits. I'd make you sweat. Don't even look at me."

Dopey did not take the trouble to listen. He fawned upon his master and waited for something new to turn up. Why not make a night of it?

In a low, monotonous voice Tim continued to scold his dog as he passed through the box of a serving pantry and crossed the dining room. It was not until he had reached the portières separating this room from the lounge that he became aware he was an object of intense interest to five pairs of seemingly fascinated eyes. He looked up and to his disgust discovered that the room had been invaded by five persons, all of whom he disliked. At that moment their faces were registering a disconcerting blending of amusement and surprise. Tim stopped cursing and, with admirable presence of mind, reached out and drew the nearest portière to him. This draped picturesquely over the lower half of his body. The remainder of him went unimproved. From a soot-streaked face his dim eyes peered out malevolently at the silent group facing him.

Close by his side Dopey crouched and indulged in a few inhospitable growls. The dog was extremely nervous. It had all been so sudden. Sudden changes were unsettling. Dopey was frightened.

Then the rich, lazy voice of Carl Bentley made itself heard. It would. The man had a way of making his voice heard. Not that it ever said anything. It was just that sort of voice.

"Well," said Mr. Bentley, beaming down from a great height on a strangely diminished-looking Mr. Willows, "if it isn't Tiny Tim himself—Tiny Tim in all his glory."

Tim offered the group a wan smile, such a smile as might distort the lips of a man gamely but unsuccessfully fighting off an attack of sea sickness.

"Yes," he replied. "Yes, indeed. So it is."

Silence greeted this lame effort. The company continued to gaze. Mr. Willows began to grow a trifle uncomfortable. He hated being looked at as if he were some particularly noxious specimen of bug life.

"Indeed, yes," he continued, for lack of anything better to say. "Here I am. Been making a bit of a fire in the furance." At this point he displayed the shovel as if to forestall any attempt at contradiction. "The other one went out," he added feebly. "There wasn't any fire at all."

Were these people either dumb or dead? Were they deliberately trying to upset him even more than he already was? The silence continued unbroken. The eyes continued to stare. Were parts of him sticking out, perhaps? He looked down at himself. Yes, lots of him was sticking out. Redraping himelf furtively he essayed another smile and swallowed hard. How oppressive it was in that room . . . the silence and those eyes. Once more he sought cowardly refuge in the sound of his own voice.

"It was too bad," he went on, his thin words trailing away into infinity. "I mean about that fire. The first one. The one that went out." What the devil did he mean, anyway? Taking a fresh grip on himself he continued, "There should be a law about fires going out at this time of night." Here he laughed meaninglessly. "Ha ha! Not a bad idea, what?"

No one else laughed. Obviously the idea was not so good. The graven images remained unimpressed. They refrained from committing themselves either for or against it. Tim had feared as much. Then, suddenly, the spell was broken—snapped. Blake Watson had done it. Blake was the slave of a furnace of which he was inordinately proud. At the mention of the word "furnace" life always took on a new interest for him. He became a changed man—changed for the worse. Snappily stroking his military mustache he glared at Tim severely.

"Can't understand that, Willows," he said accusingly.

"And that's not all you can't understand," Tim shot back. "Do you think I put the damned thing out on purpose just for the fun of making a new one?"

"Come, come!" admonished Mr. Watson. "Don't trifle. Now, I have a furnace and the fire never goes out. Does it, my dear?"

My dear, being his wife, Helen, an exhausted blonde with attractively bad eyes, languidly agreed with her husband in a voice that proclaimed she wished to God it would go out occasionally, thus relieving her of the unexciting company of the military mustache for a short time at least.

"You're a regular vestal virgin, Blake," Tim retorted. "And I don't intend to become one. No, not for any furnace."

"Good!" put in Helen briskly. "Don't become a vestal virgin. But tell us. What are you trying to become, Tim? From your attractive little costume I take it you've joined something pretty snappy."

"I'd like to take a look at that furnace of yours," cut in her husband in an executive voice he carried somewhere in the neighborhood of his boots.

"Go right ahead," said Tim. "Take a look at it, but I won't accompany you. If I see the miserable thing again I'll slit its throat from ear to ear."

"You know, old boy," Carl Bentley observed, still being his whimsical self, "we had no idea you were building a fire. You looked as if you'd just been picking lilies."

Nobody laughed much at this, and Bentley looked wistfully at the door leading to the hall. His stuff needed the right sort of audience, people who appreciated subtleness. Tim's voice recalled him to the room.

"No," he was saying quite seriously, "I really was building a fire. When I pick lilies it will be for a much more welcome occasion than this, but you won't be alive to enjoy it."

"Bur-r-r-r," muttered the irrepressible Bentley, turning up his coat collar and going through an elaborate pantomine of a shivering man. "That ought to hold me for a while."

Mr. Willows looked at him coldly, then turned to the others.

"And now," he continued, "if you don't mind I'd like to know how in hell you all got in here."

"Oh, we don't mind in the least," drawled Vera Hutchens. "We were barging by like a bunch of lost scows and we thought we'd just drop in. Make a night of it. Break out the flasks, boys."

"That was a no-good thought, Vera," observed Tim slowly. "In fact it was just too bad. And that little part about making a night of it is all wet. It's a washout. Don't trouble about taking off your things. If you want to make a night of it why don't you go out and build yourself a great, big snow man?"

"Oh, I say," complained Carl Bentley. "This is no go. We've just dropped in, you know."

"Yes, I know," said Tim, grinning, "and you can just drop out again. And I don't quite understand how you managed to drop in, to begin with. You must have damn well broken in. I locked the door myself."

"Wrong again," retorted Bentley in a gloating voice. "We were invited in most cordially."

"And who was so ill advised as to do a mad thing like that?" demanded Tim.

"Sally," trumped Bentley.

Tim was momentarily stunned.

"Where do you get off calling my wife Sally?" he got

out. "So far as I know you've only met her twice in your life."

"You never can tell," insinuated Vera. "It's a small world, you know. Small and wicked, Tim."

Tim cast the speaker a mean look.

"Viper!" he said. "You'd be writing poison-pen letters if you knew how to write."

"Listen, Tim," chimed in Helen. "Don't be such a crab. We all live in the same town, don't we?"

"Unfortunately we do," snapped Tim. "Wish we didn't. If we all lived on the same street, I suppose, according to your way of thinking, we'd be entitled to sleep with each other as a sort of neighborly gesture?"

"Something like that," said Helen.

"How do you mean, something like that?" demanded Tim. "It must be that or nothing."

"Oh," replied Helen. "Is that the type of man you are? No half measures for you."

"You can see that for yourself, my dear," put in Vera. "Look how he's dressed. Always ready for something to turn up."

"Come, come!" exclaimed her husband, a thickset, well-dressed gentleman, solid, successful, and sly. Ted Hutchens felt that he had at least one valid claim on local immortality. He had played polo at the Westchester-Biltmore once and only once. "Come, come!" he repeated, as if rebuking a child, as he looked heavily at Tim Willows. The look and the admonition infuriated Tim.

"Go, go!" he shouted. "Everybody go. Get out. Beat it. Do you think I'm going to hide behind this curtain the whole damn night?"

"That was your own idea," drawled Vera. "For my part I think you looked sweeter in your simple little shift."

"Vera!" cried Mr. Hutchens.

"Sally!" exclaimed Carl Bentley. "At last."

"Why are your voices raised in unseemly dissent?" asked Sally with easy good nature as she came gracefully into the room. "Oh, I see. It's only Tim," she continued, looking curiously at her husband. "You do look brisk, dear. I thought you'd died in that basement ages ago."

Tim was bereft of words. He clutched at the curtain and stared at his wife. She was clad in a flaring pair of pajamas and was wearing a short, silly-looking little jacket that did not seem to mean anything. He recalled having seen such outfits featured in newspaper advertisements.

"Sally!" he called in a hoarse voice. "Are you walking in your sleep? Look at yourself."

"What do you mean?" she retorted, sidling up close to the statuesque Mr. Bentley, who was looking at her with glowing eyes. "Why don't you look at yourself?"

"I mean those things you're wearing," said Tim. "They're not decent for public display. Go up immediately and put something on."

"Don't be dull, Tim," his wife replied. "These are hostess pajamas. They are supposed to be worn on informal occasions. Just such occasions as this—among friends."

"You're putting it mildly," replied Tim. "They don't encourage friendship. They invite ruin."

"Perhaps you're right," said Sally, smiling up slowly into Mr. Bentley's eyes. "I've a remote idea myself that one seldom sleeps in them."

Mr. Bentley favored his audience with a laugh not unlike a neigh, a significant sort of a neigh.

"All right!" cried Tim, thoroughly aroused by this little exchange. "I can play, too." With this he stepped out from behind the portières and stood revealed to the company in his disheveled shirt. "This garment, ladies and gentlemen," he announced, turning slowly round with his arms extended, "is what is known as a host's slip-on. It may not look so good, but it's a damn sight franker and more practical than my wife's costume."

Taking advantage of the small panic created by his sudden unveiling, Tim limped to a nearby table, from which he snatched a hip flask and helped himself to a powerful drink, a gesture which gave to his shirt an amusing frontal elevation. Amid the appreciative giggles of the women and the subdued expostulations of the men he turned his back on the company and, with as much dignity as he could command, limped painfully from the room, the shovel still in his hand and Dopey at his heels. In the hall he placed the shovel in the cane rack, to the everlasting humiliation of several snooty walking sticks, then slowly mounted the stairs, his modesty becoming more assailable the higher he proceeded. Even the violent slamming of the bedroom door failed to shut off from his ears the pent-up frenzy of a jazz orchestra avalanching from the radio. For a moment he stood looking irresolutely at the door, then, opening it a little, he listened, Dopey doing likewise.

"Whoopee!" came the hearty voice of Carl Bentley. "Come on, gang. Let's go."

"I wish to God you would," muttered Mr. Willows. "You big, inane bastard. Having a real nice time, aren't you? Seeing life in the suburbs. Wildfire! Aw, go to hell."

Once more he closed the door, this time quietly, and, hobbling over to a cabinet, took from it a glass and a bottle of whiskey. Thus equipped he sought a chair and sat staring vacantly at Dopey sprawled out at his feet.

"It's a good thing, stupid, you don't drink," he observed. "You're sufficient of a damn fool just as you are."

Dopey tried, but failed to understand. It didn't matter. Everything was all right. He was comfortable.

"Listen," continued his master, choking over his drink. "I've a good idea to get drunk and beat you up . . . within an inch of your useless life . . . to a pulp . . . a regular jelly."

The dog's snakelike tail thumped against the rug. His master was being funny. He was such a nice man. Dopey felt himself moved to kiss him, but was too comfortable to make the effort. Some other time. Wearily his eyes closed. He sighed. Things always worked out for the best.

Tim Willows arranged himself another drink and sat listening to the radio. Gradually his feet began to tap time with the music. He had forgotten about his toe.

CHAPTER III

Good Clean Fun

IN THE LOUNGE BELOW, EVERYTHING WAS GETTING better and better. That is, if noise counted. Something in the nature of a celebration in joint honor of modern and ancient days was in progress. It was rather a loose, heavy-handed affair, but those present seemed to enjoy it. Figuratively speaking, Diana was dancing improperly on the belly of a prostrate Volstead, while Bacchus poured gin in his eye. This interesting blending of Dionysian and suburban rites was, as a matter of fact, nothing more nor less than a typical cocktail-necking party such as many find it necessary to attend in order to discover if sex still appeals. The Pagan and Christian eras endeavored to merge while still retaining the worst features of both. The result was an evening of nice clean fun. After all, what is a neck more or less, plus adjacent territory, among friends? Wives were not so much exchanged as released on short-term loans. This was the modern touch, the smart thing to do. The festivities over, these fair ladies would be returned to their husbands a little bit thumbed and dog-eared and more than a little drunk. It was one of those sportive occasions at which enmities are inevitably aroused and sordid recriminations incubated, for by the very nature of things there are few husbands and wives whose limits of conduct and powers of self-control register exactly the same. One or the other member of the tandem is sure to go too far. Then all hell pops.

Husbands and wives who intend to carry on together at all permanently should never attend the same cocktail-necking party unless one of them passes out and is unable to know what the other is doing. Otherwise it

31

either cramps the style of both or furnishes the divorce courts with fresh customers.

Really, it's the devil and all to be modern—much too much of a strain. It involves, oddly enough, a swift return to a primitive state of arboreal promiscuity. Few people can follow this path with linked hands and light hearts. Each side is too heavily weighted with inhibitions and prejudices. Each side is vainly endeavoring to nibble the icing of the cake in order to retain the whole. The result is rather crummy.

Into Mrs. Tim Willows's party half a dozen fresh votaries had been introduced. They had been rung up and called in, and among them were a couple of unattached young women.

There is nothing like the presence of a couple of young women, unattached, among a number of not too old matrons to accelerate the tempo of a party. The young matrons were immediately put on their mettle when Joy Tucker and Agatha Green appeared. Then the married ladies started in to prove to the world that they had found in the matrimonial state a great deal more than they had lost. As a corollary of this they naturally had more to give. On the other hand the virgins hinted of fair but difficult, although not impassable, territory still unexplored. This, of course, was a challenge to the adventurous. Altogether it was a stimulating and healthy form of competition from which the males as usual profited, adding thereby to their already overflowing reservoirs of complacency.

Naturally there was little conversation. Under the most favorable circumstances there would have been little conversation. These people were not so constituted. However, everybody talked a great deal and shouted even more. Risqué stories which were neither risqué enough nor funny enough occasioned sporadic gales of laughter. And through it all, above and around it all, piercing the smoke and perfume and the good old American tang of gin, the tireless-tongued radio lashed dancing couples into fresh paroxysms of activity.

It was just as well that Tim Willows remained alone in his room save for the companionship of Dopey and

Mr. Ram. To begin with, at such parties he was not so good. He generally drank too much and observed too much, and the more he drank the more he observed, until at last he saw things that were not there at all. Then, again, his ideas of necking were disconcertedly crude. . . . He believed in treating a girl like a human being entitled to an intelligent exchange of ideas. Frequently women who had been gamely prepared to offer almost unlimited necking facilities were surprised to find that they had actually been talking for at least half an hour with Tim Willows, and enjoying it. This rather frightened them. They became a trifle subdued. Several stiff drinks of gin were required to bring them back to their former state of carefree animalism. On the other hand, there had been several occasions when only the intervention of Sally and several husbands had prevented him from dragging some woman upstairs and teaching her what for, as the English insist on having it. He steadfastly refused to remember these occasions, claiming that he had been too far gone in his cups to know what he was doing. Tim Willows was too simple and direct a person to be a successful modern. He belonged to a vanished era when people talked and played and loved with effortless enjoyment.

For another reason it was just as well that Tim remained in his room. It was Carl Bentley's evening. By tacit consent the women of the company had left that gentleman to Sally. He was her man. Not even the young women attempted to horn in. Had they tried their efforts would have proved fruitless. Carl Bentley was now hot on the scent. He had put in some of his best work on Sally and he had reason to believe that his campaign would soon be crowned by a complete capitulation. Sally was the pick of the lot, by far the most desirable woman in town, with no exceptions.

So Carl Bentley danced with Sally, drank with Sally and whispered suggestively in Sally's small pink ear. Above stairs Tim just drank and sought comfort in Kai Lung, than whom there is hardly a greater comforter, thanks to Ernest Bramah. When the unattached young women began to tap dance more with their abdomen than their toes, Bentley took advantage of the occasion.

Everybody was present and accounted, for, although neither clean nor sober.

"Sally," said Mr. Bentley in a voice almost as low as his intentions, "let's go out to the kitchen where there aren't so many people. You can't hear yourself think in here."

Sally looked indifferently round the room and carelessly moved off kitchenward. The blood was racing in her veins and her head felt delightfully dizzy and confused. Nothing much mattered except a good time . . . a little life. This man, Bentley, was so much more dominating and possessive than Tim. She liked that. Tim, in spite of his horrid ways, was rather too much of a gentleman. He made no parade of virility. He did not endeavor to master her. Sally decided he was not quite big enough. She preferred the size of Carl Bentley. He could smother her, and at the moment she felt like being smothered. It must be said for Sally that she was far, far from being herself. Modern gin is not a good thing for good girls, although it is awfully good for bad ones. Carl Bentley, well knowing this, followed her with a bottle.

What happened in the kitchen is nobody's business. It should be stated, though, that Tim Willows and his dog descended into the small pandemonium of the lounge only a few minutes after the disappearance of Sally and Carl Bentley. He was just in time to witness Vera Hutchens slapping her husband in the face because that unfortunate gentleman had remonstrated with her for kissing the same man too long and too often.

"He always gets like this," she complained to the company at large. "Because he has a nasty mind he thinks everybody else is like him. Insults me, he does. Well, just to satisfy you, my dear,"—and here she laughed recklessly—"I'll kiss him as much as I like and you won't stop me."

This she proceeded to do. Throwing herself into the arms of a tall, quiet person who was extremely well heeled with grog, she satisfied herself and her husband as well as the man she was kissing. It did not matter so much to the man. He hardly knew whom he was kissing. He was just kissing some woman and so far that was all right.

"Suburbia at play," observed Tim in his quiet, sardonic voice. "Don't you girls and boys ever learn any new games?"

Tim was regarded with interest, particularly by several women in the room. He had managed to struggle into a pair of pajama trousers and was wearing a magnificent dressing gown. His feet were encased in a pair of comfortably padded slippers. He had done things to his hair and tidied himself up generally. Few persons if any realized how binged Tim Willows really was.

"Carry on," he continued pleasantly. "Some of you men who are able had better do something about Hutchens or we'll be having a murder on our hands."

This was nearly the truth. Hutchens, Vera, and the man of her choice were involved in an unseemly tussle. Vera was beginning to scream and cry, and the men were calling each other some pretty bad names. It was not a thing to see, yet at these parties it was always being seen.

Tim, whose dim but all-observing eyes had noted the absence of his wife and Carl Bentley, moved quietly toward the kitchen. Dopey, his ears flat against his head, followed fearfully. Quietly Tim passed through the pantry and opened the kitchen door. So engrossed was Bentley in his occupation that he failed to note the presence of an observer. Tim gazed thoughtfully at the man's back for a moment, then lifting Mrs. Twill's heavy rolling pin from the rack close at hand, he brought it down violently on Mr. Bentley's head. That misguided gentleman swayed gently on his feet, then crumpled to the floor.

"Sorry," said Tim, looking coldly at a white-faced Sally, "but really, you know, the kitchen is no place for this sort of thing. One doesn't play with fire here, one actually uses it. But, of course, you know nothing about that."

He rummaged about in a drawer and produced a long sharp knife. With this he approached the prostrate figure.

"My God, Tim," breathed Sally as the room spun round and round her, "what are you going to do?"

Tim was cold white drunk and his words seemed to proceed from an ice box rather than from a man's chest.

"I'm going to cut his damn head clean off," he told his wife, "and throw it in the faces of your friends. That will teach them to behave themselves—fighting and screaming and semi-fornicating all over my house . . . what a way, what a way. Yes, off goes this one's head. Want to kiss it good-bye while it's still on?"

With a shuddering cry Sally dropped to her knees beside the still figure of Mr. Bentley. She placed a hand over his heart and looked up at her husband with a drawn face.

"Tim," she said at last, "you've killed him. His heart has stopped beating and he isn't breathing any more."

This information considerably sobered Tim. He walked over to the kitchen table and picked up a bottle of gin, from which he drank deeply. After this he passed it to Sally, who followed his example.

"Lock the door," he said, and seated himself on the table.

Sally obeyed and then seated herself beside her husband. Together they gazed down upon the victim of the rolling pin.

"He wasn't much of a guy," observed Tim, hoping thereby to comfort his wife.

"I know," replied Sally, "but if every guy that wasn't much was murdered there wouldn't be many guys left."

"I wouldn't mind that," said Tim. "What did you want to go messing round with him for?"

"He was all right," answered Sally. "Big and strong and passionate. You know how it is."

"Yes," said Tim rather gloomily. "I know how it was. Did you like him better than me?"

"No, not so much, but a girl gets that way on gin."

"Sally, these parties are rotten things. This should teach us a lesson." Tim looked at her seriously.

"Sure they are. I'm through with all of it," said Sally. "Everything."

"So is he—through for good, and so am I."

Sally passed him the bottle and Tim drank mechanically. So did Sally. Both of them by this time were quite too numbed to realize the seriousness of what had happened.

"Guess you're a murderer, Tim," said Sally at last.

"Sure I am," agreed Tim. "A confirmed murderer. What do you do in such cases? Telephone the police or just send for an undertaker and try to sneak him into a grave?"

"They'd be the last persons I'd telephone to," replied Sally. "Under the circumstances."

"Which are murder," added Tim with almost morbid enjoyment.

"Murder most foul," Sally managed to extract from some dim recess of her memory.

"He certainly does look murdered," reflected Tim. "Never saw a man look quite so dead. And just to think he was kissing hell out of you only a short time ago. By rights you should be stretched out beside him."

"If you're not more careful of what you're saying I'll turn you over to the police," replied his wife. "That would be a good joke on you."

"You've got a hot sense of humor. What are we going to do with his nibs?"

Sally took a sip from the bottle and considered this in silence. From the lounge came the clatter of the radio and the hubbub of many voices.

"Bury him," she said at last. "That's what they do with bodies. They bury them."

Mr. Willows regarded the erstwhile Carl Bentley distastefully.

"We'd have to dig a regular Panama Canal to tuck that body in," he observed. "Why didn't you philander with a dwarf if you had to amuse yourself?"

"Wish I had now," said Sally. "By the time we've finished a trench for this one, the neighbors will think we're getting ready for a barbecue."

"A quaint whimsey," murmured Tim. "The bottle, please."

While Tim was drinking, the handle of the kitchen door rattled violently and a man's voice called out, "What goes on in there, a murder or something?"

"Something," called back Sally. "Go away and rattle another door."

"Oh, Sally," came a girl's voice. "What we know about you."

"What she doesn't know won't hurt her," murmured Sally.

"That wisecrack about murder wasn't so dulce," remarked Mr. Willows. "We should be doing something about this body of ours. So far we're safe. Dopey was the only other witness and he crammed himself so deep in his box I doubt if he saw anything. He hasn't opened his eyes since. Guess he never will. Dogs don't like murders."

"Well, I don't exactly gloat over them myself," said Sally. "Somehow or other I don't feel like the wife of a murderer, but never having been the wife of a murderer before, of course I don't know. How do you feel?"

"Just like a murderer," was Tim's moody reply. "Like Landru, Bluebeard, and Jack the Ripper. That's how I feel."

"It must be awful."

"It is. Break out another bottle, Sally."

Sally went to the cupboard and extracted from its recesses another bottle of gin. Tim opened it and drank.

"Ugh!" he muttered. "Rotten stuff. At least he won't have a hangover."

"Yes," said Sally, reaching for the bottle. "He's got you to thank for that."

"You know," observed her husband, "what gets the best of me is that we're taking this murder altogether too calmly. From the way we sit here and discuss it you'd think we polished off some guy every night of our lives."

"It's the gin," explained Sally, nodding wisely. "And then again, people make too much fuss about murders. They're not nearly so bad as they're painted. I've felt much more upset over a game of bridge."

"You're heartless as hell. One of us should feel sorry for this body."

"Oh, I feel sorry for it, but that doesn't help any. It was a good body."

"You seemed to enjoy it."

Sally looked at him reproachfully.

"Don't rub it in," she said. "I'll never have anything to do again with any person's body except yours."

"And you won't have much to do with that if we don't get rid of this one."

"I'm too dizzy to start in grave-digging right now," complained Sally. "Wow! I can hardly stand. Let's put it in the basement for the time being. No one goes down there but yourself."

"That," replied Tim admiringly, "is what I call a swell idea. We'll hide the beggar in the basement."

And hide the beggar they did. It was not a pretty sight to see as they pushed and dragged the body across the floor. Dopey, aroused by the noise, took one horrified look at what was going on, then disappeared from view. He decided to give the incident a miss. One had to draw the line somewhere.

Difficulties arose on the basement steps. They were steep steps, and Sally, who had gone first, found Mr. Bentley's feet pressing with undue emphasis against the pit of her stomach. She felt herself being shoved off into space.

"Can't you hold this body?" she gasped. "I can't stand its feet."

"What's wrong with his feet?" Mr. Willows inquired in an interested voice.

"There's nothing wrong with his feet, you repellent ass," replied Sally. "They're coming down too fast, that's all. Hold on to the body."

"Can't do it," groaned Tim. "It's too much. I can't hold on to my own body. Do you think you could hang on while I got a drink of gin?"

"Listen, sweetie," said Sally. "This isn't my murder, you know. It's all yours. If you don't stick around now I'll wash my hands of the body and call the whole show off. You can have the body."

"I don't want the body," replied Tim.

"Well, you can't wish it upon me. Do you think I want the body?"

"No," replied Tim. "But someone must want a body. I wonder who?"

"Don't be ridiculous," said Sally. "You can't go round asking people if they happen to want a body."

"I guess not," admitted Tim. "They might ask me how I got the body in the first place."

"Exactly. And then where would you be?"

"I'd be rid of the body if they wanted it."

"But who wants a dead body, I'd like to know?"

"Well, I don't, for one," declared Tim emphatically. "I'm tired of dead bodies. Wish to God I'd never killed this one."

"Are we going to stand here all night in idle conversation?" asked Sally.

Tim was not standing. By this time he had flattened himself on his stomach and was clinging with aching fingers to the shoulders of the much discussed body. Dopey, who had been unable to restrain his curiosity, mistook his master's strange behavior for alluring indications of playfulness. Evidently everything was all right, thought the dog. That terrible still figure was going. Quietly he emerged from his box and with one bound landed in the middle of Mr. Willows's back. With a cry of utter horror Tim momentarily released his grip and the body began to slip.

"Hey!" called Sally. "What are you trying to do?"

Her question was never answered. Mr. Willows was too busy. Desparately he seized the body again, but it was too late. Mr. Bentley had evidently decided to take matters into his own hands without any further shilly-shallying. He began to descend purposefully into the darkness of the basement. Tim Willows was right behind him with Dopey on his back.

"I'm done for," panted Sally as the pressure of Mr. Bentley's feet grew irresistible. "Here I go and here it comes."

She abandoned all further effort and the body descended swiftly upon her as she slid down the steps. Mr. Willows and Dopey were close behind and then on top.

"I'm through," came Sally's discouraged voice in the

darkness. "You might as well bury me too. There's not a whole bone in my body."

"Dopey did it," declared her husband. "Damn him."

"Whether Dopey did it or President Hoover, the result would be just the same," said Sally. "I'm a gone girl, that's all I know. Heave this body off and let me die in peace."

It was a ghastly position to be lying there in the darkness on and under a dead body with a demented dog scraping briskly about the place. Neither Sally nor Tim ever forgot it. It was one of the low lights of their lives.

Tim staggered to his feet and, after some painful groping, switched on the light. Then he bestowed upon the rump of Dopey one of the most venomous kicks ever received by a dog. After he had rolled Mr. Bentley off Sally and lifted her to her feet, they both stood swaying above the body and gazed down at it with reproachful eyes.

"That's no way for a body to act," complained Tim. "It's more dangerous than a thing of life."

"Well, if that rolling pin didn't finish him this certainly has," remarked Sally. "Let's get the cadaver out of the way. I'm sick of the very sight of it."

"Hadn't we better cover it up in the coal bin?" suggested her husband.

"Not a bad idea after all we've been through," remarked Sally. "Between us we'd make one competent murderer."

Between them and with the interference of Dopey, who had come to regard the body with jovial familiarity, they succeeded in dragging the remains of Mr. Bentley into the coal bin. Tim Willows found a shovel and began to sprinkle coal over the unpleasant object.

"This is awful," he said, wiping the sweat from his forehead. "I can hardly bring myself to do it. If people only knew how much trouble a murder involves they'd resort to some other method."

"You should have killed him outside the house," replied Sally, "or in his own bed."

"You're worse than Lady Macbeth," retorted Mr. Willows, with a slight shudder. "By rights you should be taking this murder very much to heart, yet here you go complaining because I didn't kill him in his own bed. I could never do a thing like that."

"Why not?"

"What, wake a chap up only to put him to sleep for good? Horrible."

"Why wake him up?"

Mr. Willows paused, with shovel lifted, and looked at his wife.

"Hadn't thought of that," he admitted. "But just the same it doesn't seem such a nice way to murder a person."

"And I suppose you consider whanging a man over the head with a rolling pin, shooting him down a flight of steps, and then sprinkling him liberally with coal is a nice way to do him in?"

"No, I don't," replied Tim, "and that's a fact, but you see, this is my first murder and I didn't have any time to plan it. It just happened on the spur of the moment, so to speak. In I come and down he goes. He dies and I'm a murderer. It seems too damn simple to suit me."

"Then order your murders better in the future," said Sally. "Do hurry up. I'm getting the horrors down here. The gin is wearing off."

"Keep the damn dog out of my way. He's trying to dig this body out," replied Tim.

Moved by a sudden inspiration he pulled off Mr. Bentley's shoes, then proceeded to submerge him in coal until the last of the body was seen. He was about to turn away when he paused hesitantly.

"Shouldn't we say a little something?" he asked Sally. "Some sort of prayer."

"Name one," challenged that young lady.

"Well, I don't know exactly," he hedged. "Seems sort of cold-blooded to leave him here without some little thought. How about, 'Now I Lay Me Down To Sleep'?"

Sally laughed unpleasantly.

"He didn't lay him down, dearie," she explained. "He was jolly well bashed down."

"We might pray to God to forgive him for making me a murderer," suggested Mr. Willows.

"He's your responsibility, not mine," said Sally indifferently. "Go ahead and take the matter up with God. I'm going to get a drink before I throw a fit."

"You're a hard woman, Sally," murmured Tim regretfully, "but perhaps a drink would be the best thing after all."

Picking up the shoes of the departed Bentley, he switched out the light and followed his wife up the steps to the kitchen. Dopey sought his box while they sought the bottle.

"Now," said Tim with satisfaction, "you're as much a murderer as I am. You're an accessory after the fact. We can both get the chair. What do you think of that?"

"I don't think so much of that, you worm," she answered. "As a matter of fact, I think so little of that that I've a good mind to go in right now and call up the police."

"That would make you a squealer," Tim informed her scornfully.

"What do I care?" she retorted. "I'll squeal like a pig if I feel like it."

"Go on and squeal like a pig," said her husband. "Squeal like a couple of pigs, for all I care."

"I can't squeal like a pig," Sally replied sadly. "I don't know how. Give me another spot of gin or I'll squeal like a mouse."

"Then," said Mr. Willows, passing his wife the bottle, "the wisest thing that you can do is to go back to that bunch of drunken morons and make out that Bentley's gone home. Tell 'em he left by the back way and that I've gone to bed. Get his coat and hat out of sight as quickly as possible, then break up the party. I'm going to put on those shoes and make misleading tracks in the snow. Lock the kitchen door and remove the key after you. I'll lock the back door when I return."

The moment the winter night struck Mr. Willows full in the face, reason forsook him. For a long time he wandered round in the snow, leaving what he hoped

were misleading tracks in his wake, but presently he
forgot all about this, and finding himself standing in
front of a house of vaguely familiar aspect, and suddenly realizing he was exceedingly cold, he mounted
the steps and unceremoniously entered the front door.
In the vestibule he dimly remembered that a very
pretty woman lived in this house, a Mrs. Claire
Meadows, whose husband was ever absent and whose
moral and social status was ever a subject of interest to
those who had little interest left in life. He had met this
shapely, vivid-lipped creature on several occasions and
on this occasion he met her again.

As he entered the softly illuminated sitting room he
saw her lying in nothing very much on a large divan.
Eyes, lips, and silk stockings formed his first impression. Gradually he became aware of an aura of
flame-colored hair and a dead white throat.

"Hello," she said rather huskily. "I knew you would
come sometime."

"How'd you know that?" asked Tim suspiciously.

"Because you're the most interesting man in town
and I'm the most interesting woman," he was told.
Then she caught sight of his feet, burdened as they
were with the huge shoes of a dead man. "God in
heaven!" she exclaimed. "Why the Charlie Chaplin effect and why the pajamas and dressing robe? Did you
come here to sleep, by chance?"

"Yes," replied Mr. Willows. "By chance."

She watched him with her deep blue shadow-
touched eyes as he crossed the room and picked up the
book she had been reading.

"*Alice's Adventure in Wonderland,*" he read,
seating himself beside her as it were the most natural
thing in the world. "I've always liked that book. I'm
glad you do too. I like you, you know."

"I need a little liking," she said in a low voice. "I
don't deserve it, perhaps, but that doesn't keep me
from needing it. This world is not overkind. I much
prefer Alice's."

He reached out and stroked the cool skin of her
white throat, and all the time the woman's eyes were

upon him. Her hands lay open at her sides, their palms upturned.

When Tim Willows left the house of Mrs. Claire Meadows some time later he had completely demolished still another commandment, for, as has been previously suggested, Tim Willows could not tolerate half measures.

"I feel that someone is dreaming me," she said as he left. "and that when the dreamer awakes I won't be here any more."

"When you awake," he told her, "perhaps I, too, shall be gone."

Sally was in bed and peacefully sleeping when Tim turned into his. His mind was in utter confusion, filled with blank and vivid patches, with slowly revolving colors that comforted and accused. The events of the night formed themselves before his eyes and whirled blindingly like some weird effect seen on the screen. His thoughts were drugged to sleep.

A few hours later when the light was dirtily dim he awoke to find a tall, ghastly figure standing by his bed. The figure was wavering unsteadily as if moved by a spirit wind. Tim recognized the figure only too well, but no face of a living man could be as white as the face that Carl Bentley held down to him now. Tim was electrified with horror. He was shocked even more when words came out of the face . . . dull, mumbled words with a far-off sound.

"Move over," moaned the apparition. "Move over. I must lie down."

"Move over?" said Tim incredulously. "Me move over? Good God! I'll do more than that. I'll move clean out. You can have the whole damn bed."

He sat up with a springlike snap and the figure started back, its eyes fixed with terror on the face of Tim Willows. A sudden, fearful memory gripped the tall, wavering shape. The face it saw was the face of a man it associated with the most deadly peril—death itself. One wild shriek pierced the silence as the figure turned with fluttering hands and fled from the room. Sally woke up in time to see it go. Immediately she disappeared beneath the coverings at which her husband was clawing with frenzied fingers.

"Oh-o-o-o-o dear, good little God, what was that?" she chattered. "Don't pull those covers down. Stop it! Stop, I tell you!"

"I've got to pull those covers down," said Tim, tremulously. "That horror actually wanted to get in bed with me. Imagine that. He might come back and try to do it again."

"But if he sees you over here," she protested, "he might follow and try to get in."

"He won't get a chance to see me," said Tim, "and if he does we'll just tell him flat there isn't any more room."

"You'll tell him," retorted Sally, letting her husband in. "I'll have nothing to do with a ghost, particularly with one of your making."

Tim pulled the covers securely over his head.

"Of all the nerve," he murmured. "The appalling thing tried to get me to move over."

"Pretty clubby for a man you've just murdered," said Sally. "Magnanimous, I calls it. Sinister."

"Shut up! He mightn't know."

"Spirits know all," said Sally bleakly.

"Perhaps this one is dumb," replied Tim, reaching for a straw. "I hope to God we're still squiffed and merely imagining things. Of all the damned nights."

Mr. Ram gazed disapprovingly down upon the headless bed. Things were getting out of hand . . . going far too far.

CHAPTER IV

Mr. Gibber Leaves the Room

TIM WILLOW'S PIOUS HOPE THAT HE WAS IMAGINING things fell far short of fulfillment. Not only was it totally disregarded, but also virtually flung in his face.

Rising with a clamorous head the next morning, he gulped down some coffee, and leaving Sally still painfully sleeping, rushed from the house and along the too familiar ways that led to the station. He had had neither the time nor the inclination to visit the body in the bin. Sally would have to see to that. He scarcely cared whether she saw to it or not. Tim Willows was so nauseatingly sick and disgusted that he would have greatly preferred a quiet cell in the death house to a weary day at the office.

Of all the ghastly trips he had ever made to the station—and he had made many—this morning's was by all odds the most like that. Never before had he achieved such abject and unqualified depths of physical, mental, and spiritual demoralization. Never before had he carried to the office such consciousness of guilt and awareness of impending evil. His body was sick and his soul was sick. He was unable to meet the eyes of the meanest of living creatures. Think as he would, he could find no redeeming quality within himself nor could he see any hope of salvation in the future. The sky ahead was drenched with ink and aggressively sinister. Soon it would swoop silently down and blot him out—smother him lingeringly. One circumstance alone saved him from going completely mad and running around in frenzied circles before the disapproving eyes of his fellow commuters. He was too physically debilitated to care a great deal whether or not he was a murderer. His mind had not yet had the opportunity to grasp the terrible significance of what he had done. That would come later in all its stark, blinding reality. Yes, there were many unpleasant things Tim Willows had to face. At the moment his reactions were merely mechanical. His conduct was dictated by sheer force of habit. Automatically he moved and thought, and with the nice instinct of a sick animal he isolated himself as well as he could from the main body of commuters exhaling frosty puffs along the station platform. A through train swept by. It was headed in the opposite direction, leaving New York behind. There was a dumb appeal in Tim's eyes as he watched the swift passage of that train. He wished he himself were aboard it, bound away to parts unknown.

A few minutes later his own train glided in and came to a clanking stop. Like a man voluntarily approaching his own doom he climbed wearily aboard, found a seat next to a window, and arranged the protective screen of his newspaper round the upper half of his body. So far he had successfully avoided exchanging a word of greeting with a single acquaintance. He prayed that his Jovian aloofness would remain inviolate.

"Well, here goes nothing," he said to himself as the train pulled out. "I wonder who's missing Mr. Bentley now? Probably the whole damn lot of them."

He had been such a hale and hearty commuter, Bentley, one of the most depressing types. And back home in the coal bin Mr. Bentley's body was getting worse and worse. Involuntarily Tim shuddered. That lifeless body was looming larger on his horizon. It was taking more definite shape and growing more fraught with menace. Slow waves of horror churned up the nausea within his system. Print swam before his aching eyes as he strove to return to reason through the medium of an advertisement announcing a drastic reduction in the price of fur coats. Sally needed a new coat. She could wear it to the trial. A woman with a soft white throat, and a figure that shrieked in the night. Why had there been no blood?

A heavy man sank down beside him and Tim edged over closer to the window. He dreaded the sound of a voice, but no voice was forthcoming, only a ponderous sigh. Apparently his companion was mortally weary. Tim vaguely wondered what could be the nature of the trouble that had produced such a sigh. Another one fell like a swooning body on the lap of his meditations. This was awful. The man must have committed a whole series of murders. Probably wiped out an entire family. Decapitated it. Tim feared that if the man did not stop sighing he would begin to sigh himself. Then he decided that he had not sufficient energy to heave even the ghost of a sigh. The mere business of breathing was difficult enough. His lungs felt burdened. Not so his companion's. His lungs continued to bellow forth sighs of increasingly tragic mournfulness. Tim had never heard such sighs. They seemed to proceed from the grave itself. He turned his eyes to the snow-patched fields and tried to forget the sounds. But no one could forget such sighs. They made themselves felt as well as heard. They were the palpable expression of misery. Unable to bear up under them any longer Tim turned from the window and appealingly confronted the man. One glance was all that was needed to galvanize him into panic-stricken action. Apparently the man's reactions were exactly those of Tim's. Both made a convulsive effort to remove themselves from the seat with the utmost possible speed. Both were pale and trembling. Both were desperate men. Their minds were so thoroughly atrophied that they failed to realize that if either one of them would only remain quietly seated the other would most willingly withdraw. As it was, in their passionate scramble they effectively succeeded in wedging each other inextricably in the narrow space. Perhaps no two men in all the world were less desirous of such propinquity. Tim's haggard face thrust itself out into the aisle as if detached from the rest of his body. The man's feet were shuffling busily on the floor of the car. He was running in spirit if not in body. He wanted to run with both.

"Water!" gasped Tim, to anyone who might happen to be theoretically interested in thirsts. "Wanna get water."

"Water!" inanely babbled his companion, apparently too far gone to think up anything for himself. "Must go get some water."

"Then I don't want any," said Tim hurriedly. "I'm not thirsty. You go get water."

"I can't," panted the man. "You're holding me back."

"Holding you back?" exploded Tim with a short hysterical laugh. "I wouldn't touch a hand to your mouldering body for all the gold in the mint."

"That's all right, then," said Mr. Bentley, sinking back on the seat and carrying Tim along with him. "I thought you were going to strike me."

The sudden revulsion of feelings caused by finding alive and kicking the man he had thought to be lying at that moment stark dead in his coal bin moved Tim profoundly. Even now he was not sure of his ground, yet it must be so. Spirits did not get wedged between seats or try to escape the blows of mere mortals. No, Carl Bentley was real enough, and Tim Willows almost collapsed on the spot under the stress of his emotions.

"Strike you?" he managed to blurt out. "I haven't the slightest desire to do such a thing. I'd much rather hug you."

"Don't do that," said Mr. Bentley stiffly. "You've done quite enough to me already."

"All right," replied Tim rather humbly. "I won't, but are you sure you're not murdered?"

"No," said Mr. Bentley. "I'm not sure. I might die at any minute. I feel that way. I feel very much that way, let me tell you."

Tim considered this information for a moment and took comfort in it.

"I'll let you tell me," he observed at last. "And you can die at any minute for all I care just as long as you're out of my coal bin. I wouldn't mind it at all. As a matter of fact, I'd like to see you die. I'd enjoy it."

"Don't work yourself up to a pitch," the other put in hastily. "I feel very, very ill."

"I will work myself up to a pitch," retorted Mr. Willows. "I'll work myself up to a terrific pitch. What the hell do you mean messing round with my wife?"

"That is easily explained," replied Mr. Bentley. "It

was all a mistake. Simply and truly a dreadful mistake."

Tim Willows laughed nastily.

"I hope you discovered your mistake," he said.

"Oh, I did," the other replied. "The moment I came to and found myself buried beneath a lot of nasty coal I knew some mistake had been made."

"It had," remarked Mr. Willows. "I should have put on more coal."

"Well, I managed to dig myself out somehow and to crawl upstairs. My head ached terribly."

"Good," quoth Tim feelingly.

Ignoring his companion's elation Carl Bentley went on with his story.

"I was terribly confused," he said. "Nearly dead. Quite actually nearly dead. You can imagine. To come to one's senses beneath a pile of coal in total darkness and with a head that feels twice its normal size is not an agreeable sensation."

"That's what happens to men who get gay with my wife," Tim Willows told him. "That and worse."

Mr. Bentley chose to disregard this unfriendly remark also.

"There was a bottle of gin on the kitchen table," he continued, "and I finished off what was left of it."

"I must have overlooked that," observed Tim regretfully.

"Yes, it was there," said Carl Bentley, "and I drank it. But the doors were locked and I had no shoes. No shoes at all. Have you seen my shoes by any chance, Willows?"

"One can hardly help seeing them," replied Tim. "Go on with your story."

"Well, I went up the back stairs," Bentley resumed, "and then my mind must have gone blank. I don't remember anything after that. Apparently I contrived to get home somehow, but I was minus my hat, overcoat, and shoes."

"You tried to get in bed with me," said Tim accusingly.

"Then I must have been drunk," Mr. Bentley declared. "Couldn't tell one bed from the other."

"What the hell do you mean by that?" demanded Tim.

"Nothing," said the other hastily. "Absolutely nothing. Don't know what could have made me say it. I'm still frightfully confused and upset and all. For God's sake don't work yourself up to another pitch, old man. I'm not strong enough to stand it."

"Pitch, me eye," muttered Tim. "I'd like to pitch you out in the middle of the aisle. That's what you deserve."

"Don't do it," pleaded Mr. Bentley. "I beg of you not to do it. You should be grateful to me for freeing you from the stigma of murder."

"I have your thick skull to thank for that."

"Yet the skull belongs to me."

"But you're not responsible for its thickness."

"Then you can't blame me for that."

"For what?"

Mr. Bentley looked perplexed.

"I don't quite know myself," he replied. "I seem to have lost the thread."

"Damn if I know what we're talking about," said Tim Willows. "Don't let's talk."

"Perhaps it would be better," agreed Carl Bentley. "Then you won't work yourself up to a pitch."

"That doesn't matter at all," snapped Mr. Willows. "I can work myself up to a pitch whether I talk or not."

"Try not to," murmured Bentley soothingly. "Be calm. You don't look at all well."

"Is that so?" retorted Mr. Willows brightly. "Well, you look fit for a hospital, yourself—you and your stomach-ripping sighs."

"Better that than an inquest," said Carl Bentley significantly.

With an inner tremor Tim turned back to the window and allowed Carl Bentley to have the last word. The man was right. His, Tim's, escape had been a narrow one. Just an ounce or two more energy behind Mrs. Twill's time-honored rolling pin and he would be sitting there a full-fledged murderer, a murderer with hardly any prospects of escape. Sick as he was he still felt that it was good to be at large and alive. Accordingly it was a greatly relieved Mr. Willows who dismissed Carl Bentley with a wave of his hand at the station and made his way up Park Avenue to the office building in which the Nationwide Advertising, Inc. awaited whatever it might devour.

The layout of this flourishing establishment was designed to submerge the ego of the most arrogant of mortals. If any caller chanced to have a wee bit of an inferiority complex lurking about his sytem the atmosphere of this place immediately brought it to full bloom. On entering the offices a prospective client who had been prepared to spend fifty thousand dollars in advertising hastily decided to spend at least fifty thousand more for fear of being snubbed by the reception clerk, cut by the office boy, and sneered at by the president's secretary.

Everything was gorgeous. Everything was superior. Rich leather, subdued lighting, and wrought-iron work merged themselves into endless vistas of harmonious opulence relieved here and there by a slightly exotic touch of color. One gained the impression that unlike almost any other kind of writing the creation of advertisements required an environment of ease and refinement.

It was into this environment that Tim Willows stepped, feeling neither at ease nor consciously refined.

"Good-morning, baby," he said to a gorgeous girl at a gorgeous desk. "I'd like to use the lounge in your rest room if none of the girls objects."

"You're not a good man, Mr. Willows," she told him. "You're a bad, bad man. I'm sorry about you."

"Then give me a spot of something, sweetheart, or I'll die right here before your eyes on this lousily gorgeous Persian rug."

The girl gave him a critical look, then, opening a drawer in her desk, hastily poured some whiskey from a pint flask into a paper cup, which she passed to Tim.

"Go over to the cooler," she said in level tones, "and pretend you're getting a drink of water."

"Thanks," answered Tim, eagerly seizing the cup. "I already know the technique thoroughly."

He tossed off the drink, crumpled up the evidence, and accepted a mint tablet from his calm-eyed benefactress.

"I wouldn't have done that for everyone," she told him.

"And you're quite right, too," agreed Tim Willows. "The rest of these copy writers are a lot of dogs. Don't have a thing to do with them. Don't give them an inch. Just me."

"Don't hang around here any longer," she said. "You look like the devil to-day. I wish you'd behave yourself for a couple of months. Better pretend you have a bad cold."

When he had gone the girl gazed musingly at the spot where he had been.

"All the interesting ones get married," she thought, "and all of the interesting ones are bad, thoroughly bad. He isn't really bad, though. He just doesn't understand about morals. He's too good for this place. He doesn't belong here."

Meanwhile Tim, no little resuscitated, tossed his hat and coat at a friendly office boy and joined a file of his confreres making its way into the conference room.

"What's up?" he asked Steve Jones. "Are we praying for rain and prosperity this morning?"

"Same old thing," replied Steve bitterly. "Just talk, talk, talk. The Old Man's getting gaga. Damned if I know what it's all about. You've been drinking."

He looked at Tim with an enviously accusing eye.

"Lots," agreed that gentleman. "I've been through a great deal, Steve. Altogether too much."

"And you're going through a lot more," muttered Steve, "before he's finished with us."

They passed into the handsomely appointed conference room and found seats at a long table, at the end of which stood Mr. Gibber beaming good-morningly.

Mr. Gibber was a large man. He gave one the impression of being almost too large a man. He had a large, well-fed face coated with an expensively acquired tan. Mr. Gibber collected tans. He brought them back with him from diverse parts of the globe he so ornately decorated. He brought back his tans from

Bermuda, from Florida, and from various sections of the Riviera.

"There's nothing like travel," he would tell various members of his staff, "to keep a man physically fit and mentally alert. I wish we could all run across to the Continent at least once a year. But everything comes with time—with time and hard work."

"How true," Tim had once replied to this optimistic utterance. "Even death itself. You know, Mr. Gibber, they tell me that all good Americans go to Paris when they die. Perhaps that's how we'll get there."

Mr. Gibber was not amused.

And Mr. Gibber had hands. Large, brown hands that he rubbed and rerubbed. He was always immaculately dressed, impeccably manicured, and crisply groomed. It was almost as if he wanted to prove to the world that he was a clean man with nice, neat habits.

Tim regarded the man with something akin to affectionate contempt, and Mr. Gibber returned his gaze with the tolerance of one who realized it was in his power to discharge the impertinent young puppy on the spot. As he looked at the gentlemen seated round the table Mr. Gibber's eyes seemed to be saying, "I bought that new tie for you. Those socks are indirectly mine. And you there, down at the end, had it not been for me you'd never have got that suit of clothes. You're all mine, the whole lot of you, down to your very drawers."

However, he greeted them all with what he fondly believed to be just the right balance of benign paternalism and presidential authority. Behind his most sunny words there always seemed to lurk the suggestion of a sudden cold snap with thin days ahead. He played, for all there was in it, the part of the upper dog.

"Gentlemen," he began this morning. "Fellow workers in this vast organization. Men of the Nationwide Advertising Agency—and that includes you, Miss Meades, ha ha, ahem—hope you don't mind—where was I? Oh, yes—co-creators of national prosperity," Mr. Gibber's voice dropped impressively, "We must not waste words. Words are valuable. The flashing wings of thought. We must not waste them."

Mr. Gibber then proceeded to give a loquacious dissertation on the virtues of brevity. Leaning far over the table on which his hands were spread, he swayed slightly from the vibrations of his powerfully controlled emotions.

"Nationwide Advertising Agency," he repeated with almost sinister intensity. "Men, do you get the full significance of that? Do you realize what it means—nation wide—those two words? Do you grasp it?" Here Mr. Gibber grasped it, opened his clenched fingers and examined it, then, with a forceful gesture, flung it rather rudely in the faces of his listeners. "It means this exactly," he continued with awful calmness. "Take the nation in all its length. Take the nation in all its breadth. Take the nation in all its thickness." He looked piercingly round to assure himself that everyone had taken the nation in the manner he had suggested. "Then take this organization," he went on. "Take it in all its ramifications and superimpose it upon the nation. It means, men, putting the two together, that we're just as wide as it. Sitting here in this gorgeously appointed room we are exactly as wide as America. Hence our name—the Nationwide Advertising Agency."

Mr. Gibber sat down with disconcerting suddenness and tried to look exactly as wide as the nation. He very nearly succeeded. He did look almost as thick. In the face of such a huge conception the members of his staff appeared considerably shrunken. Having achieved the desired effect and for certain reasons of policy having to do with the discouraging of requests for raises it now pleased Mr. Gibber to look both severe and injured.

"Now, gentlemen," he resumed, rising to his feet and towering above them, "I hate to say it. I'm actually ashamed to say it, but I fear, I very much fear, all of you have been wasting words. Mr. Bunce informs me that of late the copy mortality has been alarmingly high." Pause. "Dangerously high." Another pause. "Disgracefully high." A most portentous pause. "This can't go on. There will have to be changes. You have ceased to look for the fundamental idea upon which every campaign and every piece of copy in that campaign should be based and must be based. Words have been wasted—squandered shamefully. You have done it, this thing."

Like criminals the men of the Nationwide Advertising Agency looked at the outraged Gibber, then accusingly at one another. Who had been wasting all those words? Who had been squandering Mr. Gibber's most precious commodity? Tim Willows felt that he could do with a great deal less of what was going on. His head was full of rebellious thoughts and stale fumes of gin. Surely this man Gibber deserved to be murdered most brutally and finally. There was no justification for his continued presence on earth. The man was speaking again. He had them all at his mercy. Tim groaned spiritually as well as physically.

"Men," resumed Mr. Gibber, "brevity is the breath of conviction, terseness the bone, and briskness the blood."

He interrupted himself at this point to jot down a note about his last utterance. It was good, he thought. Good enough for that book he was writing, that sensational book showing how Christianity had been handicapped and its rapid spread retarded because the Nationwide Advertising Agency had not been in existence during the time of Christ. His note finished, Mr. Gibber fixed the table with a threatening eye.

"Now listen to me," he said slowly and distinctly. "I want more punch in your copy. I want more hooks and"—he pawed the air as if sifting it for the right word—"I want more pith."

Mr. Gibber's last want almost finished Tim Willows. He fixed the man with round, incredulous eyes and asked in his blandest manner: "You want more what, sir?"

Mr. Gibber hesitated, then faced the situation like a man.

"I said pith," he replied with painful distinctness. "I want more pith. I must have more pith."

"You mean the stuff that goes into helmets?" Tim continued innocently.

Mr. Gibber's thoughts were somewhat confused. Tim's unexpected question had thrown him off his stride.

"What do you mean?" demanded Gibber gropingly. "Only heads go into helmets."

"I know," said Tim. "Only heads should go into helmets, but lots of things could go into them, things like pith and all."

"How should I know what goes into helmets?" asked the exasperated Mr. Gibber. "Why should I care what goes into helmets?"

"Oh, of course," replied Tim in a hurt voice. "I didn't know you felt so strongly on the subject. Let's say no more about helmets."

"I don't know why anything was said about them in the first place," said Mr. Gibber, striving to control himself.

"It was in connection with the word 'pith,'" observed Tim helpfully. "We were just wondering if it went into helmets."

"Do I understand you to say that I was wondering whether pith went into helmets or not?" asked Mr. Gibber.

"And heads," added Tim.

"But of course heads go into helmets," said Mr. Gibber. "That's what they're for."

"I hope you don't think I didn't know that," replied Tim, laughing deprecatingly.

"But I made no implication that you didn't know what went into helmets," said Gibber.

"Of course I do," answered Tim brightly. "We all know. It's heads. Not pith, but heads. Did your head ever go into a helmet, Mr. Gibber?"

The good man was immediately mollified. His vanity was stimulated. It pleased him to be regarded as an extensively traveled person.

"Time and time again," he replied. "As a matter of fact I have one at home right now."

"And is there any pith in it?" asked Tim hopefully.

Mr. Gibber's tan took on an apoplectic glow.

"I don't," he replied in a voice choked with emotion, "I don't know what's in that helmet, and frankly, Mr. Willows, I don't give a damn." He took a deep breath and added, "Will you excuse me, Miss Meades?"

"Do you mean you want to leave the room for a minute?" asked that young lady innocently.

"What!" ejaculated Mr. Gibber. "And why should I leave the room?"

"Mr. Gibber," said Miss Meades reprovingly, then lowered her eyes in confusion.

"You don't understand, Miss Meades," Tim explained politely. "Mr. Gibber doesn't want to leave the room. He doesn't need to leave the room. That is, I don't think so. He was——"

"I didn't say he needed to leave the room," Miss Meades interrupted hotly. "If he needed to leave the room I hope he'd have sense enough to go."

"Of course he has," answered Tim soothingly. "He knows when he needs to go."

"Well, I need to go right now," gasped Steve Jones. "Excuse me a minute. Must telephone to a client."

Mr. Gibber was looking at the table with appalled eyes. Was it possible they were making sport of him? Willows was at the bottom of it all. Willows was responsible. How in God's name had the situation got so out of hand? It was like a bad dream.

"It's all right, Mr. Gibber," he heard Tim saying in an encouraging voice. "She knows now that you don't need to leave the room and that you were simply asking her pardon for using a lot of bad language. Funny how things crop up like that—helmets and pith and leaving the room and all. Really, it's quite confusing. Where were we, Mr. Gibber?"

"Where were we?" repeated that gentleman, wearily passing a hand across his eyes. "I hardly know where we are much less where we were."

"It had something to do with brevity," supplied Tim. "It was all very interesting even though most of the others didn't seem to understand it."

"I understood every word he said," stoutly declared Miss Meades. "Even about leaving the room."

"Certainly you did," put in Tim pacifically, "Mr. Gibber isn't so childish. He'd never do a thing like that."

"Like what?" snapped Miss Meades in a stubborn voice.

Tim looked at the girl with admiring eyes.

"Well, I wouldn't like to say," he hedged. "Hadn't you better ask Mr. Gibber?"

"Don't ask me a thing," Mr. Gibber shouted. "I won't listen to another word."

"He doesn't like to talk about it," explained Tim. "You know how it is. Nobody does. No gentleman, that is."

"But I will talk about it," Mr. Gibber cut in. "I'll talk about it as much as I like."

"Is that quite necessary?" inquired Miss Meades, elevating her eyebrows.

"Yes, by God, it is," gritted the president of the Nationwide Advertising Agency. "It's necessary for my sanity. It's nobody's business whether I need to leave the room or not. And if I do need to leave the room—which I don't—I'll get right up and walk out of the room and stay as long as I like."

"What did I tell you?" said Tim triumphantly to the table. "He knows how to act."

Miss Meades turned on him with battle in her usually calm eyes.

"I won't let you put me in a false light," she retorted. "From the way you go on one would get the impression that I deliberately accused Mr. Gibber of not knowing when he needed to leave the room. I meant no such thing. I know he isn't a baby and furthermore——"

"Stop!" cried Mr. Gibber. "For God's sake, stop! I must put my foot down somewhere. This can't go on."

"Certainly not," agreed Tim sympathetically. "Of all things."

Mr. Gibber cleared his throat and once more flattened his hands on the surface of the table. With an earnest eye he searched the faces confronting him. He would win his listeners back.

"Boys," he addressed them this time, playing the part of just a pal. "Boys," he repeated, then his expression underwent a startling change. "Oh, dear," he muttered. "Now I do have to leave the room."

And leave the room he did, very rapidly and without looking back.

Miss Meades made a face and thrust out a small, red tongue at Tim Willows.

"Smarty," she said. "Mr. Know-it-all. He did need to leave the room all the time."

"I'm sure I don't know what you're talking about," Tim told her with tremendous dignity. "I attribute the man's strange conduct to nothing more nor less than the power of suggestion."

"Which means," retorted the girl, "that he needed to leave the room."

"You win," said Tim.

CHAPTER V

The Malicious Magic of Mr. Ram

MR. GIBBER DID NOT RETURN TO THE CONFERENCE ROOM. Few men would have in the face of such overwhelming odds. Instead, he sought the privacy of his office in which he did some highly concentrated fuming. Gibber's skin was thick but not impenetrable. Tim Willows and that Meades girl had done terrible things to him that morning. He would not forget the pair. When the trees began to fall they would be the first to go.

Meanwhile the conference, relieved of the presence of its presiding officer, was rapidly assuming the aspect of a meeting of convivial friends from which those earnest spirits in whose nostrils advertising was the very breath of life promptly disassociated themselves amid the maledictions of the harder-boiled.

Tim Willows and Miss Meades were among the last to leave. They decided it was no more than their duty to await the return of Mr. Gibber. They were conscientious about it. While so doing there was nothing to prevent them from discussing the more important things of life such as books and plays and places to go and the numerous persons they disliked. It was a quiet, restful morning and Tim was both surprised and delighted to discover upon consulting his watch that it was time to be doing something about luncheon. Accordingly he took Dolly Meades to a lunch club at which they prolonged the conference well into the afternoon. Tim drank ale, which Dolly was unable to stomach. She had to be satisfied with rye. And she was. Back at the office Tim spent the remainder of the afternoon listening to the bedtime stories of several newspaper and magazine representatives, all of whom displayed a sort of well-bred pride in the quality and size of the circulations of their respective publications.

In this manner Tim passed his last day, had he but known it, at the Nationwide Advertising Agency, an organization to which he had already given almost all of his self-respect in return for just sufficient money to enable him to exist in comparative ease, what with buying things on time.

Sally did not meet him at the station, but she was waiting for him at the door. As a matter of fact, when he opened it she almost popped out of the house.

"It's gone!" were her first words, her eyes round and fearful.

"What's gone?" asked Tim, his mind on other matters, chief among which was the possibility of getting a drink.

"The body," replied Sally. "It's gone. It's not there."

Tim then deliberately did a little husbandly tormenting.

"What are you talking about?" he demanded. "Whose body has gone where?"

"Don't be dull," continued Sally sharply. "The body in the bin. The body of the man you murdered in cold blood. The body you struck down in its prime."

"Oh, that body," exclaimed Tim comprehendingly. "That body never had any prime."

"Well, it would have had a prime if you hadn't struck it down," retorted Sally.

"How do you know that?" her husband asked. "Some bodies never have any prime."

"Yours, for example," said Sally. "Your withered mean, little rat of a body."

"Come, come," protested Tim Willows. "That's no way to refer to your husband's body. Why, only last night you were swearing to high heaven you were never going to have anything to do with anyone's body save the one you are now so harshly criticizing."

"Well, prime or no prime," said Sally, "I've got to make the best of it such as it is."

"You mean the most of it," he told her crisply. "And I do wish you'd stop referring to my body as if it were a rather questionable rib of beef. Now tell me about this other body. You seem to miss it. Do you want it back in the bin? I should think the disappearance of that long lugubrious stiff has saved us no end of mental anguish, not to mention unremunerative labor."

"I know," she said, "but we can't have a dead body knocking about the streets. People will begin to talk."

Tim laughed shortly.

"I suppose they'll criticize us for not knowing how to entertain a dead body," he remarked. "Well, if that dead body has left my bed and board I wash my hands of all further responsibility for it. It's not my dead body if it goes visiting neighbors."

"But suppose it hasn't gone visiting?" asked Sally in a hushed voice. "Suppose it tries to crawl in bed with one of us to-night? That's what's burning me up."

"Then it will be a doubly dead body," said Tim, who, having diverted himself of his hat and overcoat, was strolling in the direction of a cocktail shaker gleaming cheerfully on the sideboard. "By the way," he called back casually over his shoulders, "that dead body rather intimated to me that he mistook my bed for yours this morning."

"The nerve of the thing," said Sally, then, suddenly grasping the full significance of Tim's remark, she asked, "What do you mean by that, you grub?"

"Nothing," the other replied. "Merely that the grub rode into the city this morning in the poisonous company of that dead body."

"What!" gasped Sally. "Do you mean the body has taken up traveling?"

"Just that," returned the other. "The body was most unappreciatively alive. Only the body, though, for as you yourself know, it never did have any brain."

Sally sank down in a chair and considered this new situation. The dead body of Mr. Bentley was one thing. His live body was quite another.

"A body like that doesn't need any brain," she said at last. "Make it snappy with that cocktail, you shadow of a midget."

Tim rang for Peter and immediately that aged creature appeared. He was small, sharp, and unbent, and he gave the impression of having been kept too long in front of a drying machine. He had swapped all of his hair with the years in exchange for a face full of wrinkles. From somewhere near the center of this complicated system a thin hooked nose projected itself and on either side of this object two small eyes glittered as brightly as a thieving sparrow's. Peter had a way of swinging his arms at his sides as if he were keeping them in readiness for immediate action. Unlike the majority of domestics, he enjoyed being summoned to duty. If Tim did not call for him in the course of an evening he would invent an excuse to call on Tim, because, as he expressed it, Mr. Tim was his personal responsibility with whom he had spent many pleasant days in the past when both of them had been a whole lot younger.

Tim now fumbled in his vest pocket and produced three cigars, the day's gleanings from the visiting representatives.

"Here's your share, Peter," he said, extending them to the old man. "They look pretty good to-night. Better than usual."

Peter subjected each cigar to the expert examination of his nose, then permitted himself a smile of appreciation.

"Fifteen cents straight, at least," he gloated. "This one looks like a quarter. I shall smoke them, Mr. Tim."

"I know damn well you will," said Tim. "but in the meantime can you do a little something helpful about orange juice and ice?"

When the shaker had ceased its shaking and the cocktails had been poured, Tim turned to Sally.

"I don't know whether I'm to be congratulated or not," he told her, "but the fact is I don't happen to be a murderer any more. It all comes from not putting on enough coal. That body came to life some time after we went to bed, finished off a bottle of gin, and went barging drunkenly about the house before it went home."

"Was it—I mean, was he—in great pain?" asked Sally a little timidly.

"Yes," said Tim complacently, delicately moistening his lips at the rim of the glass. "He was in excruciating pain. Agony, I'd call it. I made him feel even worse."

"You would, you scorpion," his wife replied. "Does he know all the things that happened to him—the part I played?"

"Not yet," he smiled. "I'm saving that for some future occasion, my dear little accessory after the fact."

Sally remained thoughtfully silent.

Because of a great lassitude induced by the high revelry and nervous tension of the previous night the Willowses did not linger long in the lounge after dinner had been served. Dopey appeared footily for a brief review of the events of the day, which he immediately forgot upon suspecting the presence of a few pieces of candy concealed in a bowl. After mouthing these individually and collectively he discovered they were not so good. Accordingly he left them messily on the rug and clumped back to his box in the kitchen and the soothing conversation of Mr. and Mrs. Twill. Tim and Sally proceeded to their room, where they became busy about going to bed. Tim was always a little puzzled at the speed and ease with which Sally completed these preparations. At one moment she would be fully clad, at the next there would be just Sally, unadorned, then amazingly she would appear decked out in some tricky nightgown all set for the sheets. Tim decided that she must wear practically no clothes at all to be able to disrobe with such breath-taking precision and dispatch. For him the business of getting undressed was a long, involved, and laborious one necessitating no end of searching for this thing and that. The good Mrs. Twill believed in putting everything in some place but preferably not in the same place twice if a new one could be found. To-night, for example, he eventually found his slippers resting on a row of books on the lowest shelf of the bookcase. It was a good place, he had to admit, a splendid place, but then any place would have been good had he but known where it was. Thus cogitating on the strange ways of Sally and Mrs. Twill he came at last to his socks, and at this point he seemed to run down. After a few tentative pluckings his fingers ceased to work. He was thinking of Claire Meadows and wondering what she was thinking. That had been a queer experience, too. Like a song growing fainter in a swiftly fading dream. It seemed quite apart from life and the ordinary affairs of life. It was as if Time had suddenly remembered a moment it had forgotten to give him and had tossed it back at random. It could never be recaptured. He knew that, and strangely enough he was not disappointed.

"Tim," he heard Sally saying, and her voice sounded grimly determined, "if you don't stop doddering over those socks I'll come over there and drag them off."

"So you feel as strongly about it as that, do you?" replied Tim Willows, looking at her with a slow, irritating smile. "Well, what I want to know is, why should I take off these socks?"

"It's customary to take off one's socks before going to bed," his wife replied with withering dignity. "Gentlemen don't sleep in their socks."

"How do you know that?" Tim shot back. "From the way you talk one would gain the impression that you'd made a life study of sleeping gentlemen. Thousands of gentlemen are sleeping in their socks every night of the year. Sleeping in everything—clothes and all, even their hats. And here's another thing. These socks are my socks and these feet are my feet and that bed is my bed. If I want to take these feet, clad in these socks, and tuck them into that bed I don't see that it's anyone's business save my own. What do you say to that?"

"I have nothing to say to that," replied Sally. "Nothing at all. Just the same, you and your socks constitute a form of mental torture that would fully justify a divorce in any enlightened community. You're so gross, so utterly common. You—you revolt me, you and your socks and your shirt and your thin flanks and——"

"My toes," interrupted Tim hotly. "Go on and pick on my toes. Say things about my toes. Your own toes are so damn crooked you look as if you were walking backward."

"That's a lie," said Sally, deeply insulted. "I have perfect toes and you know it. Take a look at other women's toes and see what scrambled monstrosities they are."

"I don't keep my eyes on the ground under such circumstances," said Tim virtuously.

"No doubt you don't," said his wife, "you lecherous little animal man."

"If anyone overheard this conversation," remarked Tim bitterly, "they wouldn't believe it possible. They'd put you down as mad."

"And I suppose you'd be considered an abused husband," said Sally, with elaborate sarcasm.

"That's stating it mildly," answered Tim. "All day long I've been working at the office, standing on windswept platforms and traveling on badly ventilated trains with the body of a man I almost murdered. I'm tired. I'm unstrung. I'm in a highly nervous condition. And all you can do is to throw my socks in my face."

"I think more of your socks than to throw them in that face," said Sally. "You'd bite a hole in 'em and swear I did it."

"Speaking figuratively," continued Tim in a weary voice. "You should know when I'm speaking figuratively."

"You're such a liar," broke in his wife, "that one never can tell just how you're speaking."

"And with the knowledge of murder in my heart," continued Tim as if he had not heard her. "I get up in the morning and carry on. I go to the office, by God, and put in a full day's work. Catch any other husband doing it. And you talk about socks."

"Exactly," Sally hastened to answer. "You wouldn't catch any other husband doing it, not even the lowest. You murder a man in the evening and the first thing in the morning you rush out of the house, leaving a dead body on my hands. How would you like to be cooped up in the house all day with a dead body? Pleasant, isn't it? Lovely."

"Why didn't you take a walk?" he demanded.

"And leave the dead body behind?" asked Sally.

"You couldn't very well have taken it with you," replied Tim. "And certainly a dead body doesn't demand much in the way of entertainment. You don't have to play games with a dead body."

Mr. Ram on the bookcase was rapidly losing patience. This constant, futile bickering was doing things to his usually tolerant and friendly disposition. He felt like taking the two of them and knocking their heads together. They deserved even less considerate treatment than that. Upon hearing Sally's next contribution the little man decided to go the limit.

"You and your work and your stuffy trains," she was saying. "It's a lot of bunk. Horses couldn't have held you in this house. I'll bet you didn't draw an easy breath until you shut the door behind you. I guess you know what I mean now when I say I'd be glad to change places with you. I wish I could. I'm tired of being left alone in this house with dead bodies and clownish dogs and doddering old people who might die on my hands at any minute and add to the dead bodies. I want to change——"

"I daresay I'll come home some night and see you sitting on top of a pile of dead bodies," remarked Tim. "You'll be literally swimming in dead bodies. And by the way, lay off that dog of mine. He's far from clownish. I'd like to change places with you if only for the pleasure of being able to stay home and keep him company. He's a damn sight more agreeable than you."

"That settles it," said Mr. Ram to himself. "I'll have to take steps this very night."

"Then why don't you go and sleep with your dog?" Sally demanded. "You're just like a dog, yourself. You've got no more shame than a dog. Might as well sleep like a dog."

"I wouldn't talk about sleep if I were in your place," said Tim. "You're a horrid sloth yourself."

"I'm not going to talk about sleep," answered Sally. "I'm going to do it. Keep your damn socks on and your great mouth shut. Good-night!"

"Sweet woman," observed Tim Willows as he watched, with a feeling of defeat, his wife curl herself up in bed.

"Miserable little man," she murmured, and that was the last word. It was all Sally's.

Mr. Ram, however, won the last trick.

The slumber of this happily married couple was troubled that night by strangely realistic dreams. Vague and intangible figures seemed to be flitting noiselessly about the room. There was much peering into faces, and Tim got the impression that his body was being critically inspected. Sally later admitted that she had experienced the same feeling. And through all these dreams and dim imaginings the figure of Mr. Ram was inextricably woven. The little man had grown to full stature and appeared to be directing the activities of the other figures that peopled the darkness. Occasionally he would pause to exchange a few words with a group of Egyptian friends and at such times Tim distinctly saw Mr. Ram's white teeth bared in a malicious smile. Once or twice when the god glanced over at the twin beds Tim could have sworn he heard a subdued chuckle. Then amazingly the figures melted away and in his dream Tim saw Mr. Ram returning to his former size on the bookcase. It was all disturbingly vague and confusing. So much so, in fact, that Sally for the first time in her life woke up before her husband and immediately appropriated the bathroom, knowing full well that this would irritate him beyond measure and precipitate a morning row.

A few minutes later the sound of running water brought Tim back to consciousness. He sat up with a start, glanced suspiciously at the figure of Mr. Ram, who seemed to have changed his position during the night, then promptly rolled out of bed. Stripping off his shirt he stood before a pier-glass mirror to ascertain if his body was as ill-favored as Sally so eloquently made it out to be. The moment he did so he received a decided shock. In some manner unknown to him his wife had managed to get to the mirror first. He had not seen her do it, yet nevertheless there she was, standing in front of him and cutting off his view of himself.

"Please get out of the way," he told her irritably. "I can't see a thing of myself. And, furthermore, you're a nice person to be talking about nakedness. Here you are flaunting yourself totally nude in front of this mirror. You should be ashamed."

He was surprised at the sound of his own voice. It was unnaturally soft and had a distinctly feminine quality in it. He cleared his throat and tried again.

"Go on out of here," he said. "I've got to get to my office."

The woman seemed to be mocking him silently. Every time he opened his mouth to speak she very cleverly mimicked the movements of his lips.

"How childish of you," Tim exclaimed, and was petrified on the spot by a wild cry issuing from the bathroom.

"What the hell!" began Mr. Willows, then said no more.

A figure looking strangely like himself came dashing out of the bathroom as if pursued by all the devils in hell.

"Oh, look!" chattered the figure in a voice reminiscent of his wife's.

Tim looked incredulously at the figure before him, then quickly surveyed his own body. The sight that met his eyes almost unhinged his reason.

"My God!" he gasped. "Oh, my God! What has happened to us, or are we both going mad?"

"Oh-h-h, I don't know," breathed the other. "It all seems terrible to me. Here I stand talking to myself and yet I am you—you to the last detail. I can't stand it, I tell you, I can't stand it."

"Well, I suppose you think I'm tickled to death to be occupying your body," said Tim. "How do you fancy I feel?"

She looked ruefully at the body of which she had been so mysteriously deprived, and her heart sank.

"I had such a beautiful figure," she murmured. "And now you've got it. I suppose you'll put that silly-looking shirt on it when you go to bed at night?"

"No," replied Tim triumphantly, "I'm going to wear your best and most expensive night dresses."

"What!" exclaimed Sally. "You're going to start in wearing my clothes?"

"Naturally," replied Tim. "Do you want me to make your body look ridiculous? You don't seem to realize that in the eyes of the world I am you."

Tim was treated to the unnerving experience of seeing his own body wringing its hands.

"Oh, this is just terrible," moaned Sally. "It's the worst thing that ever happened. You won't know how to wear anything and you'll make me look all sloppy and probably end up by becoming a loose woman."

Tim laughed hatefully.

"You know what I'm going to do?" he asked. "I'm going to torture Carl Bentley. I think he deserves it."

"You leave that man alone," cried Sally furiously. "Keep your hands off him and be careful what you do with my body. First thing you know you'll be presenting me with a nameless child. I could never bear that."

This thought sobered Tim Willows. He was truly in an extremely precarious position. Once he had been able to take his chances with the best of them, but now if he slipped from the path of virtue he would have to be continually worrying about the consequences. This was a most disagreeable realization. It wasn't fair. What a devil of a thing to have happened to a full-grown man! And how the devil could it have happened? Tim very much wanted his body back.

"You won't have to bear it," he said slowly. "I'd have to bear it. Wouldn't that be awful?"

"I don't see why," replied Sally. "I think it would be just dandy. It would teach you what women have to go through in this world. Please put something on my body and try to hold it a little better. I can't stand seeing the poor thing the way it is."

She passed Tim her abandoned night dress and that shrinking creature allowed it to be draped over his nakedness. The ordeal proved too much for him. He sank down on the bed and refused to meet his wife's eyes.

"I've never been so ashamed of myself in all my life," he murmured. "To think of me in this." He plucked at the diaphanous material with nervous fingers. "In this of all things."

"You're the living image of myself," said Sally, sitting down beside him and slipping an arm round his waist. "You certainly are a sweet little thing. I think you're about the most attractive woman I've seen in years."

"Take your arm away from me," gasped Tim in a strangled voice. "And for God's sake, don't be common. I'll stand for no monkey business. The sooner you know that the better."

He sprang to his feet and stood looking down at himself with outraged eyes. Then something occurred that humiliated him to the very depth of his being. Sally picked him up in her arms and tossed him back on the bed.

"I'll settle your hash later," she said, and swaggered over to the mirror. After gazing into it for a moment she turned to the rumpled figure on the bed. "This vapid face of yours needs a shave terribly. What are we going to do about that?"

"Don't give a damn what you do about it," came gloomily from the bed. "You can cut the face to ribbons if you like. It isn't any good to me any more."

"Well, as bad as it is," replied Sally, "it's the only face I have and I'm certainly not going to allow whiskers to grow all over it."

"I wish you'd stop talking about my face as if it were a mere thing," Tim almost sobbed. "It was always a good face to me. If you don't take care of it I'll make such a fright of yours that babies will have convulsions and mothers will pass out the moment they clap eyes on me. You'll hear people saying, 'that hideous Willows woman.'"

"You'd never do a thing like that," said Sally in a shocked voice. "I'll hang this body of yours in the attic."

"I will if you're not mighty good to my face," replied Tim, "and put in a new blade."

"Oh, I'll be good to your face," promised Sally. "I'm going to try to try to improve it. God knows there's enough room."

Tim sat suddenly up in the bed and looked at his watch on the night table.

"Cripes!" he exclaimed. "You'll be late at the office. Hurry up and get dressed."

"What! Me go to your office?" Tim's former face was starched with amazement.

"Who else?" he demanded. "I can't go. You've got to carry on. We can't starve, you know."

"Do you mean that I actually have to go to work, catch trains and be on time and all that?"

"Certainly," replied Tim, beginning to enjoy the situation.

"But Tim," protested Sally. "I don't know the first thing about it. I've never written a word of copy and I won't even know the people at the office."

"You'll catch on quickly enough," said Tim reassuringly. "Luckily I'm working on a chain of women's shops at present. You'll probably be able to write that copy a whole lot better than I could. And just pretend you know everybody. Be particularly nice to the girl at the desk and also to Dolly Meades. They're pals of mine. Also Steve Jones."

"How pally are you with the two women?" asked Sally.

"Not consummated," said Tim briefly.

"Then I'll consummate," replied Sally.

"Lucky dog," observed Tim. "And they'll blame it all on me."

"But it is you," said Sally. "I'm only inside."

"Yes," remarked Tim moodily, "and the trouble is you haven't any gentlemanly instincts. You'll do the first woman dirt who comes your way."

"You shouldn't be so irresistibly attractive," explained Sally. "It won't be my fault."

"I have always exercised remarkable self-control," Tim told her. "And that's more than you will do."

"I'm exercising it right now," said Sally, looking darkly at the figure on the bed. "I've a good mind to have my will with you, young lady."

"Don't!" pleaded Tim. "Don't! Even in fun it's too much."

"So that's what you think of yourself," said the other with a sneer. "Do you wonder I've been revolted?"

"I'm all right," replied Tim. "Only thing is, I haven't gotten used to being you yet, that's all."

"Then you'd better make it snappy," replied Sally. "Remember, from now on, I am the dominant male."

But by the time Sally had got herself shaved and dressed she no longer felt quite so dominant. Her mind was full of misgivings. She was loath to face the world alone.

"I just can't go to your office," she protested, sinking down in a chair. "I won't know what to do or what to say or anything. I'll just be a mess."

"But that's what you've been claiming all along you wanted," replied Tim gloatingly. "Every night of your life you've kept dinning in my ears how much you'd like to change places with me. Well, now you've got your wish. Make the most of it."

"Tim," said Sally in an awed voice, "that must be it. We've kept wishing to change places with each other so long that someone has granted our wish. Only they've let us retain our personalities so we'll know exactly what's happened. Wonder who could have done this thing?"

"I rather suspect Mr. Ram," Tim replied slowly. "There's a funny look about him this morning and I seem to remember having met him in my dreams last night."

"So do I," exclaimed Sally. "I recall him now quite distinctly."

For the first time since they had owned him Mr. Ram refused to meet their gaze. His position was changed so that he now stood looking innocently out of the window at the house across the way.

"I guess we had it coming to us," remarked Tim. "God knows you wished it often enough."

"Who wouldn't," said Sally, "if they had to live with a creature like you?"

"Go on, get to your office," answered Tim, crawling back into bed. "I'm going to have a nice, lazy drowse. And by the way, you'd better try to do something about your voice. You sound awfully ladylike. Speak from your chest like I do."

"But you shouldn't speak from your chest."

"Then I'll practise feminine elocution while you work hard at the office," Tim replied, yawning lazily.

Sally stamped over to the bed and stood there looking down at him.

"Do you mean to say," she demanded, "that you're going to lie there in that bed and let me go out to work for you, you worm?"

"Why not?" inquired Tim. "Isn't that just exactly what I did?"

"And you're not even enough of a gentleman to drive me down to the station?" she continued.

"Certainly not," replied Tim smilingly. "I'm not supposed to be a gentleman. You never drove me down. You've changed places with me and got exactly what you've been asking for—now make the best of it."

"Then do you know what I'm going to do?" she demanded in a voice cold with fury. "I'm going to give you a baby and I hope it's twins. You just wait and see if I don't."

"I won't be the mother of your children if I have to hang myself," declared Tim. "I'll jump in the river first."

Sally paused at the door. She was laughing to herself.

"Then you'll have to do one or the other," she told him, "because I'm going to do you in. You just wait."

"Get to your office," shouted Tim, white with anger. "And I won't be here when you get back. Remember that."

"Good!" exclaimed Sally. "I'll call up one of your conquests and get her to come over."

"And I'll divorce you flat," threatened Tim. "I'll drag your name through the mud."

"It's your own name you'll be dragging," said Sally. "Don't forget that." She paused and blew him a kiss. "See you later, cutie."

The howl of a maddened animal followed her down the hall. The terrible sound died away and the person who had once been Tim Willows lay chattering on the bed. He was not going to be a mother. He was dead sure of that.

"Damn you, Ram," he muttered. "You dog-faced Egyptian crook."

CHAPTER VI

Tim Tries to Be a Lady

AFTER THE DEPARTURE OF SALLY IN WHAT HAD RE-
cently been his body Tim Willows found himself unable to enjoy that nice lazy drowse he had anticipated.
He could not even entertain the idea. He got out of bed
and forced himself to a shrinking inspection of his
newly acquired anatomy.

"If I know anything at all about women," he decided
at last, "I certainly am one. There's no getting away
from the fact. And the worst of it is I'm supposed to
act like a woman. If I fail to act like a woman I'll be
disgracing my own name. Too bad I'm so blastedly for-
getful. I'm sure to break out at some critical moment
and make a mess of it all."

This line of thought naturally brought him to the
problem of his voice. At present it sounded like a voice
that was still undecided whether to become a grunt or
a squeak. It was neither one thing nor the other, being
too deep for a woman's and too high for a man's. Sitting on the edge of his bed he industriously practised
the art of vocal elevation.

"This is about the silliest thing I've ever done," he
observed moodily to himself as he listened critically to
the peculiar sounds issuing from his lips.

"Good-afternoon, my dear," he heard himself saying. "What a perfectly sweet dress! It's just simply too
attractive. Isn't the weather foul? I loathe foul weather.
Simply loathe it! It makes one feel so—so lousy. Oh,
hell," he broke off, his voice dropping several degrees,
"it's no good. I could never go through with it. Suppose they ask me things, fiendishly personal things? I
know women do it. They always do. They have to. It's
their specialty."

He shrank within himself and stared bleakly at Mr. Ram, who steadfastly avoided his gaze.

"Wonder if she meant what she said," Mr. Willows continued to muse, his thoughts once more reverting to his wife's parting threat. "Wouldn't put it past her. She's like that. It would tickle her pink to do it. Gad, what a fix I'm in—no knowledge of female wiles."

He went to the bathroom and made a great to-do about water and soap.

"Don't have to shave," he observed, critically surveying his wife's pert face in the mirror. "That's one good thing at least, but I do have to make up a little and arrange my hair some way. How does one manage that?"

But manage it he did. Sighing deeply, he returned to the bedroom and began to rummage through his wife's bureau. A black piece of lace network caught his eye and he became idly interested.

"Guess I'll put this on," he muttered.

For five minutes he sweated over the delicate fastenings of the brassière, then, admitting himself baffled, he compromised by putting it on backwards. He had not the courage to bring himself to look at the result. After that, he went slinking about the room, furtively getting himself into this thing and that until finally he was fully if not any too securely arrayed. The garters had been a struggle. These, too, he put on backwards and dragged the straps round to the front. This weird arrangement made him feel rather peculiar and uncertain about the waist and upper legs, but he decided it was better than wearing no garters at all. By the time he had finished with himself, virtually every article of wearing apparel his wife had possessed was scattered about the room. Then with a deep sigh he seated himself at the vanity dresser and proceeded to do things to his face.

"I never thought she did this thing right," he said to himself. "Think I'll make a good job of it and make her feel envious when she comes home to-night."

But by the time he had finished with lipsticks and eyebrow pencils and mascara and rouge, there were few women in the world who would have envied him his face. The lipstick was the first difficulty. In endeavoring to achieve a symmetrical and well-balanced effect, he kept adding color first to one side of his lips and then to another, until at last even he himself grew alarmed at the size his mouth was becoming. Abandoning this feature of his face as hopeless, he applied himself to his eyelashes, with decidedly streaky results which did not add to the neatness of his already untidy face. He then penciled his eyebrows heavily, unevenly, and, being of an experimental nature, curled them up at the ends.

"The exotic touch," he murmured. "I've always been strongly attracted to exotic-looking women. I'll make an exotic face of it."

However, instead of making his face look exotic, as he fondly believed he was doing, he merely succeeded in making it look chaotic. To be truthful it was about the most chaotic-looking face that had ever been worn by a human being. This became even more apparent after he had liberally applied rouge to his cheeks and sprinkled several beauty spots in what he considered to be appropriate places.

"Must have earrings," he muttered, now thoroughly engrossed in his artistic endeavors. "Got to have earrings and a sort of necklace thing."

After emptying several small boxes of their contents, he found what he wanted and thus further adorned his person. With the earrings he experienced some difficulty, but was finally able to make them stay put. These last embellishments gave to his already miscellaneous appearance the suggestion of a frivolous but slightly smeared gypsy fortune teller. The general effect was exceedingly confusing. In his absorption in the decoration of his features, Tim Willows had overlooked the point that he was creating a face that was supposed to be worn in a civilized community. If seen at a masquerade at about five o'clock in the morning when everyone's faculties were numbed by overindulgence, it might possibly have got by, but in a quiet suburban home it was a most astounding face to come upon unexpectedly.

Certainly Mrs. Jennings found it so when Tim, still fumbling with his rebellious garters, descended the stairs and made a rather crablike entrance into the lounge. Tim was no less astounded. To his memory he had never seen this person before. He did not want to see her now. And the look he directed upon her eloquently expressed his feelings.

"Oh, my dear," began Mrs. Jennings, "whatever has happened to your face?"

"Nothing that I know of, madam," replied Tim with deep-voiced dignity. "Is my face in need of a shave or are you under the impression that the thing has slipped?"

Suddenly remembering that this was not at all the sort of answer that was expected of him, he laughed a trifle hysterically, then attempted to look coy.

"I'm practising a part in a play," he told the almost stupefied woman. "Don't know when it's going to be but it's going to be—that is, I think it is. The part calls for a deep-voiced woman. Don't ask me why. It just does. Did you ever practise being a deep-voiced woman? It's most remarkable what one can do. You should try being deep-voiced, my dear. Really you should. Just excuse me a minute. Be right back."

Tim hurried to the dining room and, opening a closet in the sideboard, extracted a bottle of rye, from which he drank deeply without even troubling about a glass. Wiping the tears from his eyes together with much mascara, he rang for Peter, and returned coughingly to the lounge once more to confront Mrs. Jennings.

Mrs. Jennings, it developed after much astute fishing, was a neighbor who on the pretext of borrowing a meat grinder had dropped over to exchange a lot of dirt. She was young, attractive, and in every respect desirable, but, handicapped as he was with his present body, Tim did not know what on earth to do with the woman.

"Well, you certainly should have been an actress," Mrs. Jennings observed. "When you first came into the room, I could have sworn a man was speaking. Thought perhaps it was your husband, although I've never met him. Only this morning Jack was saying to me, 'Flo,' he said, 'I want you to meet Tim Willows. He's one of the few interesting men in Cliffside.' "

This last declaration of Mrs. Jennings was a great help to Tim Willows. It enabled him to discover that the woman called herself Flo, and by the process of elimination, he decided that her last name could be none other than Jennings. Feeling a little better equipped to continue this unequal contest, he was about to reply to the woman when one of his earrings became detached and slipped down the front of his dress.

"Damn these earrings to hell!" he exclaimed gruffly but sincerely. "Why don't they stay where they belong?"

Snatching irritably at the neck of the dress, he succeeded not only in unfastening his brassière, but also in ripping open the dress itself. As a result of this, he was almost naked to the waist.

At that moment Peter presented himself in answer to the bell. As Tim turned towards him, that venerable domestic was startled beyond measure. Tim, noticing the old man's embarrassment, hastened to put him at his ease.

"Pardon me, Peter," he said girlishly. "Just a slight accident. You can serve breakfast now."

"Yesem," replied Peter, hurrying from the room and thinking strange thoughts to himself in his flight.

"Of course, you'll stay to breakfast, Flo, dear," continued the spurious Sally. "At least have a cup of coffee."

Flo Jennings stayed. She wanted to talk about Beth Johnson's operation and she intended to talk about Beth Johnson's operation. Nothing was going to stop her. She hoped to be able to talk about that operation for a long time and in great detail.

Meanwhile, out in the kitchen, Mr. Peter Twill was endeavoring to relieve his feelings through the unsatisfactory medium of words.

"All she needs is feathers to make her look like a red Indian," he informed his good wife. "Painted wild like a heathen savage and nearly as naked. Doesn't seem to mind. 'Pardon me, Peter,' she said, as cool as

ice, just like it was the most natural thing in the world
for a woman to be going about that way. Something's
come over her and the master, too. He gave me the
coyest look this morning when he asked for a little
pick-me-up. Then he said—and very nastily, too—that
a woman's place was in the home, but that instead of
having a woman we had a lazy bum in bed. He never
went as far as that about Miss Sally before."

Dopey, gathering from the excited voice of Peter
that rare and interesting developments were afoot, oo-
zily emerged from his box and, pushing open the pantry door, presented himself in the dining room. The
sight of his dog caused Tim once more to forget that
he was a lady.

"Come here, you old son of a hooker," he called out
in a rough, vulgar voice to the confusion of Flo Jennings. "How's every little thing?"

At the sound of his master's voice issuing from his
mistress's body, Dopey stopped dead in his tracks and
with reproachful eyes gazed at the speaker. One look
at the face sent the hair up along the dog's spine.
There was something wrong here, something radically
wrong with that face. God knows what it all meant.
Unable to trust his legs, Dopey sat down and broke
into a gentle sweat.

"Come here, damn your craven heart to hell,"
grated the painted woman.

The dog could stand it no longer. He elevated his
muzzle and pushed through it a howl of sheer bewil-
derment and mental anguish, then, turning, the great
beast endeavored to crawl away on his stomach. The
howl of the dog had already disconcerted Flo Jennings,
but that which issued from the madly painted lips of
her hostess froze the poor woman in her chair. Already
Tim Willows had been through a sufficiently trying
morning. He had stood enough for ten men. In the face
of overwhelming odds he had done his best to be a
lady. It was as if fate had conspired to defeat his efforts. His garters were all wrong and his breasts refused to work. Then this Jennings woman had greatly
added to the difficulties of the situation. These things
had he stood with fortitude. Even with the threat of

motherhood hanging over his head, he had tried to remain calm, but when his own dog turned tail and denied him, Tim Willows went temporarily mad. With a howl even less agreeable to hear than his dog's, Tim sprang from the table and hurled the nearest glass at the busily slithering body. Dopey, still close to the floor, gasped and, looking back over his shoulder with despairing eyes, gave himself up for lost. Then Mr. Willows heaped upon the head of the animal a flood of vile abuse in which he brought to light every defect in the creature's character and every crime he had ever committed. Dopey longed to put his paws to his ears if only to muffle this horrid impeachment, but he was too busy scraping with them on the kitchen door to interrupt his frantic efforts. Succeeding at last in opening this he sneaked from the room.

"No wonder the poor thing is terrified," said Mrs. Twill to her husband. "Hear her swear. Why she's just like a man, she is. Worse."

"Something strange has come over this house," old Peter replied, with heavy assurance.

Dopey fully agreed as he collapsed into his box, where he lay shivering fitfully.

Back in the dining room Tim was trying to pull himself together.

"It's my temperament, you know," he explained, bestowing a smile of suffering upon his unwelcome companion. "I get this way when I act—lose myself in the part—forget at times who I am. What were you saying, my dear? Something awfully interesting. It was all about Beth Johnson and a lot of knives and blood."

Flo Jennings, vainly trying to understand what had come over Sally Willows, soon lost herself in the ghastly narration of Beth Johnson's operation. Tim, listening with shrinking ears, struggled as best he could to choke down the bacon and eggs which Peter had timidly set before him. The woman went into the most revolting details and dwelt gloatingly on the pain inflicted on what had hither-to been for Tim unheard-of organs of the body. With mounting consternation he wondered if he had all those organs inside him, and if

he had, were they all okay. And all the time he was
thinking to himself, "Why, this woman is no better
than a ghoul—a horrid vulture. And they say men are
crude, evil-speaking creatures. This Jennings person
here has the worst of us licked. Wonder if she drinks
blood instead of orange juice for breakfast?"

When Flo lightly passed on to the subject of cancer-
ous growths and their prevalence among women Tim
was reduced to the consistency of a submerged sponge.
Rising unsteadily from the table he excused himself for
a moment, with a feeble smile of apology. In the
kitchen he seized Peter with shaking hands.

"Sneak that bottle out of the sideboard," he told the
old gentleman, who was himself beginning to shake.
"That woman in there is killing me."

Peter returned with the bottle, and Tim poured himself a stiff bracer.

"Take one yourself," he told Peter, "and give one to
Judy. We all need a little to-day."

When he had returned to the dining room Mrs. Twill
turned to her husband with frightened eyes.

"Sounds exactly like Mr. Tim," she said, "and does-
n't look much like Miss Sally."

Peter nodded in silence and swallowed down his rye.

Tim led his guest to the lounge, where he absently
selected a cigar from the humidor. After carefully
lighting the cigar he politely offered one to the woman,
who was looking at him with a peculiar expression.

"I've never smoked a cigar in my life," said Mrs.
Jennings in declining the offer.

"Oh, you should, my dear," Tim replied with false
sweetness. "George Sand did, and in Germany it's all
the rage among smart women. We'll all be doing it
soon. That, by the way, is who I'm supposed to be—
George Sand. I've just remembered. Famous writer.
Lived with a lot of men. All different."

Flo hesitated. She dearly wanted to be a smart
woman.

"I might try," she said at last. "Now that there are
no men about to see. Hope it doesn't make me sick."

"What a silly Flo you are," scoffed Tim as, with

grim satisfaction, he selected the blackest cigar he could find and lighted it for the unsuspecting woman.

"You know," said Flo Jennings after she had finished coughing, "what I really came over here for was to borrow your meat grinder."

"That's just what she would borrow," said Tim to himself. "She and a meat grinder should get along splendidly together." Aloud he remarked graciously, "Certainly, Flo. I'd be delighted. What sort of meat are you going to mutilate?"

"Roast beef," replied Flo, struggling with the cigar.

"I'll bet it's nice and rare," said Tim.

"It is," replied Flo with gleaming eyes. "I like it rare."

Tim shuddered and left the room. He was sorry for the roast beef. While getting the grinder he helped himself to another drink, then returned to the lounge. He found Flo Jennings looking very pale and wan. The sight gave him no little satisfaction.

"I think I'll be going," she said weakly. "This cigar seems to have done things to me. Don't feel as if I could ever eat again. Do run over to see me, Sally. It's been such a lovely chat."

"Hasn't it just?" replied Tim. "It was really too simply sweet of you to have let me in on Beth Johnson's operation. Try to dig up another one."

Flo was too far gone to be aware of the irony in Tim's words. She seized the grinder and made a hasty exit. Tim sank down in a chair and broodingly considered his breasts.

That afternoon, a trifle exalted, Tim took a walk, and in his reckless frame of mind allowed himself to be picked up by a couple of passing automobilists. When the machine turned down an unfrequented road and his companions attempted to become forcibly familiar, Tim's immediate reactions both pained and surprised them. Seizing a spanner from the floor of the car he knocked one of the gentlemen out, then incapacitated the other with a well-directed kick. Realizing he was no longer welcome he got out of the car and trudged off down the road. It was five miles to home, and Tim, in his light, high-heeled pumps, felt hardly equal to the task.

"To think that such a thing should ever have happened to me," he mused bitterly. "What a good girl doesn't have to stand for in this world! I'm a damn good girl, myself, but it strikes me that no girl's honor is worth a five-mile walk. On a good road it might be, and in the summer, but not on a road like this."

Thus moralizing, Tim continued to plod through the slush and the gathering dusk. Behind him on the road two stricken automobilists were examining the extent of their injuries and radically revising their opinion of the weaker sex.

Gradually Tim began to chuckle.

"I certainly did that beggar dirt," he muttered. "He'll never be any earthly good. Serves him damn well right for trying to get rough with a lady. Hope the other one isn't dead. Anyway I've still got my honor—whatever that is."

CHAPTER VII

A Man in Body Only

WHILE TIM WILLOWS WAS HAVING HIS DAY, SUCH AS it was, Sally was also having hers in full measure. The poor girl was doing her best to be a gentleman. In this she succeeded only spottily. There were moments when she was quite good and others when she was very poor indeed. Her trip into town, for instance, was most unfortunate. Especially for Mr. Carl Bentley.

Sally should never have taken that pick-me-up from old Peter. It did more harm than good. Dashed down as it had been on an empty stomach it seemed only to make her disinclined to remember for any length of time the reversed position she was now so amazingly occupying. She preferred to be herself.

And, of course, she should never have sat down in the train beside Mr. Carl Bentley. This was a mistake. Almost anyone who sat down beside that insufferably boring gentleman anywhere was making a mistake, as was very speedily and painfully realized, but for Sally, in her mood of reckless elevation, the mistake could easily have proved disastrous. As it was, the young lady in her excited condition completely lost both poise and perception, and for an apparently case-hardened commuter conducted herself completely unlike the accepted conception of that unblessed creature.

Carl Bentley himself did a little long-distance poise-losing. The moment he became aware of the fact that he was going to have as a seat-mate the man who of all men he most desired to avoid, he became demoralized in all departments. Turning slightly he viewed with alarm the features of the bogus Mr. Willows. Carl's temerity was rewarded by a smile of infinite tenderness as he looked for a startled moment into his companion's brimming eyes.

"Good-morning, dear," fell lightly from the other's lips.

Mr. Bentley started and then tried to convince himself that he had both heard and seen wrong. He fervently hoped he had. If Tim Willows wanted to be friendly, so much the better, but there was no need for him to be gushing about it. Mr. Bentley felt called upon to make some sort of reply.

"We seem fated to be thrown together," he observed a little resentfully as, with great ostentation, he unfolded his morning paper.

"Lucky fate!" exclaimed Sally with a rush. "You great big beautiful man."

Carl Bentley blushed to the roots of his hair even while his blood ran cold. This is an extremely unusual feat and very difficult to do. But Carl Bentley, so great was his perturbation, achieved it with remarkable ease.

"I said," continued the voice, this time a little louder, "you great big beautiful man."

"Don't keep on saying it," Mr. Bentley pleaded earnestly. "People might begin to talk."

With this he plunged his head in his paper and gave himself up to bitter thoughts. Was this man put on earth merely to torture him? Just because he, Bentley, had tried to dishonor the creature's home, was that sufficient reason for carrying the feud into public life? Funny thing, too, he had never noticed before that Tim Willows had such a shockingly effeminate voice. It was either that or else the man was displaying the worst of bad taste in trying to be funny in such a questionable manner.

"What do I care how people talk?" he heard his companion proclaiming. "What do we care? For the first time in my life I am enjoying complete sexual freedom. I recognize no barriers."

Sally was beginning to enjoy the situation hugely. All women are born with a well-developed desire to make men feel uncomfortable whenever possible. This retaliatory impulse compensates them in part for the long years of oppression heaped upon them by the self-satisfied male. It gave Sally infinite delight to make this large man squirm. And this feeling did not at all conflict with the fact that at the same time she found him passably attractive. For this reason her conversation was half in earnest and half in play, a most unfortunate combination for the peace of mind of Carl Bentley.

"Perfect sexual freedom," she repeated defiantly. "Sex without let or hindrance. Everything! All!"

Carl Bentley shivered.

"Practise your freedom with someone else," he told her in a low, hurried voice. "Don't try to drag me down with you. I wish for neither everything nor all!"

"You're right," continued Sally resolutely. "It's time we stood back to back and faced the world—threw our love in its ugly snoot. Why should we hide our guilty secret? I fear nothing, sweetheart, with you at my side."

"I fear everything with you at my side," groaned Mr. Bentley. "Won't you go away from it?"

"All the seats are taken. All the seats are taken," sang Sally in a happy voice. "It's just as you said, Carl, dear. Fate has conspired to keep us inseparable."

It was remarkable how uncannily the man could imitate his wife's voice. It was terrible. Carl Bentley looked furtively about him and was convinced that his eyes encountered the amused and scornful glances of his fellow commuters. In particular he noticed a pretty stenographer who was looking at him in a most peculiar way. Then, for the first time, he realized that the heavy fragrance he had been smelling ever since he had boarded the train emanated from his companion. It was true. While shifting into her husband's clothes Sally had been unable to resist spraying on herself a dash of her favorite perfume. It had been an instinctive action, a long-established habit, but Carl Bentley did not take this into consideration. He was very much upset.

"Why in heaven's name did you put that stuff on you?" he demanded. "You smell like the loosest of women. People will begin to suspect me."

"Let 'em suspect," retorted Sally. "Why shouldn't I

perfume my body? I'll anoint the damn thing with oils if I want to. I tell you I'm free—free!"

She tried to fling an arm round his neck, and for a moment they struggled unbecomingly together, to the delight of several spectators.

"I want to hug you," gritted Sally through her husband's teeth as she struggled manfully back. "Come on, handsome. Let me give you a hug."

In the small turmoil from Sally's amorous efforts she succeeded in yanking Mr. Bentley's tie out from under his vest and in completely upsetting his carefully arranged hair. The man was in a pitiful condition, almost on the verge of collapse. Sally might have felt sorry for him had it not been for the fact that the drink was dying on her, and she could feel sorry only for herself. Recklessly she tossed discretion to the winds.

"You weren't so backward the other night," she flung at the discomfited Mr. Bentley as he struggled to rearrange himself. "You were only too anxious then to have me put my arms round your neck. Don't try to deny it. You've been after me for weeks."

"What!" gasped the stricken man. "Me after you? Are you mad or am I?"

He slumped down in the seat and buried his head in the newspaper.

"I'm mad about you," he heard the soft voice say as its owner slipped affectionately down beside him and made a snatch at one of his hands. Then he became horribly aware of the conductor looking down at them both with ill-concealed distaste. What was the man thinking? Probably the worst.

Sally seemed to be the first to recover her poise. She realized that here was a situation in which she might as well act as a man.

"Hello, there," she said in the voice of Mr. Willows, thereby driving Bentley into even greater confusion. "How are you to-day, officer? Meet my boy friend."

The conductor punched the extended commutation ticket, then transferred his attention to Carl Bentley, and to that gentleman's horror addressed him in a ladylike voice.

"Will you please show me your ticket, miss?" said

the conductor to Carl Bentley. "I hope you won't think me bold."

Mr. Bentley guiltily held up his ticket with a trembling hand, and so great was the power of suggestion that when he tried to answer the man his voice cracked on a high note and he was forced to abandon the attempt. Well pleased with the success of his humor, for Sally had laughed heartily and deeply at the conductor's words, the man passed on and, bending low over the passenger in the next seat, whispered a few sentences, then chuckled coarsely. Mr. Bentley felt sure the man must be pointing at him. He sank even lower down in the seat and became completely hidden by his paper.

"You've ruined me," he muttered. "I'll never be able to live this down. It was a sad day when I first laid eyes on your wife."

"Oh," replied Sally, lapsing into her feminine way of speaking. "Well, I'll try to make it up to you for her."

Bentley made no reply to this, and for several blessed minutes he was allowed to read his paper in quiet if not in peace. His respite was short-lived. From the tail of his eye he presently made out the face of Tim Willows peeking coyly round the edge of the paper. Then the face giggled and spoke and a long finger pointed at an advertisement.

"How'd you like to see me in those step-ins?" asked the face. "Wouldn't I look cute?"

Carl Bentley shrank back, nearly overcome by his emotions.

"Wouldn't I?" persisted the face. "Tell me, Carl, or I'll make a scene."

"Oh!" gasped Mr. Bentley. "This is too much. This time you've gone too far—overstepped all bounds."

He tried to rise, but Sally clung desperately to the tails of his coat. Mr. Bentley, as he sank back, decided that this was one of life's most embarrassing moments. People were looking at him, going out of their way to look at him. They were bending out into the aisle, peering over the backs of seats.

"Say yes," continued the hateful voice. "If you don't I'll break into tears. I'll sob. I'll moan. I'll growl."

The thought of occupying a seat with a sobbing, moaning, growling Tim Willows completely cowed Carl Bentley. He would submit to any form of torture rather than have that occur.

"You would," he managed to get out, nearly sobbing, himself. "You'd look just dandy. Here, you take this paper and read it to yourself."

"You're so sweet," murmured Sally. "But I already have a paper."

"Then for God's sake read it," snapped the baited Mr. Bentley. "Do you intend to drive me mad?"

Sally burst into a fresh, girlish laugh.

"Now you're joshing me," she said, slapping him playfuly on the cheek with her husband's gloves. "You tried to crawl into my bed the other night, didn't you? What a bad, bold man you are."

Bentley gathered himself for action, then, before Sally had time to realize what he intended to do, he sprang from the seat and sped down the aisle. For a moment she looked after him, then she, too, sprang up and hurried in pursuit, imploringly calling his name. Sometimes she called him by both names as if to make sure that the whole trainload of commuters should know all about Carl Bentley. She was still dogging his footsteps when the train pulled in at the station. Bentley was the first to alight, and as his feet hit the long ramp they instinctively started to run. So did Sally's. The man fled through the gate to the huge waiting room and streaked across the floor. For a time Sally hung on, then decided it was hardly worth while. The last Mr. Bentley heard of the voice that had made him an outcast among men was, "Good-bye, dearie. Don't do anything I wouldn't do myself." This parting shot lent speed to his already flying feet.

Sally turned and was immediately disconcerted by the suspicious scrutiny of a policeman. At that moment a man she knew only slightly was so unfortunate as to pass by. Sally slapped him so violently on the back that the cigar he was smoking popped out of his mouth with such speed that for a moment the man thought his assailant had snatched it. Seizing the stunned man's hand Sally pumped it vigorously.

"Hello, Jennings!" she cried in a deep, masculine voice. "How are you, old scout? Well, good-bye."

And with that she swaggered off, leaving the old scout and the policeman feeling that a few words of explanation were due them both.

When she stood before the door of the Nationwide Advertising Agency Sally braced herself and prepared for the worst. She realized that now or never she must act the part of a perfect gentleman. Then Tim's admonition to be nice to the girl at the desk returned to her. She thrust open the door and stood for a moment studying the girl's face. Sally's first glance was sufficient to assure her that few men would find it a difficult task to be nice to this fair creature. She was a luscious specimen of womanhood, fresh and in full bloom. Looking at her Sally gained the impression that the girl was wasting her time most shamefully when not engaged in amorous occupations. She was that type of girl.

"Good-morning, young man," said the girl to Sally. "Why the enraptured gaze?"

"I'm looking at you and running a temperature," replied Sally, in a fair approximation of Tim's voice and manner. "You're such a warm number you make me feverish."

"What!" exclaimed the girl. "At this time of day?"

"Grandpa Willows was just that way," explained Sally. "I've an uncle who's even worse."

Sally thought the responsive glow that sprang to the girl's eyes should be prohibited from public demonstration. It was a menace to mankind.

"All of which, I presume, is leading up to the fact that you'd like your morning spot," said the girl. "Tell me if I'm wrong."

"I have nothing to say," replied Sally.

"Come over here," commanded the girl as she deftly filled a paper cup with a stiff drink from the seemingly inexhaustible flask in the desk drawer. "Toss that off and beat it."

Sally tossed it off, then stood swaying slightly on her feet as the tears streamed from her eyes and strange sounds emerged from her throat.

"Very old and rare," she gasped. "The person who drinks that should never suffer from baldness of the chest."

"I don't suffer from that disease," the girl replied. "I glory in it."

Sally, now invigorated by what she had received, felt truly thankful. She walked back to the desk and, bending down over the girl, neatly kissed her on the mouth, and was surprised to discover that she was more of a man than she had thought possible. In spite of her surprise the girl responded avidly. And this was what Mr. Gibber saw when he arrived at his office that fine, bright morning—his reception clerk being roundly kissed by one of his most troublesome copy writers.

"Mr. Willows!" snapped Mr. Gibber.

"It's himself," muttered the girl.

Sally was surprised at the sound of her own voice, or rather, Tim's voice. It was deep, cool, and collected as she replied to Mr. Gibber.

"One moment, sir," she protested, painfully pressing a thumb into the girl's right eye. "I think I've got it. No, that's odd. It was there a moment ago. Does it hurt much?" This last to the girl.

"Too much," came the feeling reply.

"I'll bet Mr. Gibber's eyes are sharper than mine," Sally announced, straightening her husband's body. "Look, Mr. Gibber, the poor girl's eye is all inflamed. There's a cinder in it or something."

"It's a thumb," said the girl under her breath.

"I'm sorry," replied Mr. Gibber, as he examined the girl's eye, which by this time was quite convincingly inflamed. "I misunderstood the situation, perhaps. You must be terribly nearsighted, Mr. Willows, or were you trying to bite the cinder out?"

"Ha, ha!" laughed Sally falsely, "you jest, Mr. Gibber, you jest."

Leaving Mr. Gibber with the girl's eye, Sally escaped from the reception room, and after wandering experimentally along various halls and passageways eventually located Tim's office by seeing his name on the door.

No sooner was she seated at the desk than a man

walked briskly in and brought a hand down crashingly on her back. Sally pitched forward on Tim's face and lay among the pencils and pads.

"Morning, you sot!" cried the man. "How do you come up and fall off to-day?"

"I fall off," said Sally feebly, "but I don't come up. My good man, you've ruined me."

Sally felt convinced this would be Steve Jones. No other man would take such a chance with Tim. She knew how he objected to back-slapping both in theory and in practice.

"What's wrong with you?" demanded the man. "Are you weak to-day?"

"Very," replied Sally. "Very weak to-day, Steve. Help me to resume the sitting posture you so brutally interrupted."

When Sally was once more erect in her chair she looked at Steve with tears in her eyes. Steve was a likeable enough looking chap—dark, stocky, and with alert black eyes bright with bad thoughts.

"You owe me two dollars," he announced happily. "Gold Heels lost."

"I'd like to check that with Tim." she began, then quickly checked herself and drew two bills from her pocket. "Here's your dishonestly won spoils," she hurried on. "You'll excuse me, I trust, if I seem to dash away? That blow on the back did terrible things to me."

"Double or quits," Steve Jones suggested, flipping a coin in the air.

"What do you mean?" asked Sally, pausing on her way to the door.

"You know," the other replied. "Don't be dumb."

And because Sally did not know she nodded vaguely and, taking a coin from her pocket, flipped it into the waste paper basket.

"Does that win?" she asked hopefully.

"Wait!" cried Steve. "Don't touch it. I'm matching you."

He flipped his coin again, caught it dexterously as Sally watched with admiring eyes a little tinged with envy, flattened the coin on the edge of the desk, then peered greedily down into the waste paper basket.

"Ah!" he exclaimed. "Good! It's heads. You owe me another two dollars."

Sally's, or rather the face she was wearing, grew blank.

"What?" she demanded. "Already?"

"Don't stall," said Steve, "you big stiff."

"All right," replied Sally. "Seems very strange to me. I'll have to owe it to you. Is that all that we do, or is there more?"

"Not unless you want to double it or nothing," observed Steve.

"Let's play nothing," said Sally. "I really must be going."

As she absently made her way to the ladies' rest room she decided that hereafter she would shun the company of Steve Jones.

"It cost me just four good dollars," she thought to herself, "to get pounded on the back. That's not as it should be."

The ladies' room when she found it was a place of many partitions, which arrangement accounts for the fact that at first the presence of one they had good and sufficient reasons to believe to be a man was not noticed by several girls busily engaged in tightening their stockings upon their well-turned limbs. The conversation of these girls interested Sally and made her still further forget herself. It had to do with the price and quality of stockings and the best places to purchase them. So interested did she become, in fact, that she innocently approached the girls and attempted to join in the conversation.

"My dears," she began in the most friendly of feminine voices, "where do you buy your——"

Her question was neither finished nor answered. Never before had Sally realized that women could work up so much noise at such short notice. The air was pierced by a series of ear-splitting shrieks. Partition doors slammed and the figures of frantic women dashed clutchingly about the room. Sally stood appalled as she saw these figures break for the exit and heard excited voices carrying the name of Mr. Willows to the nethermost recesses of the Nationwide Advertising Agency. It was only a matter of moments before she had the room to herself, or nearly to herself.

"Oh, God, I've done it now," she groaned. "I'll never be able to live after this. What happens next?"

Unable to bear this thought she dragged at a partition door, only to have her efforts rewarded by a fresh outburst of shrieks and lamentations.

"Be quiet!" gasped Sally. "I'm a woman myself at heart."

"Oh, what a liar," came the voice. "You're just a nasty man and you should be ashamed of yourself."

Sally threw open another door, jumped in and snapped the catch just as Miss Reeder, the president's personal secretary, bounced into the room with an expression of set purpose solidifying the wrinkles on her sharp, faded face. At the moment she was in her glory. She was hounding a man. At last she had the goods on one of the members of the sex that had neglected her for so many barren years.

"Mr. Willows," she called in a harsh voice.

"He's not here," said Sally from her place of concealment.

"Oh, he is so," cried the girl in the other compartment. "Make him go away, Miss Reeder."

"I know where he is," replied Miss Reeder complacently. "I can see his big feet. You might as well come out, Mr. Willows."

"I can't come out," said Sally sadly.

"And why not, pray?" demanded Miss Reeder.

"I don't feel like it," replied Sally desperately. "Can't you see I don't feel like it."

Then followed a period of silence which was even more unnerving than the shrieking of many voices.

"Well, Mr. Willows," came the voice of Miss Reeder presently, "are you ready to come out? I'm waiting."

"I'm never coming out," declared Sally.

"Then I'll send some men in," said the determined woman. "They'll break the door down and drag you out."

The prospect of being besieged in a ladies' rest room

proved too much for Sally. She opened the door and with great dignity walked past Miss Reeder and out of the room where an informal reception committee was awaiting her arrival. Disdaining any words of explanation Sally averted her gaze from the faces of the interested group and walked slowly back to her husband's office while the eyes of all the stenographers and clerks in the world seemed to be following her progress with hideous concentration. A memorandum was waiting for her on the desk. She picked it up mechanically and read:

Mr. Gibber will continue his talk on Brevity at 10:30 A.M. in the conference room.
                              Signed: G. M. REEDER, *Sec'y.*

By the time Sally had located the conference room the chairs at the table were nearly all occupied. Sally's belated arrival created no little interest. The distracted girl in man's image was painfully aware of the amused glances of numerous pairs of eyes. Mr. Gibber himself regarded Sally with a stern, censorious eye as she found a chair next to Steve Jones and sank down on it.

"What's the matter?" Steve demanded in a low voice. "Are you turning into a nasty old man or did losing all that money temporarily derange you?"

"Don't ask me now," pleaded Sally. "I can't bear to talk about it yet. Maybe I've gone mad. I don't know."

"Gentlemen," began Mr. Gibber, "yesterday, as you doubtless remember, I was discussing the subject of brevity."

"Yes, sir," put in Dolly Meades helpfully. "You had just gotten to pith."

"I had left pith," replied Mr. Gibber, looking at the young woman reprovingly. "And I do not intend to return to it. In other words, we'll waive pith." He squared his shoulders, then leaning over the table, made a fresh start. "Gentlemen," he said, "do you want to know something?" From the indifferent expressions on the faces of the gentlemen addressed it was only too apparent they had no desire to know anything.

Sally felt that some answer should be made to Mr. Gibber's neglected question, but as no one seemed to give a hang she answered it herself.

"Yes, Mr. Gibber," she said. "Go right ahead. I'd like to know something."

"What do you want to know?" asked Mr. Gibber suspiciously.

"I haven't the vaguest idea," replied Sally. "Whatever you were going to tell us."

"The question was merely rhetorical," said Mr. Gibber.

"Sorry," answered Sally. "I thought you were speaking on brevity. One can hardly be brief and rhetorical at the same time."

Mr. Gibber's face turned dangerously red and his eyes looked dangerously angry. Nevertheless he got hold of himself and made his third attempt.

"Boys," he called them this time, "this is what I want you to know. It's easy enough to write words, beautiful words. It's as easy as falling off a log. It's a joke. Any one of us here could sit right down now and dash off a novel or a play. We all could do it. And why don't we? I'll tell you—we have more important things to do with our words. I know it, because I have done it. Not a year passes that doesn't see a new book or a play or a sheaf of verse that has been turned out by my pen. Why do I do it?"

"Yes, Mr. Gibber," asked Dolly. "Why do you do it?"

"Just for fun," thundered Mr. Gibber. "Just for a lark. I never even take the trouble to let a publisher have them."

"A business, a man, or an idea that can be put on a paying basis must be fundamentally sound, must be essentially moral. But the vast majority of writers—these poets, playwrights and novelists—are not on a paying basis. Therefore they are neither sound nor moral. Some of them offend us while others amuse. All very good in their way, but after all, just froth—lightweights. We read them. We use them. We dismiss them. There's no money in that sort of writing. They never get out of the red. Froth." Once more a portentous pause. "Now, boys," he continued, gaining inspiration from the sound of his own voice, "get this fact through your heads: we are the people. It is we who create the literature of progress and plan the campaigns of commerce. Right here in this quiet, gorgeously appointed conference room with my old golf trophies around us and souvenirs of the hunt looking at us from the wall——" Here Mr. Gibber interrupted himself to point at the motheaten head of a misanthropic-looking moose gloomingly surveying the people.

"He doesn't seem to be tickled to death to see us, that silly-looking old moose doesn't," observed Miss Meades.

"What has the moose got to do with this discussion?" demanded Mr. Gibber.

"I don't know, Mr. Gibber," replied Dolly sweetly. "You seemed to be presenting him to us or us to him, so I thought——"

"Don't," broke in Mr. Gibber. "What I was saying, gentlemen, is that right here in this room, moose or no moose, we are the people who are doing the real writing to-day, the real inspired creative work."

"Hear! Hear!" cried Sally enthusiastically. "You're dead right, Mr. Gibber. That's exactly what my husband always tells me. He says that a copy writer must get along on less facts than a writer of fairy tales."

"Your wife you mean, Mr. Willows," corrected Mr. Gibber, highly pleased to be supported from such an unexpected quarter. He forgave Tim Willows much.

"Of course, of course. How foolish of me." Sally's blush spread over her husband's face. "Naturally, my wife."

"Gentlemen," went on Mr. Gibber, plunging his right fist into the palm of his left hand. "It's up to us to write words that sell rather than words that please. And that's hard, gentlemen, damned hard. That's real writing. I admit it. I have done it. The famous Bingo Reversible Puppy Biscuit Campaign, one of the outstanding successes of modern advertising, was mine, all mine. But it called for work, men, work before words, push before phrase, concentration before copy. That's what I mean. That's what I mean exactly. That and more. We who are gathered here together in the presence of——"

"The moose," suggested Miss Meades.

"—are carrying on a great work," continued Mr. Gibber, brushing interruptions aside, "are shouldering a heavy responsibility. It devolves upon us to protect American capital and American industry from the insidious inroads of the deadly Red Blight. It is up to us to keep American labor contented and where it belongs—obediently on the job. It is my privilege, gentlemen, to be at the head of this splendid organization which I have created. Nay, it is my duty. I must face it. I must face it like an experienced field marshal standing in a——a——a——"

"A field, perhaps," suggested Sally. "That's where he should stand by rights."

"No, not a field," gritted Mr. Gibber.

"In a daze, maybe," put in Dolly Meades, not to be outdone in helpfulness.

"In neither!" cried Mr. Gibber. "Like Marshall Field standing—ha! Where am I? Oh, yes. Like a field marshal standing before the mast, one hand grasping the helm, the other one heaving the lead——"

"A considerable stretch, that, Mr. Gibber," observed the accurate Miss Meades. "Especially for a field marshal who is much more at home on a horse. Now if you had said, 'Like a field marshal clinging to his horse, one hand grasping his tail, the other one holding his tooth——"

Sally laughed scornfully.

"Do you mean to say that that field marshal's horse had only one tooth?" she demanded.

"No, not necessarily," retorted Dolly Meades hotly. "It might have been an old horse—a toothless horse."

"They never send a toothless horse to the front," replied Sally.

"Just a minute! Just a minute!" cried Mr. Gibber.

"We've got to settle this, Mr. Gibber," said Dolly Meades. Then, leveling her gaze on Sally, she continued. "Why not?" she demanded truculently. "Why not send a toothless horse to the front? Horses are not supposed to eat the enemy."

"I know," replied Sally. "But it's the looks of the thing I'm thinking about. Not nice to see a lot of toothless horses knocking about the front. Should retire the poor things on half pay."

"I don't see that at all," Miss Meades objected. "If Marshall Field happens to like a toothless horse I see no reason why he shouldn't ride one."

"Who is this Marshall Field, anyway?" asked Sally. "I don't seem to remember him, or is he a place where you play games?"

"I haven't time! I haven't time!" Mr. Gibber protested, looking considerably dazed. "We'll drop Marshall Field——"

"And his toothless horse," added Sally.

"Anyway, you know what I mean," Mr. Gibber struggled on.

"I don't," spoke up Sally unhelpfully, but fortunately for this victim of Mr. Ram's caprice Mr. Gibber did not hear her.

"And there's money in it," he continued. "Good money. Big money. Money enough for us all."

Mr. Gibber pronounced the word "money" so succulently his listeners could almost taste it.

"Not now, perhaps,"—and here Mr. Gibber held up a restraining hand, fearing he had awakened false hopes in the breasts of his listeners. "Not now, of course, but later. For everyone in this room who devotes his entire time, thought, and energy exclusively to the best interests of this great organization there is sure money ahead. I have your welfare at heart. I think you know me well enough to trust your futures to me. Your interests are my interests. Your hopes and aspirations are dearer to me than my own. I am satisfied to be of service to mankind. Only two things do I ask—loyalty and hard work. If you give me those you need have no fear. I will carry each one of you with me along the highroad of prosperity to a happier and fuller life."

Apparently overcome by the thought of the terrific task he had set himself, Mr. Gibber walked emotionally to a window while his prospective burdens, obviously much depressed, sat and gazed down that highroad where good money, big money, was never now, but forever and forever and for always just a little bit ahead.

Turning abruptly from the window through which he had apparently tossed his emotions, Mr. Gibber once more became his usual brisk, urbane self.

"So that, gentlemen," he clipped out, "is what I mean by brevity. I thank you. Remember!"

"Thank you," spoke up Dolly Meades sweetly. "We'll never forget."

While the conference, feeling rottenly let down, was slothfully disintegrating, Mr. Gibber was earnestly questioning Sally in a far corner of the room.

"How on earth did you manage to do it?" he asked, for Mr. Gibber was sincerely bewildered by the various stories he had heard.

"I didn't try to do it, if that's what you mean," said Sally, equally in earnest. "I didn't sneak in or plan to sneak in or await an opportunity. Can't understand it myself. I was thinking of something—oh, yes—that chain store account. Had a swell idea and just didn't pay any attention to where I was going."

"But I'm told you approached some girls and tried to engage them in conversation," Mr. Gibber continued. "Why did you do that? Why didn't you make haste to leave after you'd discovered where you were?"

This was a very embarrassing question. Sally felt her nerve slipping.

"Still thinking about that chain store account," she answered. "Wanted to get the girls' reactions to a few questions."

"You pick out a somewhat singular place for your investigations, I must say," observed Mr. Gibber.

"No time like the present, I always say," was Sally's lame defense. "And of course legs mean nothing to me. I'm a married woman, Mr. Gibber, like yourself."

"I'm not a married woman," Mr. Gibber stoutly protested.

"Aren't you?" replied Sally, genuinely surprised. "Funny, I always thought you were. Then you must be a merry widow or a divorcee."

Sally smiled at the man archly and his face grew blank with amazement.

"I'm neither," he said at last.

"Then all I can say," replied Sally, "is that you must have a rather peculiar nature."

Mr. Gibber almost swooned at this. His face grew red with indignation and Sally began to fear that his body was going to pop at any minute.

"I tell you, young man," he thundered, "I have no relations with men."

"I can't help that," said Sally calmly. "It's your loss not mine."

"But I don't want to have relations with men," said Mr. Gibber in a tortured voice.

"All right," replied Sally soothingly. "No one's going to force you. How did we get where we are, anyway?"

"You said you were a married woman," said the badgered Gibber, "and claimed that I was one."

"Oh!" exclaimed Sally, suddenly seeing the dawn. "Of course I meant man. How perfectly absurd!"

"You seem to be having trouble with your genders," said Mr. Gibber, a trifle mollified, but still suspicious.

"My genders?" cried Sally in alarm. "Why, Mr. Gibber! I'm sure I don't know what you mean. Do I show any symptoms of gender disease? Is it fatal, Mr. Gibber?"

"I mean you're getting your sexes mixed," the man explained wearily.

"Oh, that," replied Sally, feeling greatly relieved. "Sex makes no difference to me. Man or woman—all the same. I'm practically sexless myself."

Mr. Gibber received this gratuitous piece of information in a state of stupefaction.

"Listen," he said at last. "I don't want to talk with you. I can't stand it. The things you say revolt me. They do indeed. But I will say this, and you can thank your stars it isn't more serious. Keep out of the ladies' rest room. I feel very sorry for you but more sorry for your wife."

"You should feel sorry for her," replied Sally feelingly. "She's having a tough time of it."

"I'm glad you realize that, at least," said Gibber. "You may go."

Sally went and had a solitary luncheon. The rest of

the day she spent rehashing Tim's advertisement of the Ducky Chain Stores, incorporating some ideas of her own. These advertisements were later okayed without a change and Tim Willows's stock as a copy writer continued to rise.

Sally arrived home in time to find Tim tenderly nursing his feet, or rather the feet that had once been hers.

"I got these saving your honor," he growled. "And I'm not going to do it again."

"Well, I just about ruined yours, to-day," replied Sally in a pleased voice. "I forgot myself and barged into the ladies' rest room."

Tim became interested, indignant, then amused.

After dinner that night they compared notes, and because they both felt strange and lonely they occupied the same bed.

CHAPTER VIII

How Not to Behave at a Church Supper

PETER, SEATED ON A KITCHEN CHAIR, WAS DOING nothing more important than scratching his venerable pate with a long, reflective finger. In the fullness of time this heavy operation would produce a vocal reaction. It did. Peter spoke.

"Judy Twill," said Peter, "this house is going plumb to the dogs. Lately it's been all cockeyed."

"Something unnatural has come over it," agreed Judy, turning from the stove and regarding her husband darkly. "And that's certain sure. Some sort of a curse."

" 'Tisn't a curse so much," pursued Peter academically. "It's more like an intermingling, if you get what I'm driving at. It's a merger, that's what it is."

He paused and once more his finger revolved upon his head as if it were stirring up thoughts in the brain within.

"Strange and uncommon things are going on," he resumed. "Unaccountable things. The master talks like the missus and the missus talks like the master, and before you've had a chance to get used to the change they switch back again to their regular voices. It's upsetting, that's what it is, upsetting. Take that dumb beast there, for instance. Low as he is he deserves some consideration. He hears coming from Miss Sally's mouth the voice of Mr. Tim, yet sitting not ten feet away is Mr. Tim as large as life. It's too much for the dog's mind, which never was good, as you yourself will agree. What does he do? I saw it myself with my own eyes. First he starts to go to one of 'em, then he turns and starts for the other, then not knowing what the devil to do and not wishing to offend either he sits

106

down exactly midway between 'em and looks perplexed. He can't go on living and keeping his health that way. No dog could."

Mrs. Twill had a word to say at this juncture, which meant that for the moment Peter's voice was stilled.

"I can't get over yet what happened the other morning," she observed.

"What was that?" asked Peter obediently.

"Why," explained his wife, "I was having a bit of set-to with the butcher's delivery boy over a leg of lamb I didn't just take a fancy to when in strolls Miss Sally. She was nearly half naked, she was. That is, her kimono was all open in front. Might just as well not have had it on. She was smoking a big black cigar and carrying a glass of drink. 'What the hell goes on here?' she asks in a deep, rough voice. Then she notices the boy staring at her as if his eyes were going to pop out. 'What are you looking at, funny face?' she rips out. 'Something wrong with my chest? Too much hair on it to suit you?' For the sake of decency I made a sort of motion and she looks down at herself and seems startled. Then she looks at the cigar and the glass and begins to giggle. 'So sorry,' says she in the rightful voice that God gave her. 'I didn't know. You see I'm rehearsing a part. Makes me forget myself.' And with that she minces out just as ladylike as can be. I'd like to know what sort of a part she's rehearsing. It will land her in the lock-up if she ever plays it in public."

"Everything's upside down," complained Peter. "She does most of the drinking now while he stays sober. That's no way. Another thing: he's taken to smoking her perfumed cigarettes and she goes round with a cigar in her mouth—I've actually seen her pulling at a pipe. And another funny thing I've noticed. We get two morning papers now instead of one, and when he comes home at night she makes a grab for the evening paper. Never saw a woman take such an interest in the news."

"The other morning I popped in on them and he was actually dressing her," declared Mrs. Twill. "She was cursing and damning like a trooper. 'How in hell do you get this girdle on?' she asked him. Imagine that, a woman asking her husband how to get dressed. And only last night I caught him strutting around in one of her nightgowns. It gave me a fair start, it did."

"This I do know," said Peter. "I get real dizzy now when I'm serving meals. Their voices shift about so quickly that I can't tell which one of them is asking me for things. Have to keep watching their lips to see who's speaking."

"Dont know where it's going to end," quoth Judy Twill.

"Perhaps it's some modern idea," suggested her husband.

"No idea is modern," replied his wife. "These new-fangled ideas we hear so much about are just oldfangled ideas that have been tried out and forgotten or lost, but I will admit that whatever their idea is it's absolutely new to me."

Meanwhile the subjects of the Twills' conversation were busily and none too happily dressing for the evening.

"I've always had ideas of my own about the way women should dress," observed Tim, "and now that I am a woman to all intents and purposes I'm going to put them into practice."

"Do, dear," remarked his wife sweetly. "I hope they're more attractive than going about half naked in an old shirt or the top part of a pair of pajamas."

"Wish I could get those days back again," said Tim with a heavy sigh.

"You should go on a diet," Sally protested. "Honestly, Tim, I wish you would. If you don't my beautiful figure will be completely ruined. You should take better care of your wife's body."

"Well, be extremely careful what you do with mine," admonished Tim. "If I ever get it back again I'd like to find it the way it left me."

Here he looked thoughtfully at Mr. Ram. In Tim's eyes there was a respectful appeal, a mute entreaty.

"I think he's responsible," he told his wife. "I have an idea that little fellow up there is at the bottom of all our troubles."

"If he is," said Sally, "I hope he has a heart. We've

never done anything to the little blighter. In fact, we've treated him very decently. Given him the place of honor."

Tim's thoughts were on other things.

"To-night, for example," he observed, "I think I'll just wear that black georgette pleated skirt of yours and that stunning red blouse."

"Take care of that blouse," said Sally. "Don't spill soup on it. I like that blouse. Wish I could wear it my-self."

"I'll take care of the damn thing," answered Tim, "but honestly, Sally, I don't see why we have to go to this church supper. I've never been to a church supper and my technique will be rotten."

This discussion had been going on for a week, and Sally's nerves were becoming a bit frayed at the edges.

"Tim, dear," she said wearily, "I don't want to go to this washout any more than you do, but I must be there. I gave Dr. Jordan my word a long, long time ago, and now that you're me you've got to keep my word. That's all there is to it."

"What a deuce of a fine idea that is," complained Tim. "Hope you haven't dated me up for any taffy-pulling parties or sewing bees or aesthetic dancing circles. I hate like hell to go to-night. It's hard to face a church supper."

"You don't like the cocktail parties I pull here," she replied, "and you don't like church suppers. Will you kindly tell me just what you do like?"

"You might be wearing my body," said Tim bitterly, "but your brain is just as illogical as it ever was. If I go to this joyless affair I've got to be primed before I start. Scream down to Peter to bring up a bottle of rye."

Sally humored him. It was the only thing to do under the circumstances. She had to get him to the sup-per. It was going to be a superior sort of supper. All of the best people were going to be there, which meant, of course, the worst. Sally was determined that she should be seen although she realized with a feeling of dread that in trusting her body to Tim she was placing her reliance in a frail craft indeed.

"All I ask is that you don't get me—my body, I mean—all lit up," she said as Tim gulped down a drink. "And keep your own mind sober. You'll need it."

In spite of the injunction, both Tim and Sally were excessively well primed when they drove off to the supper.

"Don't forget," she told her husband, who was looking as pretty as a picture, "Dr. Jordan is a real sport, a regular hail-fellow-well-met sort."

"I know," said Tim. "He's a he-man, red-blooded and all that. I'll hate him. I'll hate everybody."

When they reached the church Tim parked the car on a side street where darkness abetted indulgence. After a steep drink from a flask that lived in one of the side pockets of the car they wiped their lips, took a couple of deep breaths, shook themselves and made for the church. Sally little suspected that beneath Tim's skirt, strapped securely round his waist and held cleverly in a little holster of his own devising, rested a small but sufficient bottle of rye whiskey. Had she known this the situation might still have been saved. Unfortunately, however, she was unaware of the existence of this potential source of danger.

"Now don't leave me," Tim breathed to Sally, smelling noxiously of strong drink. "I'm depending on you to steer me through this slaughter."

"I know," replied his wife, looking down at him from her superior height, "but the trouble is you're supposed to be steering me through the slaughter. It's all quite mad.

"And as it should be," added Tim, at which both of them laughed loudly and entered the church in high merriment for no particular reason.

The supper was held in the basement of the church. It was a great, gaunt chamber with naked brick walls that flung back vindictively the songs that were flung against them. The place was now filled with long tables and long-looking people, long people with strained faces and bright smiles. Here and there were animated little groups of the smart set, the individual members of which tried so hard to be sweet and hearty whenever

approached by a regular, bona-fide church supperite.
Yet over these little groups hung an atmosphere of
guilt and fear. For once they were out of their element,
and where the real church worker walked with a confi-
dent tread these swagger members of the damned
moved with a halting step. It was as if they felt that at
any moment they would be committed irretrievably to
something—to something dismal and demanding.

Church suppers should be. There is nothing else
quite like them. There is nothing else within a mile of
them. A person who has never attended a church supper has neither lived nor savored life. It is not wise to
refuse an invitation to a church supper. It is not coura-
geous. As a rule one gets a pretty good meal for a pitiful little piece of change. Of course one pays a
thousand times over in mental anguish. One must be
hearty and innocently merry at a church supper, and
this comes hard to most of us. Then again, one must
sing at a church supper, or at least give the appearance
of singing. Also, at a church supper one must shake
hands with people one doesn't know and whom one
doesn't want to know. One must talk with these people
and at the same time restrain the impulse to scream
piercingly and to commit murder. There are ever so
many things one must and must not do at a church
supper. Among the hardest of the things one must not
do at a church supper is to keep from making maniacal
faces and obscene gestures at people who smile upon
one with unfair suddenness and dazzling brightness.
There are lots of other hard things not to do. For example: when the faded lady at your side sighs deeply
and asks, "Don't you think poor Dr. Scraggs is over-
working? He looks so tired to-night"—when the faded
lady uncorks that one it is a very difficult thing not to
reply rudely, "Indeed I don't. In my opinion, madam,
Dr. Scraggs has one hell of an easy life. In my opinion he doesn't work half hard enough. And as for him
looking tired—stuff and nonsense! It's the bunk,
madam. The Rev. Dr. Scraggs is merely bored, and
you are partly responsible."

Of course this answer might be quite untrue, for the
Rev. Dr. Scraggses frequently are both overworked and

underpaid, yet there is a deal of satisfaction to be
derived in brutally offending one's neighbor at a church
supper. One instinctively feels like doing it.

If one stopped to consider the hard work, the high
hopes, and the tons of good will and better intentions
that go to make every church supper a horrid reality one
would be sunk in a mire of self-accusation and spiritual
depression. But one must not think of such things
unless one enjoys crying into one's soup. To enjoy a
church supper in the right spirit one must be able to
take it or leave it just like that. It's easy enough to take
a church supper, but to leave it is an entirely different
matter. It is almost impossible to leave a church supper. Houdini himself was never able to escape a church
supper. Prisons, yes. Fortresses, yes. Chests at the bottom of rivers, yes, yes. Church suppers, no. His one
great failure. They go on and on and on, do church
suppers. After a while one gains the impression that
one is going to live the remainder of one's life at a
church supper. One speculates whether it would not be
a wise thing to send for one's trunks and furniture so
as to be properly equipped to do full justice to this
church supper. The faces of old friends appear in
fancy, and well-loved places now forever left behind
float before one's aching eyes.

And yet one smiles brightly at a church supper and
keeps on smiling though not quite so brightly for interminable hours, and after it's all over one goes home
and kicks one's dog, beats one's wife, sets fire to one's
neighbor's house, and feels a great deal better.

"I seem to see," observed Tim, confronting this
church supper, "quite a number of old ladies and they
all look alike with the exception that some are thin and
tired while others are stout and tired. I suspect them of
being Supper Ladies."

"They are," whispered Sally. "They constitute the
very backbone of the supper."

"Then I don't want to eat it," said Tim resolutely.

"Those old ladies—we call them the Girls—are the
only real persons here," Sally explained rapidly.
"They've thought this supper, planned this supper,
sweated over this supper, and they'll probably be too

tired to eat the damn supper. I'm glad we came if only for their sake."

"Stop, Sally, you're breaking my heart," said Tim. "I don't know whether the Girls would be so glad to meet us."

"Oh, they'd forgive anything so long as you come to their suppers," replied Sally. "Are you swaying or am I?"

"Both of us are, but in different directions," said Tim. "That's what keeps us from falling. It seems so fantastic to be clinging to my own arm with your hand."

"I don't want to think of it," murmured Sally. "It makes me feel a little distrait."

The grip on her arm suddenly tightened and she heard him gasp.

"Look, Sally," he whispered. "Is that man a maniac? I'm frightened. Take me home."

Far down at the end of the room there was a man seated at a table and on the face of this man there was an expression, or rather, a contortion. In his eyes glowed a wild light. His mouth had achieved the limits of expansion. There were teeth, not good but abundant. Sally looked upon this man and started visibly, then steadied herself.

"It's all right," she said, "but I never can get used to it, myself. That's the Smile of Welcome and Good Cheer. You will encounter many more, but none quite so well developed. It's one of the features of all church suppers. It also sings lustily and then its eyes turn up."

"Oh, God. Oh, God," breathed Tim. "Do you think it's really happy, that it enjoys being here?"

"You couldn't drive it out," said Sally. "It eats these suppers up spiritually as well as physically."

Suddenly Tim found himself looking a black button closely in the face. The button was on a black vest on which there were still other buttons. Slowly his eyes followed the course of the buttons upward. Would they never end? They did—just under a strong, pink chin. With an effort he kept his eyes going until at last they surmounted the crest of the chin, and to his utter dismay he found them dwelling on a face that was looking down at him with a fixed glare. What eyes! What gleaming teeth! The very vitality of that face unnerved Tim. He swayed forward and grabbed two black-sleeved arms for support. At the same minute Sally, wishing to give a touch of realism to her masculine rôle slapped the owner of the arms and face resoundingly on the back.

The effect to a bystander was that of a concerted attack by Mr. and Mrs. Willows upon the body and person of the Rev. Dr. Jordan. While one held the man's arms pinned to his sides the other brutally assaulted him. It was the old army game that succeeds nine times out of ten.

The slap had disconcerted Sally far more than it had Dr. Jordan, who stood rooted firm in the faith of God. Sally had no such support. She lost all poise and began to babble in a high, effeminate voice—in her own voice, in fact.

"Oh, Dr. Jordan," she gushed, "I have a surprise for you. I've brought my husband along."

"She means our wife," muttered Tim, still clinging to the preacher's arms. "Don't listen to him."

This correction brought Sally to her senses. She dropped her voice to a deep rumble, and once more addressed the preacher.

"That's a horse with another kidney," she said jovially. "But what does it matter? Who knows?"

"Knows what?" asked Tim suspiciously.

"Why ask me?" replied Sally. "Perhaps Dr. Jordan does."

But Dr. Jordan didn't. Accustomed as he was to strange and mystifying situations he found himself for the first time unable to function effectively. Gently but firmly he pried himself loose from Tim, who, realizing that something must be done, smiled brightly up at Dr. Jordan and affectionately patted his arm.

"You see, Dr. Jordan, I kept my promise, didn't I?" he said in Sally's most seductive tones. "I did even better than that, but I knew he wouldn't behave. That husband of mine never takes anything seriously."

The great face of Dr. Jordan cleared. So that was the explanation. Tim Willows was a bit of a joker. Oh,

well, the church needed more of that sort. He could
use Tim Willows to advantage. Perhaps he might be induced to become a regular member of the congregation. True, there was a suggestion of rye in the air, but
maybe . . . He beamed his beamiest upon the pair and
spoke richly.

"Welcome, welcome, welcome, friends," reiterated
the doctor. "I need your sort behind me." Tim wondered what he meant by that. "You're a bit of a larker
yourself, Mrs. Willows, but a lark flies up to heaven, as
you, too, some day shall fly." ("How gloomy,"
thought Tim.) "Glad to have you with us to-night, Mr.
Willows. I hope it will not be the last time. Come in
some day and smoke a cigar with me. Mrs. Willows, I
expect great things from you to-night. Find tables, find
tables." His strong hand swept the room and nearly
knocked the false teeth out of the mouth of one of his
staunchest workers. "So sorry!" cried the Rev. Dr. Jordan, turning to the injured party, who was clutching or
rather muffling his mouth with both hands. And when
Dr. Jordan turned again both Tim and Sally were tot-
tering among the tables.

"Charming couple," thought Dr. Jordan, then moved
away from the gentle cloud of alcohol still floating in
the air.

"What did he mean about expecting great things of
you?" demanded Tim.

"I'm on a committee," replied Sally vaguely. "Civic
Betterment. It means nothing."

Blake and Helen Watson, Vera and Ted Hutchens,
Flo Jennings and Carl Bentley were grouped in a
depressed huddle. They all wore a beaten expression.
They were furtively critical and just a trifle superior.
At the approach of the Willowses the beaten look on
Bentley's face became almost mutilated.

"Ha!" snorted Blake Watson, pulling at his
mustache. "Hah!"

"Bah!" retorted Tim, looking at the man coldly
through Sally's brown eyes. "What a hell of a jam this
is."

At the sound of Tim's voice issuing from the sweet

lips of Sally the statuesque Mr. Bentley gave a start and began to sweat unbecomingly.

"My dears!" exclaimed Sally, squeezing Vera's and Helen's hands with her much larger ones. "So sweet of you to have come. I knew you wouldn't let me down."

And with this she kissed them both.

"What's the big idea?" cried Blake Watson, giving Sally a violent push.

This treatment of his wife immediately aroused Tim. With a small foot he neatly tripped Watson, who fell with a crash among the chairs.

"Nobody can treat my wife that way," he announced, looking down at the fallen man.

Helen, although only occasionally fond of her husband, could not permit this incident to pass unnoticed.

She clawed Tim's hat from his head and threw it on the floor. Sally, more outraged by the treatment of her hat than her husband, promptly shoved Helen down on top of Blake Watson, then, taking Tim's arm, moved majestically away, disassociating herself as well as her spouse from the scene of disorder. It had all happened so quickly that even those who had been privileged to witness the scene at close range ascribed it to an accident. Church supper chairs are constantly doing things to people. They are almost human in their perverseness, either collapsing on a person or making a person collapse. Of course the noise attracted a great deal of attention, but the false and desperate laughter of the Watsons and the Hutchenses, swelled by the hearty boom of Mr. Bentley, served to dispel any suggestion of unpleasantness. Nevertheless the numbers of the little group were dazed. The strange conduct of the Willowses had momentarily numbed their faculties.

"Both of them are as drunk as coots," said Ted Hutchens. "That's the only way I can explain it."

"She actually knocked me down," observed Blake Watson in a puzzled voice.

"And he darned well hurled me down," put in Helen. "It was a sort of mixed scuffle as far as I can make out."

"It was very interesting to watch," drawled Vera.

"The hat part was pretty. How did you ever come to think of that form of retaliation?"

"It was an inspiration," said Helen. "Sally loves her hats."

"We all do—when we get them," remarked Vera, with a significant look at her husband.

"You don't love hats," sneered Mr. Hutchens. "You bow down and fairly worship them."

A middle-aged but infinitely weary-looking woman came up to Tim and took him by the arm.

"Dear Mrs. Willows," she said in an harassed voice, "would you mind lighting that newfangled gasoline stove for us? You're so clever about such things."

Sally, with a smile of unholy enjoyment, watched the dazed Tim being dragged off in the direction of the kitchen.

"Which stove do you mean?" asked Tim of the weary woman. The kitchen seemed full of stoves, all of which were working briskly.

"That one," replied the woman, pointing to a sinister-looking object squatting defiantly in one corner.

"Ah," said Tim with the confidence born of alcohol. "I'll show you how to light that baby. It's really quite simple."

So saying, he turned on a tap until his ears were pleased by the jocund sound of gurgling fluid. Then he struck a match, pushed a button, and applied the light. There was a muffled boom, an odoriferous flame, then the room became lost in a deep, heavy pall of gaseous vapor. And from the bosom of this reeking cloud issued a volley of vile obscenities uttered in the deep voice of an infuriated male. The edges of this vocal display of frightfulness were garnished by the stifled shrieks of women. A short time later the Girls, gallantly led by Tim, debouched into the supper room like a troupe of blackfaced comediennes. Never had the Girls received such a shock and never had a church supper been so lively entertaining. First Mr. and Mrs. Watson had got themselves entangled in some chairs, and actually fallen down on the floor in a most diverting manner. This was hugely funny and furnished no end of bright conversation. But to see the Girls in battle array issuing from the smoke of the kitchen was almost too much of a good thing. Of course, the explosion occasioned a certain amount of consternation, but this was quickly dispelled as soon as the bellowing voice of Dr. Jordan assured the company that all danger was past. The Girls and Tim required a certain amount of washing, which was administered by willing and tender hands. During the process of ablution Tim found an opportunity to empty virtually all of the contents of his flask. When once more he appeared in public he was feeling decidedly set up. The Girls were much more interested in trying to discover the source of the obscene language than that of the explosion. They never did, although they entertained some well-founded suspicions.

The supper proceeded coughingly, and although the food tasted weirdly of smoke and gasoline it was consumed with true Christian humility and fortitude. Then came the singing, which taxed the Willowses far beyond their capacity to stand taxing. This was especially true of Tim. At one moment he sang lustily in a clear, unmistakable baritone and at the next he startled both himself and everyone within hearing distance by swooping up to the dizzy altitudes of a soprano. Sally was experiencing the same difficulty, only not to the same extent. It was entirely forgivable if those sitting at her table were rendered mute with amazement when they heard proceeding from the mouth of an adult male the trebling alto of a choir boy. It is even more forgivable if they gasped with incredulity when they heard those ringing notes descend to a faint, embarrassed rumble. Up and down the scales fluctuated the voices of the Willowses until at times they seemed almost inspired. During a lull in the singing a lady leaned over to Tim and said, "My dear, I don't know how you can do it."

"It's a gift," replied Tim modestly. "I don't know how I manage it myself. Nobody ever taught me."

"Nobody should," remarked an old man.

When a long-faced individual asked Sally how she accomplished the feat she passed it off by saying that her mother's great-aunt by marriage had been a professional ventriloquist. This answer only partially satisfied the man. He kept brooding over the problem of how much influence one's mother's great-aunt by marriage could have on one's voice. Not a great deal, he decided. Certainly, not enough to justify the amazing demonstration of vocal gymnastics he had just heard.

The singing ended, the speeches began, but little did Tim realize that he was to be among the speakers until he heard Dr. Jordan calling in a loud voice for Mrs. Sally Willows to address the assembled multitude on the subject of Civic Betterment.

"I'll do no such damn thing," Tim muttered to Sally.

"Don't let me down, Tim," she whispered. "You know as much about the subject as anyone else. Go on up there and just say you approve of civic betterment and all that."

Whether it was Sally or the liquor within him that prevailed upon Tim to mount the platform and stand swaying dangerously at its edge will never be known. The fact remains that he did this mad act and actually offered himself up on the altar of Christian martyrdom.

"Ladies and gentlemen," he began in a voice that snapped the supperites erect in their chairs. "Members of the Congregation," he continued in softly cooing accents. "Friends, would perhaps be better," he amended rather briskly. "I shall soon get started. A short time ago I gave a successful demonstration of how not to light a gasoline stove. I shall now endeavor to show you how not to make a speech."

Tim paused to permit his audience to become convulsed, and during that pause he lost control of his thoughts and almost lost his balance.

"Look out!" Sally whispered piercingly, and Tim swayed back from the edge of the platform.

"Friends," he began again, this time making no effort to disguise his voice, "I believe in physic betterment—I mean, civic betterment. We should have a bigger and better civic—pardon me again, I mean, physic—no, I don't—what I mean is, we should have a bigger and better betterment. Oh, yes, and a much bigger and better city. We must have much wider streets with lots of sidewalk cafés." Desperately Tim's hands sought for his pockets and, finding none, plucked impotently at his skirt. "And we should have bigger gardens," he continued. "Great big gardens running off to the skyline. Everything should be bigger, much bigger and much better. Bigger houses, bigger schools, bigger stores, bigger everything. Great big moving-picture theaters with fountains. Must have fountains." Once more Tim's hands struggled into non-existent pockets and succeeded in disarranging his skirt. Sally was beginning to get nervous. "Then there's another thing. We should have bigger and better churches. And I suggest that congregations should be drafted so that all the churches would be filled and the preachers wouldn't have to deliver their sermons to eleven or twelve dispirited-looking ladies who don't need to be saved. And I believe in free education for preachers. So many preachers are dumb because they lack the time and opportunity to continue their studies. Give 'em a chance to dig into economics, psychology, and sociology—any number of subjects. Give the poor devils a break, say I." Here the dress was strained to its utmost. "On the other hand I believe in the legalization of the ancient and honorable profession of prostitution." Gasps from the audience. Wild signals from Sally, but Tim was warming to his subject. "Many a sweet girl has gone wrong because she was not allowed to become a good, honest prostitute. Do you know that last year 2,540 girls disappeared from their homes? Why, I ask you, why? Why did all those lovely girls disappear from their homes? Because they weren't allowed to become good, honest prostitutes—that is, most of them." He paused to watch the frantic approach of the Rev. Dr. Jordan. "Prostitution is an amiable and artistic profession. It develops a social instinct and——"

At this point the dress gave up all resistance and descended with a snap. The next moment the person believed to be Mrs. Sally Willows stood before the supperites and gave them the shock of their lives. The Rev. Dr. Jordan, whether from modesty or admiration, stopped in his tracks and gazed at the lovely figure. The step-ins were becomingly short and Sally's legs were becomingly shaped. Altogether the revelation was not at all bad. The supperites were in a state of ferment. Tim was almost frantic. He was making fluttering signals of anguish to Sally. Strange to say, disgraceful to say, that hard-boiled young lady was laughing. Tim could have poisoned her. What had broken Sally down was the small flask of whiskey strapped so neatly around Tim's waist. The presence of that flask explained a lot to Dr. Jordan. In fact, it explained everything. Tim took a few frightened steps, tripped and fell. During the general commotion that followed, Sally adjusted Tim's dress and dragged the broken man from the church. Once in the car she gave him a huge drink. Then she drove him home herself.

"Well," said Tim at last, "we certainly made a go of that church supper."

"Yes," agreed Sally. "The Willowses were an immense social success—a riot, in fact."

"And the Rev. Dr. Jordan got a great deal more than he expected," added Tim.

"You opened his eyes to a lot of things," said Sally.

CHAPTER IX

A Shocking Discovery

WHEN TIM WILLOWS DISCOVERED HE WAS GOING TO become a mother he nearly went mad. Sally was forced to lock up all the grog and to take a day off from the office in order to be with the semi-demented prospective mother of her child.

"I won't be a mother," Tim assured her in a trembling voice. "I'll do something terrible to myself. A lake—that's it. You'll find me in a lake. All wet."

"Now don't work yourself up, dear," said Sally soothingly. "It will be bad for baby. Let me give you this footstool, sweetheart. It will make you much more comfortable. And I'll get you a little shawl."

In response to these tender endearments, Tim Willows unleashed a scream of rage and dashed about the room looking for something to break. He picked up a clock, considered it, then returned it to its place. The clock was too expensive. Anyway he liked that clock. Finally he selected a large china vase. It made a very satisfactory sound when it crashed against the floor. He danced madly on the fragments, then fell exhausted into a deep chair.

"I can't stand it," he gasped. "I can't. Footstools and shawls. Oh, God."

"You should be ashamed of yourself to carry on like that," admonished Sally. "One would think you were demeaning yourself to be the mother of my child."

Once more Tim's scream of impotent rage rang through the house. Springing up, he seized upon another china vase, which he shattered against the floor. The first one had proved efficacious. Why not this one?

"Thank God, they're gone," said Sally, as she led the trembling man back to his chair. "I've always felt like smashing them myself, but never could work up the courage. If it hadn't been for baby, they might have remained in the Willows family for generations. What are you hoping for, dear, a boy or a girl?"

"A gorilla," gritted Tim. "A monster. A two-headed calf."

"Don't be silly, sweetheart," Sally told him. "You should have nothing but sweet and fragrant thoughts now. I'll get you a book about it—*The Program of a Prospective Mother*. You'll love it. It will do you good."

Weakly, Tim looked round the room for another vase, then abandoned the idea through sheer physical lassitude.

"You stop calling me 'dear' and 'sweetheart' and all those things," he muttered darkly. "And if you bring that book into this house, I'll burn it up on the front lawn and dance round the fire naked, screaming the vilest words I can muster."

"But, Tim, precious," explained Sally, patiently, "neither of us knows the first thing about motherhood, or childbirth or anything along those lines."

"Don't want to know," snapped Tim. "Bring me a book on how to forestall a prospective infant and you'll be doing a guy a good turn. I feel like going upstairs and wringing that damn little idol's neck. Of all the tricks to play on a self-respecting man. It was a bad day for us when that libidinous uncle of mine conceived the bright idea of sending him to us."

"Don't talk disparagingly of Mr. Ram at this critical time," said Sally. "We'll be needing all the luck he can bring us. They say the first one is always the hardest."

"What?" ejaculated Tim. "The first one? Do you think for a moment I'd have another, assuming I have this one?"

"I see no reason why you shouldn't," replied Sally, callously. "I see no reason why you shouldn't have several. It's high time we were doing something in the line of babies. Neither of us is getting any younger."

"That's right!" cried Tim. "Make a regular Negro mammy out of me. Make me bear such a brood of children I won't know exactly how many I have. I suppose you're hoping for twins to begin with."

"Twins would be awfully cute," admitted Sally. "While you're at it, you might as well make up for lost time."

"You seem to regard me as a sort of factory," Tim observed bitterly. "If I bear one very small and reluctant baby, you can consider yourself lucky."

"Nonsense," replied Sally, cheerfully. "I expect great things from you."

"So did Dr. Jordan," said Tim. "And he got much more than he expected."

"Everyone will be so pleased and excited when they find out," Sally observed with a bright, anticipatory smile. "All the girls. Think of it."

"I'll not even listen to it, much less think of it," retorted Tim. "If you breathe a word of this to a single living soul, I'll do somthing desperate and you'll be eternally sorry. Just stick that in your hatband and keep it there as a reminder."

"Oh, we'll have to let them know," protested Sally.

"That's just what we won't have to do," said Tim. "Let 'em find out for themselves. They'll know soon enough. God, what a thing to have happened to a man. I guess I'm the first member of my sex ever to have gotten this way."

"You should be proud of the fact," replied Sally. "And think of my feelings. I'll be the first woman ever to have become a father."

Tim looked at her hatefully.

"That's right," he muttered. "Go on and gloat. Feel proud and chesty. You should be ashamed of yourself for getting me in this ridiculous, not to say dangerous, condition. Suppose you lose me?"

"We must take our chances on that," said Sally, with what Tim felt was altogether too much complacency.

"You mean I must take my chances," he retorted with mild sarcasm. "You are taking no chances. It's pretty soft for you."

"I'll be very upset and nervous," replied Sally.

"Bah!" exclaimed Tim. "You'll probably get squiffed and celebrate with Steve Jones. But believe me, I'm going to make you pay through the nose for the dirty trick you've played on me. When a woman's this way she has to be humored. You know that as well as I do. At any time of the day or night, you must humor a prospective mother. And I'm going to have cravings. I'm going to think of the strangest damn things."

"All right," agreed Sally. "That's good with me. I'd do almost anything to have a baby."

"Except have one," put in Tim.

"It's not my fault," said Sally. "It's a physical impossibility. And Tim, dear, you will continue to write copy for me to take to the office?"

"Inasmuch as our bread and butter depend on it, I guess I'll have to," replied Tim. "At any rate, it will take my mind off of the horrible condition I'm in. But tell me, don't you know the first thing about childbirth, Sally?"

"Well, I know the first thing," she admitted. "That is, how to go about starting one."

"Don't be facetious," said her husband. "I know all about that, too. What I mean is, doesn't it hurt a bit?"

"From all that I've heard," she told him, "it's not what you might call a soothing experience."

"And you get awfully large, don't you?" Tim continued, with the fascination of horror in his voice.

"Tremendous," said Sally, warming to the subject. "And sometimes sick in the morning."

"I'm that now," put in Tim. "Very."

"Then you must be a shade pregnant," Sally observed with assurance. "It's almost a sure sign."

Tim brightened a little.

"But, Sally," he said, "you're not absolutely sure I'm going to be a mother, are you? There might be some mistake. I mean it's just possible?"

"Of course, there's just a chance," replied Sally. "That's why I have to take you to a doctor."

"What!" cried Tim. "And be examined? Never in this life. I won't stand for that."

He shrank back in his chair and looked miserable. The thought of the doctor revolted him. Was ever a man in such a fix? Strange that at that moment his thoughts should revert to Claire Meadows. He wondered what she would think of the situation. A strange woman.

"But you must, Tim, darling," laughed Sally. "Don't be so stupid. Everyone goes to a doctor. It's the only thing to do. Especially with us. We don't know a darned thing about it. Have to get some honest-to-God advice. Have to learn things and find out what you must do with yourself—what to eat and what not to eat, and, most important of all, how much you can drink, if any."

"Hope he doesn't stop my grog," said Tim. "That is, not entirely. Before we go to this doctor, you've got to give me a drink or so. Otherwise I'll call the whole childbirth off."

Sally agreed because she realized that it would be in all likelihood the last time the poor devil would be able to indulge. It seemed a shame to stop Tim's grog. He enjoyed it so. Give him a bottle and a book, and life for him was complete. He demanded of it nothing more.

Peter brought a fresh bottle of rye and some glasses and a siphon. After he had deposited these on a convenient table he stood looking appreciatively at the remains of the shattered vases. He was glad, but at the same time uneasy. If they began breaking up the household effects, they'd soon be eating off the floor like animals.

"I broke them, Peter," offered Tim, in what he hoped was a sweet voice. "I did it in a fit of rage. And I knew you didn't like them. You can clear away the remains later."

"Thank you, Miss Sally," said Peter. "They were horrid things. Remember when they were bought. His great-aunt, Mrs. Ames Willows, brought them home one day. They occasioned a great disturbance. Mr. Ames went on a bender for a month. It didn't take much to send him off, he was so highstrung." Peter paused and gazed reflectively at the table. "He was fond of the bottle, too," he added significantly.

"Listen, Sally," said Tim, when Peter had left the room. "I've had something on my mind I've been wanting to tell you for a long time. Now that I'm in this serious condition, I think I will."

"Shoot, old kid," replied Sally, as she sipped the highball.

"Well, you know the night I nearly murdered Carl Bentley?" he began.

"I'll never forget it," said Sally.

"Well, that night," continued Tim, "I drifted quite accidently over to Claire Meadows' house and—and I didn't act quite right. I guess I was a bit unfaithful."

"If you can only guess about it," said Sally, "it mustn't have been much of a party."

"It was more like a dream," replied Tim in a low voice. "Like being inevitably guided in a dream. No power to control circumstances and no desire, Sally. But it was real, all right. You know I was in a bit of a fog—a dense fog, in fact."

He gulped down his drink and looked at Sally out of her own limpid, brown eyes. She in turn was regarding him with affectionate amusement.

"Pregnancy," she remarked easily, "is already making an honester man of you." She paused to refill the glasses. "You know," she continued quite seriously, "I can't find it in me to blame you for being unfaithful with Claire Meadows. To me she is the most irresistible woman in town. Anyway, I wasn't doing so well myself that night. As a matter of fact, I started you out on the primrose path. It's a funny thing, though. It's insight, that's what it is. When I first met Claire Meadows many months ago, I had the weirdest feeling that some day you two were going to get together. She's the sort of person who'd appreciate you and your silly attitude toward life and things. Yet, I had the comforting feeling, also, that she was not the woman you should have married. I'm that woman, or, at least, I was. Both of you are too hard-boiled and at the same time too idealistic. You'd burn each other up. You'd hurt each other terribly in some fool way." Once more Sally paused and a slow smile, a wicked smile, crooked the lips that had once been Tim's "Just the same, Tim," she resumed, "I'm much obliged for the tip. Think I'll drop round to see Claire Meadows some night. She must be missing you, old thing."

"And me in this condition!" Tim cried indignantly. "You'll do no such thing, Sally Willows. Now that you've got me all funny the way I am, I'll be damned if I'll stand for any monkey business. I'll abort myself, or whatever it is you do."

"Now don't get yourself all worked up and nervous over nothing," said Sally, soothingly. "Of course, I was only joking. I wouldn't think of doing such a thing."

"And you're not going about with a lot of light women, when I get all fat and ugly," continued Tim, getting himself all fumed up and excited at the ghastly ramifications of his condition. "Give me another drink. I'm terribly cast down. I'll stand for no messing about. Do you understand that?"

"Of course, I do, dear," said Sally, smiling in spite of herself. "Don't worry your head about me. I've learned my lesson. I almost made you a murderer once, and I did make you an adulterer. You're indebted to me for the latter although you may deny it."

"This is the weirdest darn conversation that ever took place between man and wife," replied Tim, somewhat mollified, as he reached for the bottle.

"No question about it," agreed Sally. "But I try not to think of it any more. You get sort of goofy if you do."

Under the influence of the bottle, and morally liberated by his confession, Tim's spirits rose until, by the time he had reached the doctor's office, they had become rather unruly, almost boisterous.

"Hello, Doc!" he cried, throwing his arms round the neck of the astounded physician. "My wife, here, tells me I'm a wee bit pregnant. Not much, Doc, not much, but enough—almost too much. What about it, Doc, do you think I'm elected? Do I look sort of preggy?"

"That's a silly word," commented Sally. "Sounds like baby talk."

Tim was almost convulsed. He released the doctor and flung himself upon Sally.

"That's just what it is," he cried. "It's baby talk, and

it's all your fault, or at least, I think it is. Somebody blundered."

At this point the doctor interposed in a suave voice while still adjusting his collar. Addressing himself in low tones to Sally, he suggested politely, "This is a mental case, I perceive?"

"Alcoholic," replied Sally briefly. "Also somewhat pregnant."

"And mental, too, Doc," interpolated Tim. "Don't forget that. I'm entirely mad, I assure you. And I'm going to have a mad baby—a regular monster."

The doctor ignored Tim and turned once more to Sally.

"And the object of your visit, sir, is exactly what?" he asked.

"Absolutely no object," put in Tim. "Just a visit. We thought you might like to know about me, that's all."

"And to congratulate us, perhaps," added Sally, who was feeling quite giddy herself.

"Yes," declared Tim. "We thought you might slip us a snifter. Doctors have lots of whiskey. They love it."

"May I ask just who you are?" demanded the doctor, his disgust getting the better of his professional urbanity.

"Oh, we thought you knew that," exclaimed Sally. "Everyone knows us. We're the Willowses. This is my husband—I mean my wife, Mrs. Tim Willows. I'm Tim, himself, in the flesh."

The doctor was undecided whether to call for assistance and forcibly eject this peculiar couple or to try to get rid of them peaceably.

"I presume, then," he observed, "that you would like me to—er—run over Mrs. Willows?"

"What's that?" demanded Tim. "Run over? Does the man think he's a lawn mower or a sort of human Juggernaut? I didn't come here to be run over."

"Are babies in your line, Doctor?" asked Sally, also ignoring her husband.

"I'm an obstetrician, if that's what you mean, sir," replied the doctor with dignity.

"He's a what?" demanded Tim.

Both Sally and the doctor looked at Tim wearily.

"You wouldn't understand, dear," she told him. "He obsteterates, does this doctor, so it seems that we've come to the right place."

"Well, that's nice to know, at any rate," commented Tim, seating himself in a most uncomfortable chair.

"Could you tell me just when you noticed you were in this condition?" asked the doctor.

"Never noticed it at all, Doc," answered Tim. "It sort of crept up on me like a—a—er—thief in the night."

"Or a wolf on the fold," added Sally.

"I don't seem to find this very helpful," said the docor, rather impatiently. "I had better examine Mrs. Willows."

"One minute, Doc," interposed Tim, holding up a restraining hand. "Before we go any further, I'd like to know how much it's going to set me back to have this baby. Because if it costs too darned much, we'll waive the baby and buy a new car."

When Tim discovered it would cost about five hundred dollars to cover the entire expense involved in presenting his wife with a child, he was terribly shocked.

"What!" he exclaimed. "All that money for the fun of suffering like hell? Why, it's a racket, a regular racket. Women should be paid to have babies, and as for a man, why he should be elected mayor, to say the least."

The doctor, becoming more aroused, informed Tim definitely and categorically that personally it was a matter of the most abysmal indifference to him whether he, Tim, had a baby or not.

"That's not very neighborly of you, Doc," Tim replied. "If women didn't have babies you'd be out of luck. You'd probably have to become a magician and pull rabbits and things out of hats. It isn't an easy life."

"I could find something better to do than that," replied the doctor, stung by Tim's remark.

"For example?" asked Tim challengingly.

"Mrs. Willows," the doctor explained, "if you and your husband dropped in merely to pay me a personal call, I must remind you that in spite of my gratification there are other demands on my time. Do you wish to be examined or not?"

"Suppose I don't pass this examination," demanded Tim, "won't I be able to have a baby, then? Is it a written or verbal examination? It doesn't matter, though, because I don't know the first thing about childbirth. Why don't you examine my wife instead—I mean, my husband? He's nearly as dumb as I am, but at least he knows something. The whole damn business is Greek to me. I was never intended to be a mother, and if it hadn't been for my innocence, which is a nice word for ignorance, I wouldn't be the way I am now. You men seem to think that all a woman has to do is to toss off a baby and call it a day. Let me tell you right here, Doctor whatever-your-name-is, it's men like you and my husband, lecherous, low-down, licentious bums——"

"Madam, madam," objected the doctor. "I've never experienced such a thing in my life. You must endeavor to calm yourself. We must endeavor to calm each other. In all my professional experience, I've never encountered a prospective mother who was quite so casual and unsympathetic, quite so hardened. It isn't natural. We must endeavor to correct your mental attitude. Do you, or do you not, wish to be examined? If you don't, well and good, but if you do, I urge you to come inside with me. Mr. Willows can come with you if you want him."

The doctor's voice was shaking a little and his nerves were beginning to jump. He realized how important it was for him to keep strict check on himself. Once let a woman get talking among her friends about the unfeeling methods of a doctor and he might just as well abandon his practice and move to another town.

"I wouldn't let that guy in on my examination for anything in the world," proclaimed Tim resolutely. "He'd gloat, that's what he'd do, and I'll have no gloating."

"Be a good girl and go with the doctor," said Sally coaxingly. "I'll give you something when we get home if you do, otherwise, no—not a drop."

Tim rose from the chair and suspiciously followed

the distracted doctor into his private office. A long, oddly twisted glass tube attracted his wandering attention.

"What's this for?" he demanded, seizing upon the tube and examining it critically.

Unfortunately the tube slipped from Tim's careless grasp and crashed against the tiled floor with a loud report. The doctor froze in his tracks and hunched his back. Low, clucking sounds came from him. His fingers were twitching spasmodically. But he did not even turn round as he asked in a strained voice, "What was that, Mrs. Willows?"

"Sorry," replied Tim casually. "It was some silly looking object. Didn't have any sense to it, seemingly. You're well rid of it, Doctor."

At this remark, the doctor renewed his clucking. He was gallantly striving to pull himself together. Sally, sitting outside, on hearing the report, naturally assumed that either the doctor had shot Tim or Tim had shot the doctor. She sprang from the chair and popped into the room.

"What's that?" she demanded tragically.

The doctor jumped and spun about, then settled shudderingly to rest.

"Don't startle me so!" he exclaimed. "I'm not at all used to such conduct."

"No," put in Tim easily. "Don't startle the doctor any more. He can't stand it. You know, I think we'd better examine him first before he examines me. He doesn't strike me as being any too good at present. No control."

This observation had the effect of starting the doctor off on his clucking again. He went to a shelf and, taking down a bottle, poured out a drink.

"A small sedative," he muttered.

"Just what we need," cried Tim, snatching up the bottle and taking an avid gulp. "A rose by another name would taste as strong."

He passed the bottle to Sally, who followed his example, smacking Tim's lips at the end of the operation. The doctor rushed up and forcibly retrieved his property.

"You mustn't do that," he chided. "It's not the way to act, not at all the way to act."

"Pardon me," replied Sally sweetly. "I thought the drinks were on the house."

At this moment Tim pressed a button on a switchboard and from somewhere in the room a dynamo began to tear through its paces. The button seemed to be in some way connected with the doctor, because he began to jump up and down as if he were riding an invisible pogo stick.

"Keep away! Keep away!" he shouted. "You'll burn yourself to a crisp. The X ray's gone mad."

"What a fascinating life a doctor leads," commented Tim, above the hum of the dynamo.

This restarted the clucking on the part of the doctor, who was sliding along the wall in the direction of the button. When the switch was turned off, he carefully mopped his face with his handkerchief and took a deep breath.

"Another mild sedative," suggested Sally, presenting herself before the weary man with a glass half filled with whiskey.

"Thanks," he muttered, as he tremblingly reached for the glass. "The effect of the first one was spoiled. I do wish we could get along with this examination."

"Directly, Doctor, directly," said Tim, in a soothing voice. "What you need is a good rest. Can't burn the candle at both ends, you know. Your nerves are all shot."

"Yes," added Sally, solicitously. "What you need is a nice long rest." She took a sip from the bottle, then passed it on to Tim. "Would you like to lie down for a moment before you go on? Must get over that shaking. You're not addicted to drugs, are you, Doctor?"

This time the physician's clucking was not only excited but also bitter. He pawed at the air.

"Please go away," he said, in a pleading voice. "Don't talk to me now."

"It's drugs, I'm afraid," muttered Sally, going to the door. "Something should be done."

When Sally had closed the door, the doctor turned to Tim and spoke in a deadly voice.

"Lie down on that table," he said, "and for God's sweet sake, Mrs. Willows, stop fluttering about."

Tim looked at the table suspiciously.

"What are you going to do to me?" he asked.

"That's my business," replied the doctor coldly.

"Not entirely," replied Tim. "I'm in on it, also."

"Are you going to lie down on that table?" demanded the doctor, advancing on Tim with a distracted look in his eye.

"Suppose I don't?" Tim temporized.

"Suppose you don't what?" continued the doctor.

"Lie down on that table," Tim replied.

"If you don't lie down on that table, do you know what I'm going to do?" asked the doctor.

"I don't know," replied Tim.

"Well, I'll tell you," said the doctor, licking his dry lips. "I'm going to damn well hurl you down on that table, Mrs. Willows. I'm going to get you down on that table if it's the last thing I do on earth."

"Oh, Doctor!" exclaimed Tim coyly.

The doctor stood clucking at Tim.

"Get down on that table," he grated.

Momentarily overawed, Tim hitched himself upon the table and sat there swinging his legs.

"Be reasonable, Doc," he said. "Let's talk this matter over."

"Flat on your back," replied the doctor implacably.

"Just give me a hint," Tim pleaded.

"Down there, down," answered the doctor.

Tim sank back on the table.

"After all, Doctor," he said, "I'm not exactly a dog. Not quite."

The doctor extended his hands.

Exactly thirty seconds later Sally was startled by the sound of a maddened scream, followed by a tremendous crashing of glass. Once more the scream was repeated, then gave way to Tim's deep-throated roaring. The door burst open and the doctor hurtled out with a look of congealed horror on his face. Immediately behind him appeared an infuriated Tim. With one hand he clutched at his clothing and with the other he carved great slices of air with a wicked-looking operating knife. The doctor jumped behind Sally and clung to her for protection.

"Speak to her, Mr. Willows," he chattered. "Reason with her if you can. The poor woman has gone mad."

The shock of suddenly confronting himself restored Tim to his senses. He halted and looked accusingly at the doctor.

"Of all the things to do with a body," Tim exploded, pointing the knife at the trembling man. "Of all the low-life tricks. He might be a doctor, but he's certainly not a gentleman."

"She doesn't understand, Mr. Willows," hastily put in the doctor. "She's just like a savage."

"What did he do?" asked Sally.

"What did he do?" repeated Tim indignantly. "What didn't he do. That guy did plenty. What a way to carry on. You're a fast worker, Doc. I'll have to say that much for you. But life is not all play, Doc. You'd better remember that."

"I thought you knew," explained Sally. "You poor dear."

"Poor dear, hell," snapped Tim. "I almost murdered the man. It's a nice time to tell me about it." He looked at the doctor and a grin spread over his flushed face. "Sorry, Doc," he said. "There seems to have been a slight misunderstanding. We were both right according to our standards."

By this time the doctor himself was in need of medical assistance. Between them they dragged him to his study and dumped him down on the sofa. He was making ineffectual passes at the air with a pair of limp hands. Sally brought the bottle from the almost demolished laboratory and she and Tim took a drink. Then they stood looking speculatively at the doctor.

"Better ring for the maid," said Tim in a low voice. "There doesn't seem to be any secretary knocking about. I thought all doctors managed a secretary by some hook or crook."

"She's sick," gasped the doctor, his professional pride forcing him to speak.

"She would be," replied Tim. "Bathe his temples,

Sally, with that grog. He'd chatter the neck off the bottle if you tried to give him a drink."

"Make a try at it," whispered the doctor. "Don't waste the stuff. It's good."

"What thrift," said Tim admiringly.

"All right now?" asked Sally, after she had succeeded in feeding the man a drink.

"Better," whispered the doctor.

"Then I guess we'd better be going," she continued, rather lamely. "We'll come back another time for that examination."

"Okay, Doc?" asked Tim.

They left the doctor clucking wildly on the sofa.

"A most embarrassing experience," observed Tim as they quietly let themselves out of the house.

"What I want to know is," demanded Sally, "how do you expect to have a baby if you won't let a doctor come near you?"

"By long distance," replied Tim. "Or like a woman of the Stone Age. I feel like eating some pineapple."

CHAPTER X

Tim Seeks Enlightenment

A FEW DAYS LATER, AFTER WOLFING DOWN A ROBUST
breakfast, Tim decided to call on his old friend, the village barber. Alfredo had lots of children, children
without rhyme or reason. Mrs. Alfredo was always
having a baby or about to have a baby or just getting
over having a baby. She was in the baby business and
seemed able to turn over her stock with surprising reg-
ularity and speed. Tim would speak with this Alfredo
and pump him about babies. He would inquire into babies, their production and their upkeep. Sally would be
surprised at his vast range of information. At the same
time he would have his hair trimmed, or rather, he
would have his wife's hair trimmed as a pretext for ac-
quiring wisdom. For the moment Tim had forgotten
that in his metamorphosed form his old friend, Alfredo, would hardly recognize him.

He slipped on one of Sally's smartest coats and
crammed a small black felt hat carelessly on his head.
Then he left the house, taking the lunging Dopey with
him.

There was a touch of spring in the air and the snow
was melting fast. The distant hills were coming through
and the sun lay warm upon them. Soon they would
arouse themselves from their winter slumber and take
steps about getting green. It was quiet along the neat,
well-ordered suburban street. Tim felt the quietness. It
got inside him. He breathed deeply and stood at the
curb, looking about him. He would like to efface all of
the houses in sight as well as all of the persons who
lived in them. Dopey lunged Tim across the street,
then paused himself to investigate nothing much. The
dog was too strong for Tim in his female body. Tim

suspected that Dopey knew it and was prepared to take advantage of his knowledge. Yes, it was a nice suburb, mused Tim. That was just the trouble with it. It was too damned nice. But the spirit of the people was not so nice. It was too imitative, too acquisitive. A man had to have exaclty what his neighbor had, or better—better if it could be managed. And a man had to live in a certain section or else exist under the burden of a steadily growing inferiority complex. It was sad about that. There were decent men and women living in other sections. Tim liked many of them. But there they were. They were just not on the in, and that was all there was to it. And women had such a way of lording it over their less fortunate sisters. It was cruel and it was senseless. He was glad Sally was not that way. She bought her meat wherever she liked. It was not her method, like so many of her friends', to establish prestige through the butcher or baker. Yes, this suburb would be better with a lot of revisions and deleting. All these real estate people with their quaint ideas and parky minds. Restricted developments and all that. They thrived on snobbery. And in New York the bread lines were twisting round corners. Men standing bleakly in the cold for the privilege of remaining miserably alive on the surface of a world that had no use for them. Yet the bread lines had thoughts and feelings. They were composed of human beings, men who wanted things and who missed things and who watched others live through eyes that were too distantly hopeless even to express envy. And right here in Cliffside men and women were making themselves miserable merely because they could not afford a car as good as Sam Jones's or a radio as fine as Bill Smith's or a home on Upper Clear View Road. It was all out of proportion. Tim realized that he himself was a selfish individual, but at least he didn't get all hot and bothered about those things. Give him a bottle and a book and leave him alone, that was all he asked. He realized that as an individual he could do nothing about the bread lines. He couldn't even help materially one individual member. But he was aware of their existence. That was a start, anyway. Idly his thoughts drifted and absently he delivered a sharp kick on Dopey's adamant rump. The dog made no protest. Tim rather suspected the beast enjoyed an occasional kick. It gave him to feel he was being noticed. Tim wondered if he was always going to be a woman, if life from now on was going to be just one baby after another. He knew he would never be clever about not having babies. He was altogether too careless and shiftless. He sighed from deep self-commiseration and started off down the street.

"Sally Willows," a voice called.

He turned with a frightened expression and saw, hurrying toward him, a woman who as far as he was concerned had never existed before. Evidently from the warmth of the kiss she gave Tim she must have known Sally quite intimately and liked her. Tim, poor soul, was not enough of a woman to know that the kisses women so liberally exchange with each other mean exactly less than nothing.

"Hello! Hello!" cried the woman.

Tim contented himself with one small "Hello."

"I've come back," said the other. "Here I am."

"Are you sure?" Tim asked her.

"Same old Sally, I see," continued the unknown.

"A trifle renovated," replied Tim. "Perhaps 'altered' would be a better word."

"What's all the news?" demanded the woman.

"The same old thing," said Tim easily. "Scandal and philandering and concealed animosity—envy and a touch of heartbreak thrown in for good measure. The merry whirl, you know."

"It's dreadful how people go on," the recently returned one contributed virtuously. "Of course Dan, my husband, doesn't know this, but I met the grandest man while I was away. I was all on my own, you know."

"Yes," said Tim, trying to keep the sarcasm from his voice. "Dan was just grinding dumbly along while you met the grandest man."

"Dan loves his work," declared the woman. "Couldn't drag him away from it."

"Did you ever try the dragging process?" Tim asked mildly.

"Don't be horrid, Sally," said the other. "Don't you believe a woman should have her own life?"

"Oh, don't misunderstand me," replied Tim. "I believe a woman should have at least nine lives, like a cat. And all the grand men she can handle. It merely occurred to me that if there wasn't a husband knocking about in the background stupidly loving his work or pretending to love his work she'd have one hell of a time struggling through one life in the manner to which she was accustomed. It was merely a passing thought."

"No doubt about that," agreed the other. "A husband is convenient at times."

"Around the first of the month," suggested Tim, thoroughly hating this woman.

"Yes," said the woman. "What a horrible dog. Where are you off to?"

"That's not a horrible dog," retorted Tim. "That's the finest mixture of canine strains that ever perplexed a bitch. And if you'd like to know, I'm going to get a shave."

"A shave?" exclaimed the woman.

"I mean a trim," Tim hastened to reply. "Did I say a shave? How stupid of me. What I really meant to say was a trim, you know, the hair."

"I'll walk along with you part of the way," said the woman. "That is, if your dog will give me some of the sidewalk."

Dopey received another kick and moved slightly in advance, gratefully wagging his tail. He hated this stopping on street corners and talking to people. It made him nervous.

"Did you ever have a baby?" Tim asked presently, with as much indifference as he could manage.

"Why, don't you remember?" said the woman in a surprised voice. "You came to see me yourself at the hospital."

"Did I?" asked Tim absently. "That was nice of me, but then I'm always doing nice things, and there are so many babies—too many."

The woman laughed.

"You're a queer duck," she said.

"Aren't I," agreed Tim. "Did it hurt much, this baby?"

"Why, didn't you know?" asked the woman. "For days they thought I wasn't going to live. I had septic fever and all sorts of complications."

Tim shrank within himself and looked at the pavement with scared eyes.

"Are there lots of complications you can get?" he asked in a low voice.

"You wouldn't believe how many there are," said the woman. "All sorts of things can happen."

Tim choked down a little gasp.

"Then it was pretty awful?" he went on.

"I wouldn't go through it again for all of the money in the world," the woman assured him. "And I'm fond of money, but I was lucky at that."

"How do you make that out?" Tim inquired.

"The woman in the room next to mine died and the one next to her went mad," replied Tim's companion. "Stark, staring mad."

Tim felt that within a very few moments he would follow the example of the woman next to the woman who died.

"Are the doctors kind?" he managed to ask after swallowing hard several times.

"Mine wasn't," replied the other. "He was as cross and callous as an old crab. It's quite ghastly," she continued. "I'm glad it's all over. Any woman who has the nerve enough to have a baby has my sympathy. It's nip and tuck for her."

Tim had no use for the woman's sympathy. She was burning him up. He parted with her on Springfield Avenue, and dragged Dopey, squatting sidewise, into the barber shop.

He found Alfredo disengaged and, after elaborate courtesies, seated himself in the glistening Italian's chair. Dopey delicately rested his head on a cuspidor and endeavored to forget everything by going to sleep. Tim was very much upset. His conversation with the unknown woman had sadly shattered his morale.

"How are you to-day, Alfredo?" he asked in a weary voice.

Alfred paused in his occupation and looked slightly perplexed. Then he glanced behind him to discover if another customer had been speaking, a customer with a strangely familiar voice.

"I am well, madam," he replied at length. "You have been here before, madam?"

The twice repeated "madam" served to remind Tim even in his preoccupied frame of mind that he was no longer the customer with whom Alfredo had been wont to deal. He smiled sweetly upon the Italian and spoke in a ladylike voice.

"No, Alfredo," he said, "but my husband, Mr. Willows, comes to you often. He has spoken to me of your family. Says you have a splendid lot of children."

Alfredo's eyes and teeth did some fairly snappy sparkling upon the reception of this compliment.

"Mr. Willows, madam," he said. "He's one fine man. One of my best. I like him very much."

"He advised me to come to you for a nice trim," continued Tim, deciding that Alfredo himself was not such a bad fellow. "About your family now—is your wife well? No ill effects?"

"My wife," replied Alfredo complacently, "she make another baby now."

"How interesting," observed Tim. "Does she find it very difficult?"

Alfredo shrugged his shoulders rather discouragingly.

"You know how it is, madam," he said. "It is never good. Like death itself."

"No, I didn't know that," said Tim faintly, sinking a little in the chair.

"It is always bad, madam," continued Alfredo. "There is nothing good about it. The first time, she nearly died."

"O-o-o-o," came shudderingly from Tim.

"Did I hurt, madam?" asked Alfredo, pausing with poised comb.

"No, Alfredo," answered Tim, rallying in the chair.

"Everything's splendid. Go right on. You say she nearly died?"

"Yes, madam," continued the barber reminiscently. "My wife she was at the death. What suffering, madam. What anguish. It is always thus with the first."

"O-o-o-o-o," gasped Tim, slumping miserably still farther down in the chair.

"I'm sure I must be hurting, madam," said Alfredo.

"No, Alfredo," answered Tim. "Not the way you think. You're doing fine."

"It was torture, madam, torture," resumed the begetter of many progeny. "She was on the wreck."

"What!" exclaimed Tim, starting up in the chair. "That's painting the lily. She had this baby in a wreck?"

"No, madam," explained Alfredo. "Not in a wreck. She was on this wreck. How do you say—the torture wreck."

Tim's thoughts dwelt broodingly on this mystifying but nevertheless chilling new item of awfulness.

"Because she wouldn't bear down?" he asked. "Is that why they did it?"

Alfredo shrugged his shoulders uncomprehendingly.

"I don't know, madam," he replied. "She was on it, the wreck."

"But they have no right to put people on wrecks when they're going to have babies," protested Tim.

"I don't know," replied Alfredo rather hopelessly. "There she was. On it."

Suddenly the intention rather than the meaning of the Italian's words dawned upon Tim.

"You mean she was on the rack," he suggested. "Isn't that it, Alfredo?"

Once more Alfredo resorted to one of his expressive shrugs.

"It's all the same," he said. "Wreck or rack, she was on it. Untold suffering and danger. Without cease." He paused for a moment, then added proudly, "Italian women have their babies much easier than American."

Upon the receipt of this information Tim's eyes grew

round with horror. The hair that Alfredo was trimming endeavored to rise up on its ends.

"You mean they have a harder time of it than your wife?" faltered Tim.

"Much," replied Alfredo generously. "Many die. Poof! They are gone. It is sad."

It was altogether too sad for Tim. When he left the barber shop he was plumbing the depths of spiritual depression. He was going to die, die like a dog on a wreck. There was not the remotest chance of escape. His number was up. Alfredo must know what he was talking about. Certainly he had had enough experience.

He stopped in front of a grocery store to consider a display of nuts. It was an attractive display. Tim was very fond of nuts. He thought of the vanished bar of a vanished Sherry's where in bygone days he had eaten tons of nuts and swallowed gallons of cocktails. Gone, all gone. His past life swam before him. He was beginning to die a little already, he decided. A baby carriage had been parked near him. With morbid curiosity he bent down and regarded the small and disconcertingly complacent face of its occupant. A nice baby with nice little old wise eyes. A potential murderer. The baby looked long at Tim, then showed him how to blow bubbles without the use of either water or soap. The baby was good at it, had mastered the technique. From the number of bubbles it made it was apparent the baby knew it was putting on a pretty good show. "Bubbles," thought Tim moodily. "For all the good we accomplish in this world we might just as well sit in a carriage and blow bubbles. I've even lost that art." Then the baby's mother appeared. Tim smiled timidly at her.

"You've a lovely baby," he said. "I envy you."

The young mother's face flushed with gratification.

"He's not so bad," she smiled, endeavoring to keep a check on her inordinate pride.

"Did—did—did it hurt much?" asked Tim, almost in a whisper.

"My dear, I almost died," said the woman.

With a choking cry Tim turned from her and hurried down the street. The woman looked after him curiously, then shook her head and dismissed the incident from her mind, for the moment. But Tim did not hurry far. Dopey had other plans. If there was anything the dog loved it was to give the appearance of ferocity without incurring the risk of putting it to the test. On such occasions he was an awful sight to behold. He foamed at the mouth and rolled his eyes. His jaws were a nest of teeth lined with hellish red. A very small dog already on the run was the excuse for the demonstration. Dopey's fury was instantaneous. He lunged after the small creature like a maniac on four feet. The pursued uttered a despairing yelp and doubled on his tracks. Dopey followed his example with an unpleasant sound of scraping toenails. Unfortunately Dr. Jordan stepped blithely into the picture at this moment. Dopey rounded the clerical legs at great speed and brought his leash against them with terrific force. The sudden shock pulled Tim to the pavement. Dr. Jordan almost immediately emulated his example. As a matter of fact, for a moment it was a neck-and-neck race to see who would hit the sidewalk first. Tim won by a sufficient margin to permit Dr. Jordan to descend heavily upon him. Dopey, suddenly realizing that he was no longer under restraint, sat down abruptly and whimpered. At any moment that small dog might change its mind and return to bite him. In the meantime from beneath the body of the stunned man of God came one of the most convincing and comprehensive expositions of the baser side of the English language that had ever been heard on Springfield Avenue, or on any other avenue, for that matter. All the bitterness and depression pent up in Tim's soul poured out through his throat and crackled venomously in the surrounding air. Even in his dazed condition the Rev. Dr. Jordan was reminded of something. It had to do with the explosion of a gasoline stove. There had been a church supper. The good man shuddered at the memory.

"Well?" came the voice from beneath him, "isn't it about time you were thinking about getting up? Do you like it here? Why not kneel on my body and offer up a prayer?"

The small crowd that had both seen and heard stolidly watched Dr. Jordan struggle to his feet and brush himself off diligently.

"That's right, you big stiff," came spitefully from the pavement. "Leave me here crushed and broken."

Dr. Jordan looked down at the small figure and was human enough to long to kick it completely out of his sight and memory. Two women stepped forward and helped Tim to rise. Then the three of them stood looking at Dr. Jordan.

"Such language," said one of the women.

"Never heard anything like it in all my life," observed the other.

"And from a man of the cloth," put in Tim. "It's not the sort of language one would expect. Dr. Jordan, I'm shocked and surprised. You have overstepped. You have put your foot in it."

"My dear ladies," rumbled Dr. Jordan, his face not unlike a grinning sunset, "I assure you I did not open my mouth. Not a word of anger or condemnation passed my lips. I heard all the terrible things you heard, the unbelievably vile language, and I was shocked to the core."

"Where is that?" inquired Tim.

"Where's what, the core?" asked Dr. Jordan.

"Yes, the core," replied Tim.

"Madam, it is merely an expression," explained the badgered man.

"Well, I don't think it's a very nice expression, I'm sure," replied Tim.

"I agree," said one of the other women. "It's a terrible thing to speak about."

"Why, my dear madam," pleaded Dr. Jordan. "It's the most harmless thing in the world. Let me——"

"We know how harmless it is," the other woman cut in sarcastically. "You'll be telling us next that babies are found in cabbage heads. What a man."

"If you've finished insulting us, Dr. Jordan," said Tim in his most ladylike voice, "we'll be going. I suggest that the next time you see a young woman on the public thoroughfares you'll make some effort to control yourself. In the privacy of one's home I could understand, if not condone, your conduct, but an assault on the main street of the town is short-sighted, to say the least. And do try to elevate your language. It's disgusting."

With this Tim collected Dopey and, with a bright smile at the two ladies, sailed off down the street. Dr. Jordan, standing amid the ruins of a shattered world, looked after him with murder in his heart. As if not knowing what to do with his hands he extended them supplicatingly to the street and turned helplessly from side to side. He seemed to be looking for someone to whom he could explain the whole ghastly affair, some reasonable, fair-minded person. Then, fearing lest he should go mad in public, he hurried home and turned on the radio at full blast. And under the cover of the resulting din the Rev. Dr. Jordan gave vent to his pent-up emotion. He could not remember all of the words Tim had used while lying on the sidewalk, but those that he did recall, Dr. Jordan made do double service. He concocted words of his own. In his desperation he even resorted to those words and expressions that are usually to be found on billboards, subway posters, and lavatories. Then, having cleansed his soul and unburdened his mind, he turned off the radio, sat down at his desk, and set about preparing his Sunday sermon in almost a cheerful mood.

Tim's last experience of the day was one he would have preferred to avoid. He would have preferred to avoid them all, he now decided, and remain in a state of blessed ignorance.

On his way home from the village, and while he was in the act of cursing Dopey bitterly for his hypocritical conduct, he glanced up to find himself looking into the clear, inquiring eyes of Claire Meadows.

"I can tell that you like that dog," Mrs. Meadows remarked unsmilingly, "otherwise, with all you seem to have against the beast, you would not be associating with it."

"This dog is a vice, like drugs," replied Tim. "The animal is so darned useless I actually feel sorry for it."

"Come home and have some tea," said Mrs. Meadows, in a surprisingly comforting voice. "You've a desperate light in your eye. I'm a pretty desperate woman myself."

She took Tim by the arm, and reluctantly he allowed himself to be led to the home of Claire Meadows.

"But I forgot," said the woman suddenly. "You might lose your reputation if you were seen on the streets with me."

"Listen," Tim declared quite earnestly, "I haven't enough reputation left to dust a fiddle with. And I don't give a damn about this town. I'd like to blow it up."

"That would avail you little," said Claire Meadows. "There are oodles of other towns like this filled with almost exactly the same sort of persons. All over the world there are towns like this. You can't escape them."

"Then I will ignore them," replied Tim resolutely.

"If they let you," said Claire cryptically. "But they won't. These towns want to know. They insist on knowing, and they generally find out sooner or later. They look for the worst."

Over a cup of tea in Clare Meadows's pleasant drawing room Tim broke down. Perhaps it was the dreamlike memory of another and happier occasion that did it. What it was he never quite knew, himself. He just found himself talking, and he didn't trouble to stop.

"I'm going to have a baby," he announced in a deep voice.

"That's nice," said Claire easily. "I wish I had mine."

"Did you ever have a baby?" asked Tim with awakened interest.

Mrs. Meadows nodded slowly and looked at Tim with unseeing eyes.

"I had a baby once," she said in a low voice. "A perfectly good baby. A little girl with sleepy eyes. She used to sigh so fatly."

"Did the little baby die?" asked Tim gently.

"No," she answered, with a hard note in her voice. "He took her with the divorce. She was old enough to go then. They said I was unfit. The law can say a lot of things it really doesn't mean. But they hurt for all that."

"Did you experience much trouble having this baby?" Tim inquired delicately.

Claire Meadows raised her eyes to heaven.

"Don't ask," was all she said.

The calm moderation of the woman chilled Tim's last hope. It lay cold against his heart. It was not so much what she had said as what she had left unsaid, what she had intimated, the awful things implied. In his self-absorption he forgot about Claire Meadows's baby and thought only of his own prospective one.

"But I'm not what I seem," he said haltingly.

"None of us is," replied Claire Meadows.

"I shouldn't be having this baby by rights," he went on. "You see, I'm a man at heart."

At this surprising statement, Claire Meadows sat up and looked penetratingly at Tim.

"You do talk like a man," she said at length.

"And I think like a man," added Tim.

"But seemingly you're not a man," the woman replied.

"It's a sort of yes-and-no proposition," Tim explained. "I don't function like a man, and now I'm in this terrible condition. Everybody says I'm going to die." Tim's voice grew shaky. "I haven't written my damn book yet," he added, "and now I guess I never will."

"Come over here," Claire's voice commanded.

She took Tim in her arms and made him comfortable. After she had heard his strange story she sat back and appeared quite charmed.

"I've always believed in magic," she remarked at last, "but I never knew it actually happened. After what you've told me almost anything is possible. I might get my own baby back. Are you sure you're not dreaming this?"

"I don't know," said Tim. "It seems like a dream."

"And you simply must not pay any attention to what other women say," continued Claire Meadows. "Childbirth is not easy under the most ideal circumstances, but it's not nearly so bad as the majority of women make out. After all, I don't blame them a bit. All men think that women exaggerate, so in order to give them an approximate idea of the truth women really do have to exaggerate. It's a vicious circle."

Presently Tim left. He was feeling greatly comforted, Claire Meadows had done it.

"You know," she said, following him to the door, "I've often longed to establish contact with a man's mind without having his body constantly interrupting the conversation. This is the first time I've had that pleasure."

It was Tim's grin that appeared on Sally's lips.

That night he related to Sally the experiences of the day. She was especially edified by his encounter with the Rev. Dr. Jordan. Later, while Tim was writing the next day's copy assignment, he sent her to the village to search for an avocado. He had yearnings.

"Here's your damned alligator-pear," she said an hour later. "I hope to God it bites you."

"What a way to speak to a person in my condition," replied Tim, delicately elevating his eyebrows.

CHAPTER XI

No Job for a Lady

SALLY'S POSITION IN THE OFFICE WAS BECOMING INcreasingly more difficult. There were times when she was called upon to dash off pieces of copy on the spur of the moment. She grew to dread these sudden demands on her depleted supply of inspiration. The results of her best efforts were usually quite unsatisfactory. There was no Tim in the offing to call upon for assistance. She was forced to rely on her own vast inexperience. What did she know, poor girl, about drop forges, lubricating oils, Never Flap union suits, and a number of other unsympathetic, not to say inimical, products thirsting for popularity through the medium of advertising? She was beginning to crack under the strain of the situation into which Mr. Ram had plunged her, and she, too, cursed that colorful little gentleman from the bottom of her heart. Grudgingly she admitted to herself that the business of being a good provider for a family even of two was not as easy as it had once seemed. There were times when she even wished that she could change positions with Tim and do things about having a baby. He was making an awful mess of it, getting himself all worked up and nervous.

All afternoon she had been laboring uninspiredly on one of these rush-copy assignments when a person no less than Mr. Gibber himself saved her. He summoned her to his presence and spoke with unwonted feeling.

"Willows," he said, "Tom Burdock is in the city and we can't get him out. He's our best client. We have to handle him with gloves. A club would be better, but, as I say, he is our most important and profitable client. Already he has both physically and morally shattered three of our most hardened account executives. It is

151

now your turn—your opportunity, I should say. Get Tom Burdock out of town and you are a made man here. The sky is the limit. Stick to him. Don't let him out of your sight. Here's two hundred dollars. Give it to him and get him to sign this slip. Draw as much money as you need yourself. It's on the house. Now, Willows, I don't hold with excessive drinking. Never have. But this is an exceptional case. I feel that any steps you see fit to take to get Tom Burdock on a train headed back home will be fully justified. After all, his wife and children might like to see what he looks like. Use drugs if necessary. And remember, he is our most important client. Be smooth, be tactful and—you know—be convivial. Above all, stick to your man."

Sally may live to witness the stars go mad in their orbits, volcanoes gush forth ill-tempered jets of flame, and the Empire State Building stand jauntily on its head, but more vivid, more demoralizing than any of these manifestations will be the memory of her attempt to stick by Tom Burdock.

He was a large, jovial man with a crop of defiant red hair, a livid face, and an all-pervading thirst. She found him sitting on the bed in his hotel room in the attitude of Rodin's Thinker. When she gave him the two hundred dollars, the great man changed his position and looked upon Sally as if she were a messenger from on high. Immediately thereafter he began to distribute largess to the hotel staff. As a result of this generous conduct numerous flasks and bottles began to make their appearance, and as a direct result of their arrival Tom Burdock was soon back where he had been on retiring the previous evening. It was in this exalted state that it occurred to him it would be a benevolently paternal act to buy a doll for his youngest daughter. As long as Tom Burdock could think he acted, and even after he had ceased to think he still continued to act. Sally found herself in the street sticking to the great man.

"Willows," he declared, "I'm going to buy me a doll—for my youngest daughter—it will get her on my side. When I get back home I'll need every friend I have on earth as well as many who have indubitably gone to hell."

Cheered by this harking back to home, Sally encouraged him in his mission. When they left the department store she found herself carrying the largest and most lifelike baby doll she had ever seen. The thing even felt like a baby as she carried it along the street, Burdock, in his impatience with details, having stripped off the wrapping, which like all wrappings had untidily come undone. The doll attracted no little attention and comment on the part of passing pedestrians, and it was this that started the trouble. Mr. Burdock conceived the idea that Sally was carrying the doll all wrong.

"Here, give me that doll," he said, looking critically at Sally. "I'll show you how to carry a baby. Watch me."

Not only did Sally watch him, but also everyone else on the street. Burdock's method of carrying the doll was brutal in the extreme. With one huge hand he seized the lifelike object round its neck and dragged it along after him, its legs dangling gruesomely against the pavements. In spite of her knowledge that Mr. Tom Burdock's burden was as inanimate as a doll could be, Sally was unable to repress a slight shudder of revulsion on seeing it thus handled. The fact that at home Tim was busily if reluctantly evolving a real baby did not help matters. Sally was sensitive about babies.

They had not progressed very far when they were accosted by an indignant but unfortunately myopic old lady who informed the genial Mr. Burdock that if he persisted in subjecting an innocent child to such inhuman treatment she would be forced to call a policeman. The situation seemed to tickle Tom Burdock. He proceeded to make it worse.

"Innocent child!" he exclaimed huskily as he grabbed the doll's neck with two powerful hands and began to choke it before the horrified eyes of the old lady. "Innocent child!" he repeated. "I like that. Why, this child has the heart of a fiend, you old owl. It won't go to sleep. It won't do a damn thing. I'm bored to tears with this baby and, madam,"—Tom Burdock lowered his voice—"I'm going to strangle it to death before your very eyes. Observe."

The old lady's piercing scream collected a crowd with such startling swiftness that Sally gained the impression its individual members must have been rehearsed in their parts and had been merely awaiting the old lady's signal to rush into action. In spite of Mr. Gibber's adjurations to stick to Tom Burdock, Sally felt strongly inclined to remove herself as speedily as possible from the neighborhood of the Nationwide Advertising Agency's most important client and to stay removed. Above the crowd Mr. Burdock towered, the doll raised aloft, its head shaking so violently that it gave every appearance of life and animation.

"I'll murder the child," gritted Burdock. "It's illegitimate, anyway. Better dead than alive."

The doll was moving so rapidly now that it was virtually impossible for the spectators to ascertain its true character. Several men covered their eyes with their hands in an endeavor to blot out the unnerving sight. The women stared as if fascinated and the old lady screamed.

"Gord," breathed a girl to her escort. "The poor kid must be used to such treatment if it doesn't even cry."

"Can't very well get used to a thing like that," answered the man. "By the time you do you're damn well done in."

Sally began to fear that the most important client was beginning to lose his head, to take his part too seriously. He was laughing like a demon and his eyes were flashing wildly. The success of his acting had overstimulated him.

"Innocent child!" he cried, addressing himself to the crowd. "Ha! See what I do with it. I choke it. I twirl it. Thus."

And Mr. Burdock began to twirl the doll above his head.

"I can stand very little more of this," gasped a well-dressed gentleman. "I'm not very fond of children myself, but such treatment of a mere baby is going altogether too far."

"Stick out your tongue at the lady," said Tom Burdock. "Go on, stick it out, you black-hearted brat."

"He's gone mad," ejaculated a woman. "He doesn't know what he's doing. For God's sake get a policeman."

But already several members of the crowd were beginning to suspect the true state of affairs. They smiled with tolerant amusement and waited for further developments.

"Are you a friend of this gentleman?" a man asked Sally.

"Merely a business acquaintance," Sally replied hastily.

"He's more than that," cried Mr. Burdock, who had overheard the question. "He's the father of this baby. He refuses to give it a name."

"Then why don't you do something about it?" the old lady demanded of Sally. "Are you willing to see your own baby murdered?"

"Yes," replied Sally in a voice that carried conviction. "I don't want it. Small children disturb me. And anyway, I can't stop this madman. He might take it into his head to twirl me about. That would never do."

"Oh!" exclaimed the old lady. "I've never experienced such cowardice and brutality in all my born days. Why doesn't a policeman come? Why don't you men do something?"

She kicked Mr. Burdock sharply on the shin, and that gentleman uttered a howl of rage.

"Stop that!" he shouted. "You're only making matters worse for the baby. I'll snap the thing's head off."

"Don't worry, lady," a spectator said soothingly to the old woman. "It's not alive."

"Do you mean to say it's dead?" she asked. "Then that means murder. And every one of you are accessories before the fact for looking on and letting him do it."

And with this she lifted up her voice and called piercingly for the police. Presently Patrolman Riley sweated a path through the crowd. At the sight of the policeman Tom Burdock redoubled his efforts. The doll fairly sizzled in frantic revolutions.

"What's going on here?" demanded Riley. "What's all the trouble?"

Apparently the members of the crowd decided to let the officer find out for himself.

"Arrest everyone," said the old lady. "Officer, they're all in it. They've let this madman murder a baby before their very eyes. And there's his friend, the father of the child."

Sally stood quakingly under the accusing eyes of the policeman, but at this moment a diversion occurred. The doll detached itself from one of its legs and described a jangling arc in the air. For a moment it poised over an open manhole in which some laborers were further confusing the electric system of the city, then dropped from sight within. Officer Riley, abandoning his tactics of tolerant inquiry, sped after the doll and followed it down into the manhole. For a moment Mr. Burdock stood looking at the leg in his hand.

"Can't do anything with that," he said at last. "Perhaps a cannibal's daughter might like it, but not mine. Here, old lady, you can have it as a little souvenir of your first murder."

He thrust the leg into the hand of the shrinking old lady and, breaking through the crowd, hailed and entered a taxi. Sally stuck to him.

A few minute later Officer Riley emerged from the manhole with a disgusted expression on his face and a disheveled doll in his arms. He approached the old lady and shook the bedraggled object under her nose.

"Here's your murdered baby," he snarled. "I've a good mind to run you in for making a fool of the law." He looked about for Mr. Burdock. "Where's he gone?" he demanded. "Did you let that man escape?"

"I couldn't stop him," the old lady faltered.

With a cry of rage the officer dashed the doll to the sidewalk and shouldered his way through the grinning crowd.

"Move on, the lot of you," he shouted, "or I call for the patrol wagon."

Slowly the crowd dispersed, leaving a bewildered old lady peering down at the doll lying crumpled at her feet.

Back at the hotel Sally was sitting on the bed and seriously considering Mr. Burdock, who was soothing himself with a bottle. She realized he presented a problem that would require some stiff solving. With the abandoning of the doll the man had severed the one tie he seemingly had with his home. She had an overnight job on her hands and a pregnant husband at home impatiently awaiting her return. Mr. Gibber had told her to stick to Tom Burdock. Her job depended on the success of her sticking powers. She would have to telephone to Tim.

"Willows," said Mr. Burdock from his easy chair, "we know all about how to buy a doll, but we're not so good at getting it home. I think I'll have the next one sent."

"I would," agreed Sally. "To the Aleutian Islands, for instance."

Disgustedly she rose from the bed and put in a call for Tim. When she heard his familiar voice coming to her over the wire she followed her natural instincts and spoke to him as a wife speaks to a husband—that is, as she speaks at times.

"Oh, Tim, darling," she called in a soft, feminine voice. "Yes, dear, of course, this is Sally. And I won't be home to-night. No, not to-night. Don't use such terrible language. It's Mr. Burdock. Yes, yes, dear. Tom Burdock, a client. What's that? A what? Oh, Tim, he's a perfect dear. Yes, simply sweet. You understand. Will you miss me, old thing? That's nice. Good-bye. Take care of Baby. It's a big thing. Of course not. I don't mean Baby."

When Sally turned back to Mr. Burdock he was looking at her with a very peculiar expression in his eyes, a mixture of fear and suspicion.

"I always call my husband Tim," she said rather pointlessly, becoming confused herself for a moment.

"But I thought your name was Tim," Tom Burdock replied.

"That's right," said Sally. "We call each other Tim just for the fun of the thing."

It was Mr. Burdock's turn to become confused. He scratched his mop of red hair and looked consideringly

CHAPTER XII

Sticking to Mr. Burdock

As the evening advanced, Sally's opinion of Mr. Burdock was not favorably revised. The man was a cosmic consumer of strong drink. Sally would not have objected to this entirely forgivable weakness had the gentleman confined his indulgence to himself. Tom Burdock was not that way. Never had been. He insisted on others drinking. He forced vile libations on Sally. What had once eaten the enamel off bathtubs now got busily to work on the lining of their respective stomachs. They attended the performance of a play the name and meaning of which neither of them was ever able to remember. They slumbered disreputably through two acts and one intermission. Finally they were escorted to an exit by a contingent of ushers who bade them godspeed as they stood in the street wearily supporting each other while they strove to accustom their smarting eyes to the kaleidoscope of Broadway. To Sally's way of thinking, the street had gone mad. Tom Burdock seemed to be trying to return to sleep by resting the upper half of his body on her head. Unsympathetically she moved away. Mr. Burdock followed. His mind was consumed with one idea to the exclusion of all others. He must get some sleep. For sleep he would commit every crime on the calendar and if necessary think up a few new ones. Sally was of a like mind.

Even then all might have gone well for the ill-matched pair had not an unemployed baker by the name of Joe Clark allowed himself to be struck down by a taxicab. The collision looked more serious than it proved to be. By the time the ambulance arrived all that remained of the erstwhile baker was a battered hat. The man himself had washed his hands of the whole unpleasant incident. After roundly cursing the spot where Joe Clark had once lain, the ambulance surgeon hastened to a nearby cigar store while the driver returned to his seat and followed with hopeful eyes the frantic leaps of an elderly gentleman who seemed determined to make up for the delinquency of the baker by hurling his own frail body beneath the wheels of as many automobiles as would accept him.

The sight of an empty and comfortably appointed ambulance presented itself to Tom Burdock as a God-given opportunity. As has already been stated, Mr. Burdock continued to act long after he had ceased to think. He did so in this instance. With the confidence born of a fixed idea he climbed into the ambulance and disappeared from sight beneath a blanket. Realizing the futility of any attempt to remove the body of the monolithic creature, Sally did the only thing left for her to do under the unprecedented circumstances. She followed him into the ambulance and sought the protection of another blanket. In the cozy darkness of the compartment Tom Burdock was chuckling like a well-disposed percolator.

"Willows," he said, in a subdued voice, "isn't this great? Wonder what they'll do when they find us in here."

"Quite a lot," replied Sally. "Even more than enough."

"I guess they'll do plenty," Mr. Burdock agreed. "You'd never have thought of a thing like this."

"Never," retorted Sally. "And I wish to God you hadn't. All I can think of is the vast quantities of dead men who have from time to time occupied the same spot in which I am now lying—probably the same blanket."

"No doubt about it," whispered Burdock. "I daresay this ambulance has had its fill of corpses and mangled bodies!"

"A nice place you select for a pleasant nap," observed Sally.

"The way I feel," replied Mr. Burdock, "I could sleep cheek and jowl with a corpse itself."

"You almost are," breathed Sally.

Further conversation was halted by the arrival of the surgeon. He swung himself into the back seat of the ambulance, looking back at the lights of Broadway. Gradually a peculiar sensation took possession of the man. He glanced into the body of the car and received the distinct impression that the blankets had come unrolled and were quivering as if with suppressed mirth. The possible significance of what he saw was not reassuring. Blankets that quivered of their own volition had no place in the general scheme of things. The young surgeon was not elated.

For a long minute he sat considering the blankets with apprehensive eyes, then, opening his bag, he produced a flask which he applied to his lips. Placing the flask beside him on the bench, he returned to the objects of his contemplation. This time it seemed to him that the blankets were threatening to lose control of themselves and to become wildly hysterical. Were those strange, gurgling sounds of human origin or were his eyes and ears playing tricks on him—dirty tricks, at that? He gazed down a long street and thought of other things. He thought of an old man who had died in that ambulance the previous evening because he, the surgeon, had cynically mistaken acute starvation for sordid alcoholism. True, the old man's breath had smelled strongly of bad whiskey, but so did nine out of ten breaths along Broadway. Had the spirit of this hungry old man returned to taunt him with his neglect? The surgeon reached for his flask and was electrified to find it gone. Gurgling noises continued to issue from the blankets. Without further delay he called to the driver to stop; then he climbed up beside him. The blankets could have the entire ambulance for all he cared. Blankets that quivered were bad enough, but blankets that drank whiskey were obviously out of the question. And, anyway, the investigation of occult phenomena was none of his business. He'd leave that to the cranks before he became one himself.

"Get more fresh air up here," he explained to the driver. "Back there the gasoline fumes from the street are stifling."

"Maybe that's what gets the best of your customers, Doc," suggested the driver. "Most of 'em seem to pass out en route."

Having no desire to be reminded of the high rate of mortality suffered by his customers, the surgeon made no comment and the drive was finished in silence.

Four powerful attendants were awaiting the surgeon's bidding.

"What did you catch to-night, Doc?" one of them inquired.

"Look in the back and see," replied the surgeon with simulated indifference.

They looked in the back and saw. What they saw was in no wise startling. Since the advent of prohibition they had grown accustomed to such sights. Two well-dressed gentlemen were sleeping peacefully and comfortably on the floor of the car. Beside them was the surgon's flask. The surgeon, himself, unable to restrain his curiosity, and fortified by the presence of others, looked long and hatefully upon the oblivious bodies. His whiskey must have been the last straw. Both Sally and Mr. Burdock had gently passed out. A look of profound trouble clouded the driver's eyes.

"I'll swear to God the pair of them were born fully dressed in there," he protested, peering over the surgeon's shoulder. "We didn't pick up one body, let alone two."

Acid bitterness then entered into the young surgeon's soul. The ethical compulsions of his high vocation vanished from his mind. To him those two still bodies were not human. They were things to be made to suffer both physical and mental anguish. He spoke confidentially and persuasively to the attendants. Those stalwart worthies nodded with unqualified approval and did all that was required.

Some hours thereafter Tom Burdock swam back to consciousness through the alcoholic waves that were beating against his brain. He found himself cold, unreasonably and clammily cold. Removing the sheet from his head, he discovered that everything else also had been removed. "Strange," he thought numbly, "I seem to have crawled into bed mother-naked. Wonder where Willows is." He reached for the night lamp but was unable to find it. Then he sat up and looked about him. What he saw was not reassuring. Along the opposite wall were numerous rows of large drawers. Certainly this was not his hotel bedroom. "Might have barged into the linen closet," he reflected, "and gone to sleep there. Damn fool thing to do." Then in the dim light he noticed a number of slablike tables upon which sheet-draped figures were apparently sleeping the unstirring sleep of the weary.

"I've got it now," he decided. "We're in some sort of a Turkish bath. They've taken all our clothes and now they're freezing us to death."

He let himself down from the table and started out to search for his friend. At that moment two gray-clad figures came swinging into the room and marched up to one of the large drawers. Mr. Burdock modestly shrank down behind a table and observed a scene that was anything but happy, although his faculties were still too atrophied to comprehend the full significance of what he saw.

The two men opened one of the drawers and snapped the body of an unpleasant-looking man into view. This they unceremoniously deposited in a basket-like arrangement.

"Well, here's the last of this beauty," remarked one of the men, as if the final removal of the beauty were a pleasure that had been long deferred.

"He's still so full of slugs he's as heavy as a graven image," complained the other.

Laying violent hands on the blanket, the two gray-clad figures half dragged and half carried it through another door.

"What a tough joint we picked out," Mr. Burdock observed to himself. "First they make a guy sleep in a drawer, then they drag him off in a basket. Wonder what they meant by that bit about slugs. Sounded sort of bad to me."

His growing feeling of solitude and uneasiness gave him the temerity to lift the end of the sheet from the figure on the table behind which he had been crouching. He found himself confronting a pair of large, aloof-looking feet.

"Can't be Willows' feet," he decided, delicately recovering the feet and moving to another table. "I'll try this sheet, but maybe they tucked him in a drawer."

This effort was rewarded by a glare from two pale, malevolent blue eyes set in a dead white face decorated with a flowing beard. Mr. Burdock, after one look, hastily dropped the sheet. This Turkish bath evidently drew its customers from the very scum of society.

"I beg your pardon, brother," he mumbled. "I was looking for my friend."

He realized it was rather improper to be going about uncovering naked strangers, and was fully prepared to have this man snap erect and tell him to go to hell with his friend. He was not prepared, however, for the silence that greeted his apology. Perhaps the man had not heard. He'd try him again. Once more he diffidently raised a corner of the sheet and looked down. A person did not usually go to sleep with his eyes wide open, no matter how tired he felt. There was something in the very immobility of the figure that arrested Tom Burdock's attention. Very gently, very reluctantly, he edged in a finger and touched the man's cold face. Mr. Burdock's hand flipped back like a frantic fish leaping from a lake. He stood there petrified, frozen to the marrow by the shock of a ghastly realization.

"Oh, my God," he breathed at last, "I'm a dead man. We're all dead men. That bit about the slugs. I see it all now. The ambulance. We died on the way. That stuff in the doctor's flask did the trick. It killed us."

In his morbid mental condition it was not at all difficult for Mr. Burdock to persuade himself that this was the only rational explanation of his predicament.

"Wonder what poor Willow looks like," he mused as he moved to the next table.

Idly he lifted the sheet and glanced down. The grinning face of a Negro seared his eyeballs. The sheet dropped from Mr. Burdock's nerveless fingers and blotted out the terrible sight.

"Dear me," he quavered, in his fright forgetting how

to curse. "Oh, dear, dear me. Oh, goodness. I can't go on with this much longer. How awful everything is."

At this inauspicious moment the sheet on the table on the other side of Mr. Burdock was seized with a sudden convulsion. Tom Burdock had often heard of a person's jaw dropping under the stress of some terrible fright or confrontation. He had never believed it, however. People did not really go about dropping their jaws. In the whole course of his life he had never seen a single jaw drop. But now as he stood looking at that wildly thrashing sheet he had occasion to alter his opinion. His own jaw swung open like a gate that had been roughly kicked. His eyes became two glassy points of fear. What horror was he now about to witness? When Tim Willows's head finally emerged from the sheet, Tom Burdock drew a quivering breath and snapped his jaw back into place.

"Where are we?" asked Sally, in a high tremulous voice which even in his dazed condition Mr. Burdock found somewhat incongruous.

"Take it easy, old man," he said in a funereal voice. "Pull yourself together. I fear we're all dead."

"Dead?" repeated Sally. "Why, you're not dead. You don't even look sick."

"I know," replied Burdock bleakly. "It must be like that. All around us lie the dead. Some of us are in drawers."

"You're not in drawers," said Sally, not looking at the great man. "Get a sheet and wrap it round you."

Absently Mr. Burdock plucked a sheet from a nearby table. In so doing he neatly unveiled the body of an oriental ax victim. Sally took one swift look, then crumpled beneath her sheet.

"Has it gone?" came her muffled voice. "What a sight!"

"It will never go," said Burdock hollowly. "It will be dragged away in a basket."

"Oh, dear God," moaned Sally, hoping to curry favor. "Do they make picnics out of us?"

"No," continued Burdock, now thoroughly enjoying his misery. "After that comes the ground—the earth. Parts of us go in bottles, perhaps."

"Well, we'll make a couple of powerful quarts," Sally could not help observing.

She ducked out from under the sheet and looked curiously about her.

"I thought it was a Turkish bath," intoned Tom Burdock, "but it turned out to be a morgue."

"From the frigidity of the temperature," said Sally, "I should say we've missed hell by several degrees."

"You shouldn't talk like that, Willows," Mr. Burdock mournfully remonstrated. "This may be merely a moment of transition—the pause before the plunge."

So far as the plunge was concerned the words of Tom Burdock were singularly prophetic. An aged man came into the room, gave one appalled look at the two strange figures, then hurriedly withdrew.

"There's a couple of resurrections in there," he told the doctor, "and they're raising hell with our morgue."

The doctor received this startling announcement with a smile of malicious glee. A few minutes later four large attendants filed briskly into the morgue and roughly apprehended both Sally and Mr. Burdock. Then came the plunge. They were transported through leagues of space and violently deposited in two tubs of ice-cold water.

"The final plunge," gasped Sally as the water closed over her head.

Mr. Burdock's amazement and indignation knew no bounds. Sally had reached that stage whereat nothing really surprised her. Dead or alive, she was still sticking to her man.

The bath over, a couple of strange-looking garments were flung in their faces.

"My God," chattered Tom Burdock, distastefully examining the article in his hands. "The things they can't think of doing to you in a place like this! Now what do you suppose this damn thing is? It looks pretty desperate to me."

"Put it on. Put it on," snapped one of the attendants. "Can't you see we're waiting?"

"How many pour souls have met their God in mine?" demanded Sally, at which Mr. Burdock's face went white.

"Plenty," said the attendant.

"It's still quite good," replied Sally.

"I can't do it," gasped Mr. Burdock. "Have men actually died in these things?"

"Suffered and died," said the attendant. "And if you don't get into yours you'll find yourself in a strait-jacket.'

"If it's a new one," observed Mr. Burdock, as he struggled into the uncouth sleeping garment, "I think I might prefer even that."

"Now, how do we look?" asked Sally after they had slipped into the nightshirts.

"Take 'em off," commanded the attendant disgustedly. "You've got 'em on backward."

"But this way seems more logical," suggested Mr. Burdock.

"I'm getting mighty tired of you," said the attendant. "Are you going to do what I say?"

"Sure he is," put in Sally. "Dress pretty for the gentleman, Tom."

The attendant gave Sally a suspicious look. She had spoken in her natural voice, which even Mr. Burdock found difficult to tolerate.

"Don't talk like that," he pleaded, "or you'll be getting us into more trouble."

Once more they were seized upon and hurried down the hall. This time they were thrust into a long ward apparently entirely occupied by the maddest sort of madmen. Wild and alarming noises filled this ward. Some men were cursing in their sleep while others preferred to laugh. The laughing was the harder to bear. Several were singing lustily on their cots, while others troubled the air with a cacophony of hard-driven snores. It was bedlam at its weirdest.

"You don't expect us to sleep in an animal house like this?" demanded Mr. Burdock in a voice of dignified reproof. "Why, damn it, I'm a gentleman."

"We don't care whether you sleep or not," replied the communicative attendant. "You can shout and scream like the others if you feel like it. Everybody's nuts in here."

"What!" exclaimed Tom Burdock. "Do you mean to say you're putting us in with insane people?"

"Why, didn't you know?" asked the attendant. "You're that way yourself. Hope you don't think we'd put you in with normal patients. You're under observation."

"I can't stand it," muttered Mr. Burdock to Sally. "I know I'll never be able to stand it. I'll go mad myself. What humiliation! And this damn silly nightgown all split down the back. That in itself is enough to make a person look and act like a madman."

Not only were they thrown into bed but also strapped down until only their heads could move.

"Well, I never in my life would have thought it possible," said Mr. Burdock, cocking his massive head at Sally. "To be strapped helplessly in bed with a ward full of raving lunatics. Can you imagine it?"

"I don't have to," replied Sally, popping up her head. "I'm experiencing it to the hilt."

"Next time I crawl into an ambulance," groaned Burdock, "I hope to God they shoot me."

"They probably will," said Sally wearily. "They can do anything they want to you in a place like this, especially if you're mad. Do you think you are?"

The great man strained at his bonds.

"Don't," he pleaded. "Don't even suggest it."

"Well, I think I am," went on Sally. "I believe I've lost my reason. First I thought I was dead and now I'm pretty sure I'm not quite all there. I'm glad I'm strapped down or else I might do either you or myself an injury."

Tom Burdock gave her a frightened look and shivered. Perhaps that explained the sudden shiftings of his companion's voice. There was, now that he came to think of it, something rather odd about Tim Willows. No normal man could talk so like a woman.

"I wish we had Mr. Volstead strapped down between us," went on Sally. "He'd make a noble experiment."

A doctor came quietly up to Mr. Burdock's cot and stood looking rather sadly down at its occupant. Burdock returned the man's depressing scrutiny half timidly and half combatively. Suddenly the doctor stooped down and examined the great man's eyes, roughly snapping back the lids.

"Don't do that," complained Burdock. "Damn it, man, you're gouging."

Slowly the doctor rose and sorrowfully he shook his head.

"It's too bad," was all he said.

"What's too bad?" demanded Burdock.

"Gone, clean, gone," continued the doctor, as if speaking to himself. "The mind . . . a case for the mad house."

"What do you call this?" asked Sally. "They don't make houses any madder, Doc."

Mr. Burdock's eyes were starting from their sockets. His face was purple from the strain of his efforts to get at the doctor.

"Do you mean to stand there and tell me to my face I'm gaga?" he fumed.

The doctor's face brightened.

"That's it," he replied soothingly. "My good man, you're gaga. Do you like being gaga?"

"You're crazy as a coot," Mr. Burdock managed to get out. "You should be where I am. You're criminally insane, yourself."

"Another sure indication," observed the doctor. "The persecution complex. Thinks everyone's mad but himself. A very sad case."

Inarticulate with rage, Tom Burdock began to whine like a dog.

"Thinks he's a dog now," went on the doctor, then, looking down once more at Mr. Burdock: "Playing wow-wow, old man?" he asked. "What sort of a dog are you?"

The whining turned to a howl of truly animal ferocity.

"Why don't you examine me, too?" Sally inquired of the doctor. "I'm as mad as hell. Much madder than he is. I'm so far gone I think I'm a couple of wow-wows, not to mention a pack of wolves. If I wasn't strapped down I'd stalk myself and then turn at bay and snarl in my own face."

"You're not mad," replied the doctor. "You're merely peculiar. An all too familiar type."

"Now I wonder what he meant by that?" mused Sally as the doctor drifted away. "It had all the earmarks of a nasty crack."

"Willows," said Mr. Burdock weakly, after he had quieted down somewhat, "Julius Caesar and Napoleon and Alexander the Great and all those famous men would be just as helpless and humiliated as we are if they took away all their clothes and made them wear these silly-looking nightshirts all split down the back, wouldn't they?"

"Sure they would," replied Sally encouragingly. "And that goes for President Hoover, Aimee Semple McPherson, and Rudy Vallee. Mahatma Ghandi is the only possible exception. He might look quite snappy for him."

"It's so demeaning," continued Mr. Burdock. "They don't give you a ghost of a chance. They strip you of dignity and self-respect and make you look like a fool. They get the moral and physical advantage over you and you can't do a damn thing. It's the worst feeling in the world. No man can look competent rigged out the way we are."

"I've never succeeded in looking like that even in a fur coat," replied Sally. "But it must be hard lines for you, the head of a great concern."

"It is, Willows. It is," said Burdock mournfully. "I don't think I'll ever regain my former self-esteem."

"My own inferiority complex," replied Sally, "has been given a terrific boost. If a worm looked at me severely I'd break down and confess everything."

At this juncture an interne presented himself and gave them what proved to be a sleeping potion, for presently their eyes closed and they fell into an uneasy doze.

Several hours later Mr. Burdock awoke and immediately wished he hadn't. What he saw caused him to shrink within his bonds. He hoped he was still dreaming. He even hoped that the doctor had been right and that he had gone mad. He hoped for any other explanation except the true one. An incredibly aged creature or thing, a face remotely suggestive of a woman, an evil face framed in an unholy nimbus of straggling, gray hair, was peering down into his, peering with the glazed, fixed stare of the demented. In the hand of this apparition was a long kitchen knife. Just above Mr. Burdock's throat the blade was suggestively poised.

"Get up, Jim," croaked the face in a hoarse voice. "Get up at once. It's time ye were rising, man."

Mr. Burdock licked his dry lips and endeavored to speak. No sound came.

"Get up," continued the terrible voice. "Get up, Jim, you hulk of a man."

"My good woman," Tom Burdock gasped. "Nothing would please me more. I long to get up. I'd give ten years of my life to get up, but unfortunately I can't get up."

"I'll make you get up," grated the old woman, tentatively pricking her victim with the point of the knife.

"But, madam, I'm not Jim," Mr. Burdock protested. "You've made some mistake. I think that man over there calls himself Jim."

"Oh, what a lie!" exclaimed Sally, who had been awakened by the sound of voices. "Don't you believe him, lady. Jim went out to get a drink."

"I'd like a drink," observed the old woman.

"Why don't you go and get one?" suggested Mr. Burdock. "We all want a drink."

"No," said the old woman, once more prodding Burdock with the knife. "You go get the drink."

"Listen, lady," he said very earnestly. "If I could go get a drink you don't think I'd be lying here, do you? I couldn't go get a drink if they were being given away in buckets. I can't even budge."

"I'll make you budge," proclaimed the old lady, growing excited. "Are you going to get that drink before I slit your throat?"

As she prodded the knife into Mr. Burdock her face was working horribly. Unable to stand the situation any longer, he lifted up his voice in one anguished cry for help.

"Pipe down in there," called a gruff voice. "Want another cold bath?"

"Yes," shouted Burdock. "That's it. I want another cold bath. Quick, for God's sake."

"If you don't hurry he'll be bathed in blood," Sally sang out. "We've got a wild woman in here. And she's got the cutest knife—about twelve inches long."

"Come out of there, Maggie," came a bored voice. Neither one of those guys is your husband. They're just plain bums. Come on and give us that knife and I'll slip you a little drink."

"That's a good girl, Maggie," said Mr. Burdock. "Did you hear what he said? He promised you a little drink. Think of that!"

Evidently Maggie was thinking of that. She seemed undecided. From the knife she looked to Mr. Burdock's unprotected throat. Maybe she could cut it and get the drink, too. A greedy look sprang up in her eyes.

"No, no," said Sally, who had been watching the old woman closely. "No cheating, Maggie. I'll tell."

Mumbling furiously to herself, Maggie turned and hobbled from the alcove.

"Who in God's name can that be?" asked Tom Burdock, the sweat standing out on his face.

"She seems to be the mascot of the troop," observed Sally.

"Well, she certainly gave me the worst fifteen minutes of my life," said Mr. Burdock. "This has been a most unpleasant night. Wish I could go home."

"Do you mean that?" cried Sally.

"If I ever get out of this place alive," replied Burdock with deadly conviction, "that's just where I'm going—home."

"Is that a promise?" asked Sally.

"It's more than a promise," said Burdock. "It's a grim determination."

Sally sighed deeply and let her head sink back to rest.

An orderly appeared and stood at the foot of Mr. Burdock's bed. He was grinning rather apologetically.

"Maggie wasn't premeditated," he said. "We didn't plan Maggie. It was all her own idea."

"She's got some mean ideas, that girl," commented Sally. "Why don't you keep her locked up?"

"Oh, Maggie's perfectly harmless," replied the orderly. "We've had her with us for years. She's a sort of privileged character. She wanders from ward to ward. Nobody seems to mind."

"I mind terribly," said Mr. Burdock. "I most strenuously object to Maggie. She may be a privileged character, but not with my neck."

At an early hour they were unstrapped and fed. Then Tom Burdock was given a heavy flat weight attached to a broom handle, and told to push it up and down the linoleum which ran the entire length of the ward.

"My God," protested Burdock. "This hall is so damned long I don't even see the end of it. I'll drop from sheer exhaustion before I'm halfway through."

"Better send Maggie along with him to keep him from getting lost," suggested Sally.

Without further protest the employer of five thousand souls set off on his long trip. Sally was set to work emptying buckets, a most uncongenial task. Whenever their paths chanced to cross in the course of their humiliating occupations the two friends' expressions were eloquent. They were weary, strained, and disgusted. Sally looked especially wan.

"Would you believe it?" demanded Mr. Burdock. "Me with this damn thing. Pushing it. And in such a get-up."

"I suppose I look quite natural," remarked Sally bitterly.

"You have all your life before you," replied Tom Burdock.

"And a sweet little bit behind," retorted Sally. "You've made history for me, Tom Burdock."

By ten o'clock in the morning both of them were convinced that they had been up an entire day. An attendant flung two bags at them and told them to clear out. Neither one of them ever achieved again such speed in dressing as they did that morning. Even then the operation seemed interminable to them. Both were knotting their neckties as they marched down the hall.

Once in the open air they breathed with voluptuous enjoyment. Never had life seemed quite so desirable. A taxi took them to the Grand Central. Sally was taking no chances.

"I'll fix it up with the hotel," she assured Mr. Burdock. "I'll pack your bags myself and see that they're sent along."

"You're a great little scout, Willows," said the large man. "What a time we've had, eh?"

"I've enjoyed every minute of it," Sally replied with a grin. "Every jolly old minute. Wouldn't have missed one of them."

"The same here, you liar," said Mr. Burdock. "We've had a nice, quiet time. Going to tell my wife all about it."

They were standing on the long platform now and Sally was watching Tom Burdock with anxious eyes. A white-jacketed porter stepped out of a Pullman and greeted Mr. Burdock with a dazzling display of even whiter teeth. Mr. Burdock returned the salutation in his large, friendly style. Evidently he was well known on this line. Sally had no desire to linger over the farewells. She wanted to see her charge disappear into the train and the doors shut against his return.

"Don't forget America's Sweetheart," she told him.

"You mean Maggie?" asked Burdock, with a slight shudder.

"Herself," replied Sally.

"Never," said Mr. Burdock. "I'm going in now and collapse in a chair. Do I look all right?"

"Surprisingly well, considering what you've been through."

So departed Mr. Burdock from the city that had so disastrously misunderstood his playful intentions. Sally stood on the platform until the train pulled out, then she hurried to the nearest telephone and made a full report to a congratulatory Mr. Gibber. An hour later she caught a local to Cliffside, hoping there to enjoy a much-needed rest. She never did. Not on this occasion, at any rate.

The excitement started when she was wearily crossing Springfield Avenue on her way home from the station. Speaking accurately, the excitement must have started elsewhere. It merely reached its highest point of activity in and around the spot where Sally was standing. It was first brought to her attention by a bitter fusillade of bullets and the sharp reports of an exceedingly loquacious revolver. As inured as she had become to the unexpected, Sally was nevertheless somewhat disturbed. She was more so when she saw Mr. Carl Bentley, clad in a dripping wet union suit, approaching her at great speed. Close behind Mr. Bentley, and covering ground much too rapidly for a prospective mother, came the metamorphosed Tim, diligently pumping an old service automatic. And close behind Tim were two leaping state troopers, their faces eloquently expressing incredulity and determination. It must have been a moment of supreme humiliation for Mr. Bentley, but the Don Juan of the suburbs seemed to have tossed all considerations of shame and modesty to the winds as being impediments to flight.

Catching sight of a person he erroneously believed to be the husband of his murderously inclined pursurer, Mr. Bentley crouched behind Sally and pleaded for protection.

"A terrible mistake," he managed to get out between gasping breaths. "She suddenly went mad. Speak to her, Mr. Willows. I'm too young to die."

This settled Mr. Bentley's hash forever with Sally.

"You were never too young to die," she told the cringing man. "You should never have been allowed to get as far along as you have."

Tim, held firmly by the two state troopers and talking loosely about his purely hypothetical honor, was hustled up to the spot.

"I'm afraid, Mr. Willows," said one of the troopers to Sally, "I'll have to ask you to accompany your wife and this—this——" The trooper seemed to be having difficulty in classifying Carl Bentley. Tim helped him out.

"Nasty-minded craven," he supplied, then added several unladylike epithets.

"Madam!" said the trooper reprovingly.

"To hell with you," snapped Tim. "If the two of you

hadn't butted in this bum would have been a corpse by now."

"May I ask what all the shooting's about?" Sally put in mildly.

"That's what we want to know," said the other trooper. "Come on down to the police station and we'll try to find out."

"If you want to know," remarked Tim, "it's all about this damned honor of mine."

He slipped an arm through Sally's and winked wickedly up at her. Sally was undecided whether she would prefer to lose her honor privately or her reputation in public. Ahead of them, held with unnecessary brutality, Carl Bentley in his dripping union suit proceeded down the street.

In, virtually, any part of the civilized world this little procession would have occasioned comment. In Cliffside it did more than that. Even to this day, it is a subject of conversation that increases in dramatic intensity with the passing of the years. Carl Bentley's dripping union suit is still as fresh in the memory of those who had been privileged to witness the incident as when that unfortunate gentleman had first sprinted grotesquely down Springfield Avenue.

CHAPTER XIII

The Baiting of Mr. Bentley

MR. RAM SHOULD NEVER HAVE DONE THE THING HE did. But, then, one never can tell about Egyptians. Especially with old Egyptians. With new Egyptians it's different. Nobody knows just what a new Egyptian is. One can't very well dig up a new Egyptian. Old Egyptains are much easier to get to know. They seem to have had a quaint idea of humor. Like Mr. Ram.

There was no sense in giving Tim Willows the body of a woman and leaving him the mind of a man. It was a flagrant example of perverted sorcery, and just what one would expect from an old Egyptian, an old and cynical Egyptian deeply steeped in all the more exasperating phases of the black arts.

One may say that in the case of Mr. Ram there were extenuating circumstances. Perhaps there were. No one enjoys less than an old Egyptian being forced to listen to the constant bickerings of a married couple. An occasional row is diverting, but a daily diet of recrimination and vain regrets wears on one's nerves and saps one's moral fibre. Even at that Mr. Ram might have tried something a little less drastic. For example, he could easily have made Sally dumb and Tim deaf or vice versa. It would not have mattered much just how he went about it. But, seemingly, Mr. Ram did not choose to act reasonably in the matter. Probably he decided that the only way to get these two unreasonable persons to understand him was to be thoroughly unreasonable himself. Either that or he suddenly lost his temper after long years of provocation, and did the first thing that popped into his head. He might have figured it out this way: Give people what they ask for and then wait and see what they make of it. Both Tim and

Sally had made a mess of it. But Tim had made a bigger mess of it than Sally. Perhaps a woman is more adaptable than a man. She must be if there is any truth in the rumor that from a mere rib—an unsightly object at best—she developed into the complicated creature of curves and nerves she represents to-day. You would never catch a man allowing a thing like that being done to him. If the process had been reversed and the rib extracted from Eve's side, that rib would have hemmed and hawed and argued and compromised until there was not a bone left in the poor woman's body. Men are like that. They have a fine sense of dignity. No real man would be willing to run the risk of having his wife turn on him suddenly and cry: "Shut up, you mere rib." A man would not stand for that, but a woman would. A woman will stand for everything so long as she gets the best of the man. Eve did not care a snap of her fig leaf about being Adam's rib, whereas Adam would have put up an awful howl had the tables been turned or the ribs reversed. Eve knew perfectly well that as soon as she got working properly, that is, as soon as she had developed her curves and acquired her nerves Adam would forget all about the rib part of it and try to get familiar. Men are even more like that. In a paroxysm of nervous hysteria she forced the apple on Adam, saying he never liked anything she picked, then with a skillful use of her curves she got the best of him as she had all along known she would even when a mere rib. And that must have been about the way of it. Adam never had a chance. Neither had Tim Willows. Nor Carl Bentley, for that matter. Certainly the latter had no chance at all when he was so ill-advised as to call on one he mistakenly supposed to be the delectable Sally Willows on the same day when that young lady in her husband's aching body was seeing the last of Tom Burdock.

Tim, thoroughly convinced that his condition justified a little self-indulgence, was lolling in bed with his morning paper and a cigar when Mr. Bentley, like the astute snake in the grass he was, telephoned to ascertain if the coast was clear. Tim answered the call in Sally's most affected voice.

"Hello. Who's speaking?" he asked.

"Sally, is that you?" came the low inquiry.

Tim's face darkened, but his tones remained just as dulcet. He had recognized Mr. Bentley's hateful voice.

"Oh, dear," he said vibrantly, emitting the while a cloud of pungent cigar smoke. "It's been ages since I've seen you."

At the other end of the wire Mr. Bentley was beginning to feel better and better. He liked to keep his women feeling that way.

"You said it, baby," he replied, in that whimsically slangy way of his that proved so effective with women. "Is it all right for me to come round now?"

"But Carl, dear," protested Tim, smiling grimly, "baby's still in bed."

"Then I'll hurry right over," said Bentley. "Don't trouble to get up for me."

"What a man!" exclaimed Tim coyly as he viciously jabbed the receiver down on its hook. "I'll make him pay for this," he continued to himself as he sprang from the bed. "By God, I'll make him wish he'd never been born a man. One of these birds who refuses to learn a lesson. All right, I'll teach him. Thinks I'm at work, does he? Ha! I'll make him sweat."

Opening a bureau drawer he examined his automatic to see if it was properly loaded, then, dressing rapidly, he deluged himself with perfume and hurried downstairs.

When Carl Bentley arrived a few minutes later and found his prey already up and dressed, his face eloquently expressed his disappointment.

"You needn't have gone to all that trouble for me," he said. "I've often been received by ladies in bed."

"Especially when their husbands are safely out of the way at their stupid old offices," put in Tim with a wicked smile.

Mr. Bentley smiled back fatuously and approached Tim with carnal intent.

"I took a day off from my office just for this opportunity," he said in a low voice. "Are you going to make it worth while, Sally?"

"What do you think?" asked Tim teasingly, then

added to himself, "You low-lived louse, you'll get more than you ever expected in your wildest dreams."

As Bentley's eager arms enfolded him, Tim managed to lock one foot back of that gentleman's heel, then, as if in a frenzy of passion, he hurled himself suddenly against the opposing chest and let gravity claim its own. It did. Carl Bentley went down with a crash, landing painfully on the sharp edge of a footstool. At the same moment Dopey lumbered in from the kitchen and, seeing a man in an apparently helpless condition, immediately attacked him. Bently emitted feeble cries of fear and suffering as Tim clumsily strove to disengage the gallent dog's teeth from the prostrate man's trousers. Eventually Tim succeeded, but not without leaving a nice big V-shaped rip. Everything was going splendidly. Tim had not counted on the collaboration of Dopey. He appreciated the dog's intervention. Kneeling down by the writhing figure he proceeded to scold it playfully for being so easily thrown off its balance. Carl Bentley's vanity was challenged. He rose weakly from the floor and hobbled over to a chair, into which he tenderly eased his injured torso.

"I know," he complained, "but I wasn't expecting an assault. You pretty nearly ruined me."

"I'm that way," murmured Tim with downcast eyes. "You make me lose my self-control and then I don't know what I'm doing. Anything might happen. You'll have to protect me against myself, Carl dear."

Carl dear had no such intentions, but he did resolve to protect himself a little better against Sally in the future.

"What am I going to do about my trousers?" he asked, looking ruefully at the rip.

"I'll sew that up after you've taken them off," said Tim, then added hastily, "Oh, dear, what have I said? What could I have been thinking about? Do forgive me, Carl. Of course you don't have to take off your trousers."

"But I will if you think it best," replied Mr. Bentley quite willingly.

"I think it best," Tim said decisively.

Before Mr. Bentley had time to reply to this one

Tim undulated from the room and mixed a huge cocktail composed of medicated alcohol. He had tried the stuff once himself in a moment of desperation and as a result had become violently and lingeringly ill.

"Sorry I can't join you," he said enviously when he had returned to Mr. Bentley. "But it's the doctor's orders. I'm off the stuff for a month, maybe longer. I'll just snuggle up close to you and watch you enjoy yourself. If you don't like that cocktail I'll know you don't love me and I'll turn you out of the house."

The doomed man tossed down the proffered cocktail, then his face became a horrid thing to see. It looked all smeared and twisted. Nevertheless, remembering Tim's words about turning him out of the house, he contorted his lips into a grimace of a smile and tried to give the impression he had swallowed wrong. For several moments he feared he was going to strangle to death. His eyes began to rove desperately round in their sockets as he wheezily sought to entice some air down the sizzling reaches of his seared throat.

"Delicious," he said at last in a husky voice, wiping the tears from his eyes. "What do you call the thing?"

"I call it a Rub-down Special," was Tim's proud reply. "It's so soothing inside. Now you can have just one more and then you'll have to be a good boy. I wouldn't think of letting you make love to me if you kept on drinking."

"As a matter of fact," Mr. Bentley stated, "I think I've had about enough already. I don't enjoy drinking alone and"—here he made a weak attempt to smile alluringly—"I'd much rather make love to you."

"I guess one more won't do you any harm," replied Tim, in a voice just a little too gruff for Sally's. "If you don't take it I'll not like you one little bit."

Once more the crippled hero of many liaisons subjected himself to the brutal punishment of a Rub-down Special, thinking as he did so that whatever favors he received at the hands of his hostess would be well earned indeed. Shortly after the consumption of this second cocktail he faintly asked to be excused for a moment to enable him to brush up a bit. When he dragged himself back to the room Tim had the satisfaction of beholding a wan and haggard Mr. Bentley. The man sank wearily into a chair and made revolting noises in his throat.

"Did the doctor tell you especially not to drink those cocktails?" he asked after he had rested for a moment.

"Yes," replied Tim innocently. "He said the things would kill me if I kept on drinking them. He claimed I was poisoning myself."

"Can't see that," declared Bently gamely. "They seem mighty fine to me."

"You're a regular old darling," cried Tim, slapping the enfeebled man so appreciatively on the back that he was forced once more hurriedly to leave the room. This time when he swayingly returned Mr. Bentley was unquestionably not in the pink. Still, he hoped against hope for better things. The fair object of his foul ends seemed to have noticed nothing. It was an odd thing, though, how everything seemed to go wrong whenever he entered the Willows house. There seemed to be a curse on the place. Again he sank into a chair and made some more queer noises, this time apologizing profusely for his little lapses.

"What you need," proclaimed Tim, "is a little fresh air. That's what we both need. I'm going to take my great big beautiful man for a nice walk and after that—ah-ha, what then?"

The great big beautiful man allowed himself to be bundled into his overcoat and pushed with playful vigor out of the front door. In some mysterious manner he missed his footing on the top veranda step and a moment later found himself sprawling at the bottom of the flight. Two stout matrons of Cliffside had the pleasure of witnessing Carl Bentley's grosteque debacle. Too dejected to put up a pretense, he lay on the walk with his head cocked at an awkward angle on the bottom step and looked at the two passing matrons from out of his dim, unseeing eyes. In the back of his throbbing mind a suspicion was growing that all these things could not happen to a man without there being some directing force either human or supernatural behind them. However, the sympathy and consternation so eloquently expressed on the face that Tim was wear-

ing as he helped the fallen man to his feet dispelled
such unworthy doubts.

"We'll go by the river path," decided Tim as he led
Mr. Bentley down a side street. "It's so lovely there
and quiet, and there are no prying eyes. We'll be quite
alone—just you and I and the river."

For some reason the way Tim brought out the words
"river" and "alone" made Carl Bentley shudder
slightly. He was the sort of person who confined his
reading to the most lurid passages of the current nov-
els. Quite naturally he had never made a complete job
of Dreiser's two-deck *American Tragedy,* but he did
recall the drowning scene, and felt no better for it. His
mind had reached that stage of morbidity at which only
the most unpleasant eventualities seemed probable.

The success Tim had so far achieved in subjecting
Carl Bentley to pain and humiliation had put him in
the best of spirits. He felt that if Sally had only been
present to witness his various artful dodges his triumph
would have been complete. He experienced no com-
punction for what he had done to Bentley, nor for
what he was going to do to Bentley. In fact, he was
mildly surprised he had not already murdered the man.
As he summed up the score between them he con-
cluded he held a decided advantage over this would-be
home wrecker. Once he had almost put an end to his
unwholesome activities for all time. Now he was about
to repeat the experiment. Tim looked forward to it.
Tim Willows was not really a bad man at heart, but
when people were mean to him he enjoyed being just a
little bit meaner.

There was still a thin coating of ice on the river. The
path that ran close to its edge was narrow, slippery,
and disagreeable—the last place in the world to select
for a walk at that time of year. Tim pretended to enjoy
it. Carl Bentley, a little revived by the fresh air, still
clung to his fixed idea. He was going to have his will
with Sally Willows. How else could he justify to himself the pain and indignities he had already suffered at
her hands? Once more he resumed his tentative endeavor. Winding an arm round his companion's waist
he slipped and sloshed laboriously along at the side of

his intended victim. In so doing he received a rather unpleasant impression. Sally Willows's waist as he remembered it had been delightfully slim and firm. The same could not be said of it now. It was still firm but most decidedly not slim. In fact, it was almost fat. It was fat. Moodily Bentley wondered if Sally was a secret eater—a greedy woman. It would not have surprised him in the least. She was so strange, so different from other women. The truth of the matter was that Tim's pregnancy was increasing by leaps and bounds. Unaccustomed as he was to pregnancy, especially as applied to his own person, each time he observed his mounting displacement he was freshly indignant with nature and Mr. Ram for the unfair advantage they were taking of him.

"Soon I'll be sitting about the house like a jovial female Falstaff unable to rise without assistance," he had recently complained to Sally.

"Well, you can't eat your cake and have it, too," had been that lady's unfeeling rejoinder.

"If the situation were reversed," Tim had observed, "and you were in my fix I'd be a damn sight more sympathetic with you than you are with me."

"That's because you're not really a woman," she had said. "A woman is rarely sympathetic with another woman for performing her natural functions. She either looks on a prospective mother with envy or considers her extremely careless."

"Well, after all, it's your figure that's being enlarged," Tim had replied.

Carl Bentley was now finding things out for himself. Sally Willows's waist was actually gross. When he attempted to elevate his grip, Tim gave a little scream and halted.

"Let's play clap hands!" he cried girlishly, skilfully maneuvering Mr. Bentley so that he was standing with his back to the river and perilously close to its edge. "My patties are awfully cold."

Without much display of enthusiasm Mr. Bentley extended his large hands and allowed himself to go through the vapid passes of this exceedingly childish game. But if Mr. Bentley was deficient in enthusiasm his companion more than made up for it. The game, which at its wildest could hardly be called gripping, seemed to stimulate his fair opponent to a frenzy of excitement. So madly did Tim's hands slap and lunge that Carl Bentley began to wonder whether the woman had mistaken boxing for a simple nursery game. At last he found himself wholly on the defensive, busily engaged in warding off blows. A sense of unreality stole over him as he strove to hold his ground. Why should he be standing there, he wondered, permitting this silly thing to go on? Unconsciously he stepped back several paces, seeking a better foothold. He never found it. At that moment Tim broke through his guard and with a cry of innocent glee gave him a violent shove. The game ended abruptly in a crash and a plop. Carl Bentley had found his foothold on the bed of the river. Only his head was visible, but that was quite enough. From the expression on the man's face one would have been led to believe that he was seriously contemplating suicide, whether life still held sufficient promise to make a return to it desirable. Never had Tim beheld such a brooding and disgusted countenance. This was good. He laughed shrilly and hysterically.

"You know," he cried, "you do look a sight. Just like John the Baptist with his head hygienically transferred to ice. Stop moping about and hurry out of there. I'm getting cold standing here on this freezing ground."

"Do the misfortunes of others always strike you in a humorous light?" Bentley demanded.

"Misfortunes, nonsense!" exclaimed Tim. "You just didn't know how to play the game, that's all there is to it. Hurry up and let me help you. I'm simply freezing."

"That's too darned bad," replied Bentley, beginning to chatter a little himself, "but please don't try to help me. You might get all wet. I couldn't bear that."

But Tim insisted on being helpful. In his eagerness he kept getting in Mr. Bentley's way and thwarting his most desperate effort to climb ashore. A dispassionate observer would have gained the impression that a very small woman was grimly endeavoring to prevent a very large man from quitting an ice-cold river. The dispassionate observer would have been quite right.

In desperation the exhausted and chilled Bentley was forced to drop to his hands and knees and literally to claw his way past the obstructing legs of his rescuer. He fell panting and shivering on the muddy bank, a spent man weary of life and of all that it had to offer.

"Hurry!" cried Tim. "I must get you home and make you strip. It's a lucky thing I was here or you might have been standing there yet."

"If you hadn't been here," replied Mr. Bentley, with the uncivil logic of the wet male, "I wouldn't have been standing there at all."

"Cheer up," continued Tim. "What's a little river between friends?"

"If the river had been between us," declared Mr. Bentley as he struggled to his feet, "it would have been a damn sight safer for me."

"Nonsense," replied Tim. "Don't go on so. You're not the first man who ever fell in a river. Thousands drown every year. Suppose you were a lumberjack."

"I have no intention of ever becoming a lumberjack," retorted Mr. Bentley.

"But that doesn't keep you from supposing you were one, does it?" asked Tim.

"No," admitted the other, "but I can't see how supposing I was a lumberjack is going to make me any warmer or drier."

"It certainly won't make you any colder or wetter, will it?" demanded Tim argumentatively.

"All right," said Bentley desperately. "I'm a lumberjack. What happens now?"

"Very well, then," replied Tim. "Come along. I knew it would be like this."

"Then why did you ever start out?"

"I wanted to make sure. Thought at least we might be able to take a quiet walk without your flopping and splashing about in a river."

Mr. Bentley could not trust himself to reply to this unreasonable observation. Instead he gave an outlet to his pent-up emotions by sneezing inartistically all over the adjacent landscape.

When Tim had hauled his visitor home he hustled the dripping creature up to the bedroom preparatory to the last act. Here he made Mr. Bentley strip to his union suit, practically dragging the clothes off the miserable man with his own two hands.

"You wear union suits, I see," Tim remarked as he yanked off Bentley's soaking trousers.

"Yes," chattered Mr. Bentley. "What does Willows wear?"

"Rags," replied Tim. "Old, unsightly rags. He picks up things about the house and tries them on."

"Tough on you," observed Mr. Bentley, his vanity getting the better of him. "I like to look nice this way. A man owes it to himself. Poor Willows. I'll never forget the night when he hid behind the portière."

It was this remark that settled Carl Bentley's fate. Not only was this great oaf laboring under the delusion that he was going to seduce poor Willows's wife, but also he was actually pitying the husband with horrid condescension.

"That tears it," said Tim decisively, in his natural voice.

"Tears what?" asked Bentley, momentarily startled out of his self-satisfaction.

"You'll soon find out," said Tim, walking over to the bureau and producing the automatic. With this lethal weapon held carelessly in his hands he turned on Mr. Bentley and grinned unpleasantly. "Instead of ruining me," he continued, "I'm going to pretty well ruin you. But before I start in I want to let you know that you look simply terrible in that union suit with its tricky little trapdoor arrangement in the back. You make me ashamed of my sex, as undecided as it is at the moment."

Mr. Bentley's amazement as he listened to Tim's voice crisply issuing from Sally's lips mounted to stupefaction. Had it not been for the blue-black automatic covering him he would have been inclined to believe that Sally was playing another trick and not a very nice one at that. The automatic, however, was altogether too convincing. Try as he would he could not find a laugh in his system sufficiently robust to do away with that disagreeable-looking object. So unnerved was Mr. Bentley that he was not even able to work up the sickest sort of a smile. Recalling his embarrassing experience on the train, he came to the conclusion that the voices of the Willows must have become interchangeable. Tim's voice continued. He was methodically lashing himself into a fury. He fully intended to make himself madder than he had ever been in his life. It would be a fairly easy matter. One short look at Carl Bentley was enough to set him going. A long look was sure to bring on a violent rage.

"You thought I looked so funny hiding behind that portière," he went on. "You'll never forget it, will you?"

Mr. Bentley was far too frightened to become further confused. He made no attempt to answer, but kept his fascinated eyes on that gun.

"Well, here's something else you'll never forget," continued Tim. "Something that will live with you to your dying day." Tim's voice changed suddenly to a note of sharp command. "Unbutton your little trap door," he snapped.

"But," faltered Mr. Bentley, wondering what on earth was in store for him, "that's hardly——"

"There's no buts about it," interrupted Tim. "I have a desire to see it flap as you go. I want everybody to see it flap."

Reluctantly Carl Bentley did as he was told. He felt as if he had been deprived of his last shred of self-respect. He was not only unbuttoned, but also undone.

"You're a sight for sore eyes," observed Tim. "Now about-face and march. Go right down the stairs and directly out of this house. Don't stop or hesitate. I'll be close behind you with this gun. Once in the street walk rapidly but don't try to run. If you do I'll start shooting. Get a move on now, and don't talk back. You can still save your useless life if you do exactly as I tell you. Off you go."

Thus it came about that Mr. Carl Bentley, clad in a dripping union suit not properly arranged in the back, was seen walking briskly along the streets by practically the entire population of that suburban town. About ten yards behind this arresting figure came Tim Willows. In his hand was an automatic.

Carl Bentley at first endeavored to give the impression of a man walking in a trance or in sleep, but as he neared the more populous quarter of the town his frayed nerves snapped and he incontinently fled. Tim, in spite of the fact that he was running for two, did his best to keep up with the fleeing man. The sight of the flapping trap door added greatly to the pleasure of the pursuit. It was then that the shooting began, which terminated only when Mr. Bentley sought protection behind Sally.

The little party, escorted by the state troopers, proceeded down the street and entered the police station, which also served as the courthouse. As Mr. Bentley was about to go in, one of the troopers rapped him smartly with his club.

"Button that up," said the trooper. "Have you no pride?"

Mechanically Mr. Bentley's fingers began to grope for the button of what Tim had been pleased to call the little trap door.

CHAPTER XIV

Much Ado About Honor

"WELL, WELL, WELL," DRAWLED SERGEANT DEVLIN, letting his pleased eyes dwell ironically on the strange figure of Mr. Carl Bentley. "What have we here?"

"Damned if I rightly know," replied one of the state troopers. "I've never laid violent hands on anything exactly like it since I've been on the force. It's all wet and nasty."

"I shall remember the revolting circumstances when recommending you for promotion," observed the sergeant, returning once more to his rapt contemplation of the miserable object under discussion. "You know," he continued, in his calm, deliberate voice, "I've sat here behind this desk for many a long year and during that time some mighty unpalatable-looking specimens have been dragged in off the streets, but this one is by all odds the queerest—the most difficult to classify as a member of the human race. It's enough to unseat one's reason." Having delivered himself of this scholarly observation—Sergeant Devlin being an exceptionally well-educated officer—he let his eyes refresh themselves on the figure of one he mistook for a small but none the less appealingly fashioned woman. Suddenly he started and a dismayed expression appeared in his eyes. "Joe," he said to one of the troopers, "what is the little lady doing with that large gun in her hand? That doesn't strike me as being quite prudent. Ladies with revolvers are notoriously irregular. However, it doesn't really matter. Everything connected with this affair seems to be somewhat irregular." Giving the officer addressed as Joe no opportunity to reply, the sergeant resumed his dispassionate scrutiny of Carl Bentley. "Couldn't you have arranged to put a little something on before getting yourself brought before me?" he inquired, with surprising gentleness. "Had it been the lady, now, I would have offered no word of protest, but then I suppose in my job one shouldn't expect too much in the way of amusement." At this point in the officer's monologue it was on Sally's stubble-covered face rather than on Tim's smooth one that the blush of modesty appeared. Tim in his vulgar manner giggled rather indecently. Sergeant Devlin was quick to note the incongruity of these reactions. "Who is that man?" he demanded, inclining his head in the direction of Sally.

"Seems to be the lady's husband," one of the troopers replied.

"He seems to be?" repeated Devlin. " 'Seems' is hardly the word. Either he is or he isn't the lady's husband. However, it doesn't matter. That may be irregular, too."

"We're man and wife," spoke up Sally, with truly ladylike hauteur.

"That could easily be possible," replied Sergeant Devlin, looking more searchingly at the male owner of the female voice, "but which is the man and which is the wife is still a question in my mind. Your attributes seem to have become strangely confused." Once more he turned his attention to Carl Bentley. "You know," he remarked easily to that individual, "your quaint idea of a gentleman's walking attire has placed you in a very unfortunate position, my dear sir. Even before this obviously involved situation has been made clear to me I feel strongly inclined to charge you with several disgusting offenses."

"I had no opportunity," Carl Bentley protested in a feeble voice. "I was fleeing for my life."

"Was it worth it?" asked the sergeant, with the detached interest of the true skeptic. "I believe things would have worked out better for you in the long run if you had lost your life. Many persons—I don't say all—but many nice-minded persons would rather be found dead than caught the way you are."

"But that woman was trying to murder me," whined the no longer statuesque Mr. Bentley, pointing an accusing finger at the cause of his degradation. "She's a terrible woman, Sergeant. You don't know. There's something strange about her."

A smothered exclamation broke from the undeniably provocative lips that circumstance had thrust on Tim.

"You horrid man!" he cried threateningly. "You just wait until I tell the nice officer all about how you tried to do in my honor. If you'd had your way with me I wouldn't have had enough honor left to dust a fiddle with."

As Sergeant Devlin smiled approvingly on Tim the miserable Mr. Bentley shivered with apprehension. The poor man seemed to realize he had not the ghost of a chance. The sergeant's next remark made assurance doubly sure.

"I can see nothing strange in the lady's conduct," Devlin observed. "I would very much like to murder you myself. Unfortunately duty forbids." He turned graciously to Tim. "Not that it matters much," continued the sergeant, "but did you have any definite reason for wanting to kill this creature, madam, or were you merely trying to perform a public service? I've always been interested in trifles."

"Well, this wasn't any matter to trifle with," said Tim promptly. "It was a good old-fashioned, free-for-all assault. Never have I been so shocked and surprised."

"Dear me," murmured the sergeant, looking severely upon Mr. Bentley. "At this late day and age do you still find it necessary to go about assaulting women? You must be an out-of-luck guy indeed. It's really too bad the little lady missed her mark. Then we might have been able to hush the matter up. Instead of being buried beneath a nice, clean, protective layer of quiet earth you will now be crushed beneath the weight of public scorn and indignation."

Sergeant Devlin was now thoroughly enjoying himself. His life as a whole was a dull one. There had not been much crime of late. He had come to look on a law-breaker as a generous gift from God. This case promised to become unusually sweet and pungent. Although it pleased him to feign ignorance he was quite well aware of the identities of his three visitors. He knew the names, residences, and social standing of each actor involved in this diverting little drama. It gave him infinite satisfaction to get his hooks into some members of the upper strata for a change. Both from report and personal observation he had formed an especially low opinion of Mr. Carl Bentley. He would make that so-called gentleman suffer for the good fortune of birth and position.

"Do I understand, then, madam," he asked politely, "That you wish to lodge a charge of assault against this prisoner?"

"I surely do, Sergeant," declared Tim earnestly. "Exaggerated assault. The worst sort of assault."

Devlin scratched his head in some perplexity.

"Just what is the worst sort of assault, lady?" he asked. "Opinions might differ, you know. One man's meat is another man's poison."

"Well, this man is all poison to me," retorted Tim. "I've always been true to my husband, haven't I, dear?"

This question, coming so unexpectedly upon Sally, completely shattered the pose of calm reserve she had been striving to maintain since her first break. A flute-like voice popped out surprisingly from between her lips, the upper one of which stood sadly in need of a razor. At the sound of a woman's voice proceeding from a man's body Sergeant Devlin looked up and scanned the speaker's face with a mystified expression in which there was a shade of mistrust. This case, to his way of thinking, bade fair to develop some rather sensational sidelights.

"Always, darling," Sally was saying in answer to Tim's question. "We all of us have our faults, but misplacing or forgetting your honor is not one of yours. That I will say for you."

"You'd have been fit to be tied to-day," Tim continued volubly. "The way that man went on was nobody's business. It was nip and tuck for a while. Didn't look as if I was going to have any honor left at all."

"May I ask how far this fiend succeeded?" inquired

the sergeant. "Merely as a matter of record, you understand, my dear lady."

"Well, I wouldn't like to go into details, Sergeant," Tim modestly replied. "No lady would, but the assault proper was a complete flop. I still have all my honor left right down to the last shred, such as it is. Still, it's the only honor I have."

Tim seemed to regard his honor as he would a powder puff or lipstick or any other small article women usually carry about with them in their handbags. Sergeant Devlin would not have been a bit surprised if the little lady had produced her honor and proudly displayed it for his inspection.

"Well," he remarked after a moment of reflection, "I'm sure we're mighty glad about that."

"You're not nearly so glad as I am," said Tim. "You know, Sergeant, a girl's honor is just about the best thing she has, and sometimes it's not so good, at that. I always try to keep my honor spick and span, right up to the minute."

"Up to what minute?" Devlin inquired, with justifiable curiosity.

By this time Mr. Bently was writhing in mental as well as bodily anguish. If this terrible woman continued to make ground at her present rate of progress he would have no more chance than the proverbially proverbial snowball in a proverbiably proverbial hell. It was high time that his voice was heard.

"It's all a lie, officer," he broke in furiously. "That woman has no honor. She's trying deliberately to frame me. Why——"

"What's that?" interrupted Tim. "Do you hear what he's saying, Sergeant? He's actually got the nerve to stand up there and tell me to my face that I haven't any honor—no honor at all. Why, you big, hulking stiff, I'll have you know that I've got the least tarnished honor of any woman in town, which isn't saying a great deal, now that I come to think of it."

"Don't you believe her, Sergeant." Carl Bentley pleaded as a man pleads for his life. "That woman, that she-dragon masquerading behind a thin veil of virtue, actually dragged my trousers off with her two bare hands. Then, still unsatisfied by that display of female ferocity, she held me up at the point of a gun and forced me to walk through the streets in this terrible condition."

"Oh, what a whale of a lie he told," Tim exclaimed in righteous indignation. "I was merely protecting this confounded honor of mine I've been telling you about. The first thing I knew that the man was feeling that way was when he came dashing into my house and began to tear off his clothes—even his pants, Sergeant—think of it—what a sight—and then he began to make noises just like an animal. That's no way to act. After that he started lunging—that's what he did—he made lunges at me, and I can't stand being lunged at. So I very quietly said to myself, 'Sally Willows, my good woman,' I said, 'if you don't do something constructive mighty quick it's good-night for your honor.' Then I took up my husband's revolver that he won the war with in Fort Leavenworth, and I made this man stop his lunging. And that's the low-down on the whole beastly affair, so help me God."

Tim stopped for lack of breath and looked triumphantly at Carl Bentley. That gentleman's pendulous jaw was hanging low. Above the cavity thus revealed peered the stricken eyes of a beaten man. He seemed to be seeing himself as he actually might have been—lunging. Sergeant Devlin himself appeared to be deeply moved. For some moments he did not speak, but sat as if in contemplation of the vivid picture Tim had painted of Carl Bentley in action. At last he stirred and spoke.

"Mrs. Willows," he said, "you have been through a most trying ordeal, from which you luckily emerged—thanks to your courage—with your honor quite okay." He paused and allowed his eyes to burn up Carl Bentley, then he spoke coldly to the man. "Do you wish me to believe," he asked, "that this frail woman, this lady of culture and refinement, was able, in spite of all your efforts, to drag the trousers off your large, fat, repulsive-looking legs?"

"Well," hedged Mr. Bentley, realizing too late the mistake he had made, "almost she did. She lured them off, so to speak. It was a trap—a snare. I tell you she was out to frame me and she stopped at nothing. She enticed my trousers off after she had first tried to drown me."

"This situation becomes more involved as time goes on," sighed the sergeant. "You now would have me believe that this lady also made an attempt to drown you. How can I believe a statement like that, I ask you? It's impossible on the face of it. Why, this little woman couldn't drown even a kitten, let alone a gorilla of a guy like you."

"That's because you don't know her," replied Carl Bentley, endeavoring to summon to his aid the last remnants of his depleted dignity. "If she attempts to lodge a charge of assault against me I, on my part, will prefer charges of attempted murder, defamation of character, and mental anguish against her."

"All of those," observed Sergeant Devlin, slightly elevating his thick eyebrows as he jotted down some notes on his record. "Well, this situation is altogether too delicate and at the same time too serious for a mere policeman to handle. I'll have to let you both tell your troubles to Judge Clark. He should be here in about five minutes if he doesn't get so furious at something on his way down to court that he forgets where he's going. He's like that, Judge Clark is. A man of sound and fury." At this point he paused, and, after adding a few cogent sentences to his report, passed the paper to a policeman, who vanished with it through a side door. "Joe," resumed Devlin, addressing a state trooper, "present this little party to Judge Clark with my compliments. He'll be tickled scarlet to see them. And just slip a coat over our friend here. His Honor would have a stroke if he saw him the way he is."

Mr. Bentley was hustled into an old police overcoat which made him look worse, if possible, than he was before, and then pushed through a door. Tim and Sally made ready to follow.

"Don't worry about your honor any more, Mrs. Willows," said the sergeant to Tim with a friendly smile. "But if I were in your place I would worry a little about His Honor. Judge Clark is an exceptionally irascible gentleman. Good luck to you."

"You've been so sweet to me, Sergeant," replied Tim. "And for your sake I'll forget all about my honor. I've a feeling the judge and myself will get along as thick as thieves."

"There's no honor among thieves, Mrs. Willows," the sergeant reminded Tim.

"What a blessed relief that must be for lady crooks," replied Tim, pausing at the door. "I'm getting pretty well fed up with mine. It's a greatly overrated encumbrance, Sergeant, believe me. Always needs protection."

At that moment Sally dug her husband in the ribs, an act which elicited a deep-throated oath, but which nevertheless made him move on. Sergeant Devlin remained seated at his desk, thoughtfully worrying his hair. "From the way that baby talks," he said to himself, "and from the way she uses those eyes of hers I wouldn't be a bit surprised if that poor sap didn't have a little something on his side after all. Just the same he deserves to be hung on general principles. I must get a look at the judge's face when he first lays eyes on him."

Sergeant Devlin leaned back in his chair and smiled broadly.

CHAPTER XV

Judge Clark Almost Loses His Temper

WHEN THE LITTLE PARTY WAS REASSEMBLED IN THE courtroom an exchange of unpleasantries immediately broke out between its contending factions.

"You're a nasty little liar," Carl Bentley flung hoarsely at Tim. "What are you trying to do, get them to hang me?"

"Yes," replied Tim promptly. "I'm hoping to get you hung by your dirty neck. Officer, this assaulter is calling me bad names and threatening me with things."

"If you call her a nasty little liar again, I'll scratch your eyes out," cried Sally in a ringing falsetto.

"Calm yourself, Mr. Willows," urged one of the state troopers. "You're actually losing control of your voice. And as for you, you big gazebo, if——"

"Quiet!" commanded the other trooper. "Here comes His Honor now."

"What's his honor to me?" expostulated Tim. "I've got my own honor to take care of. Men haven't any honor anyway. They can lose it year in and year out and still be honorable men, but just let a woman lose her honor one teeny little bit and her goose is cooked for good. She's a gone coon, she is."

"No dobut you're right," said the trooper soothingly.

"I don't know. Never went into the matter. Take it up with the judge. He's a very highstrung gentleman and he likes everything nice and orderly."

Tim subsided and turned his attention to the judge. He was a thin, little old judge and he gave the impression of having been hurriedly strung together on badly twisted wires. His sharp face was livid and shrunken, and a volcano of wrathful impatience flickered on the verge of eruption behind his small, beady eyes. As he slowly approached his desk he looked like a man who had already been tried too hard for one day. A long tuft of gray hair still clung to his otherwise bald head, the rest having been torn out during fits of judicial frenzy. Whenever the word went out that Judge Clark was enjoying one of his good moods the information was never accepted at its face value. His satellites had come to know through bitter experience that the rumor merely meant that the judge had not entered his chambers in a state of inarticulate rage.

As he now seated himself carefully behind his desk, it was only too apparent that he was not enjoying one of his softer moments. He favored the two troopers and their charges with a spiteful look from his smouldering eyes.

"What are all these people doing here?" he snapped. "They disgust me."

Briefly one of the troopers endeavored to enlighten the judge. When he had finished his sordid story, His Honor's eyes were blazing dangerously.

"Make 'em sit down," he grated. "I'll put the lot of 'em away as soon as I've cleared up these other cases."

Tim and Sally and Carl Bentley sat down, and with a feeling of increasing uneasiness watched Judge Clark's method of clearing up cases. Whatever his prisoners may have thought of it, Judge Clark's method had at least the virtue of strict simplicity and rigid impartiality. Everybody received a sentence. The first prisoner up was hardly there before he was gone again, literally whisked from the eyes of man.

"Six months," rapped out the judge. "No. Better make it seven. Next prisoner."

Business moved so briskly that finally the spectators got the impression that they were witnessing a procession of the damned rather than the administration of justice. One prisoner, a large, lachrymose Negro with hypocritically humble eyes, on being sentenced to a year less a day, endeavored to suggest to the judge that, even accepting the word in its most casual application, what had happened to him had not even remotely resembled a trial.

"Why yo' hain't even tried me. Yo' Honor," the Negro protested. "Hain't never axed me a question."

The judge looked at the Negro a long, long time—much too long for the Negro's comfort.

"Do you want me to try you?" asked the little man, in a reedy, gentle voice. "Do you want me to ask you questions?"

"Ah reckon not," mumbled the Negro. "Ah reckon ah's just as well satisfied to hurry right along now like you says."

No smile could have been grimmer than the one that twisted the judge's lips as his snappy eyes followed the back of the retreating Negro.

Although it required no little temerity to stand beneath the baleful gaze of this terrible little man perched high above her like a bird of evil omen, Sally nevertheless accompanied Tim and Bentley when they were summoned to approach the seat of justice. The judge seemed to have forgotten he had ever seen them before. When the senior state trooper respectfully started to say his little piece the judge promptly shot up a restraining hand that was shaking with indignation as he considered the weird figure of Carl Bentley.

"Don't say one word," he commanded. "I have eyes in my head, haven't I? Am I a fool? A driveling idiot?"

"Yes," replied Tim, unable to resist the insistence in the judge's voice.

"What!" shrilled the Judge. "You call me a fool and an idiot—a driveling one?"

"No," said Tim hastily. "I was saying 'yes' to something else."

"What were you saying 'yes' to?"

"I was merely saying, 'Yes, you have.'"

"Yes, I have? Speak up, you ninny. Yes, I have what?"

"Yes, you have eyes in your head."

The judge's face blanched with passion.

"Of course I have eyes in my head," he snapped. "Who said I didn't?"

"Nobody," answered Tim. "You asked if you had."

"Asked if I had? What did I ask if I had?"

"If you had eyes in your head."

Tim was growing steadily more confused.

"But I know I have eyes in my head," said the judge.

"It seemed for a moment you didn't," was Tim's halting answer. "You see, you asked about them."

"Asked about who?"

"Whom," corrected Sally.

"What's that?" cried the judge.

"The word is 'whom'," replied Sally. "You asked about who and you shouldn't have. It's whom, that's what it is."

"Hold your tongue, sir. I'll ask about who I damn please."

Sally shrugged indifferently.

"You were asking about your eyes, Your Honor," Tim meekly put in.

"Damn my eyes!" howled the judge. "I'll clear up this case right now."

The little man leaned far over his desk and peered down at Carl Bentley, who shrank beneath the gaze.

"Don't say a word," he gritted. "I see it all quite clearly. One of my own policemen caught in a raid on a disorderly house—a bawdy place. What a sentence I'll give him!" So much had Judge Clark deduced from the undressed appearance and battered condition of Mr. Carl Bentley. "I didn't even know we had such places conveniently at hand hereabouts," went on the judge in an injured voice. "What's this man doing with his buttons on? Strip 'em all off. Don't leave him a single button. These other two ran this brothel, I suppose."

"But Your Honor," protested one of the troopers, "if we strip off all his buttons the man will be mother-naked."

"Then arrest him for indecent exposure," said the judge blandly. "And why do you say 'mother-naked'? Why does everybody say 'mother-naked'? Do fathers never get naked? Do I understand that they sit about the house all day long muffled up to their ears? Expressions like that exasperate me. Don't answer. The implication is quite improper and it has nothing to do with this lecherous policeman. Hasn't he any clothes on under his coat? And what is he doing to my floor? Officer, remove that man at once! Hasn't he any better sense? Imagine!"

"Your Honor, he's dripping wet," explained the trooper.

"I can see that for myself," cried the judge. "The man's a regular human fountain—a gusher. Make him stop it."

"He can't, Your Honor," said the trooper.

"He can't?" gasped the judge. "What on earth is the matter with the man? Do you mean he can't or he won't? Where does he think he is?"

"He fell in the river, Your Honor."

"I was pushed in the river, Your Honor," Mr. Bentley corrected.

"Silence!" shouted the judge. "Or I'll push you in a cell. What's he got on under that coat?"

The other trooper pulled back the coat and Carl Bentley stood revealed. Judge Clark drew a sharp breath and blinked his eyes.

"What a sight," he managed to whisper. "My word, what a sight to behold. And to think that after all these years of honorable service on the bench I should at last be brought face to face with a thing like that. The man deserves to be put to death by torture—slowly."

The courtroom for some time past had been doing capacity business. It was obvious that word had gone out that the case of Sally Willows vs. Carl Bentley was being tried. The élite of the town was present—any number of women whose minds were not quite as nice as their frocks or their manners. And while Judge Clark was sitting back in his chair trying to devise a legal pretext for making Mr. Bentley pay the extreme penalty, one of the state troopers once more essayed to make the case a little clearer for the benefit of the bemused jurist. When finally it was borne in on that gentleman's mind that the individual he had mistaken for a policeman was merely a plain citizen he became, if anything, madder.

"Why didn't you tell me that in the first place?" he demanded, snapping up in his chair and fixing his mad eyes on Mr. Bentley. "So he first attempted to assault this woman, then he tried to murder her."

"Not quite, Your Honor," corrected the trooper. "She tried to murder him."

"What does it matter?" retorted His Honor impatiently. "Why quibble over mere details?"

"It was a case of my honor, Your Honor," said Tim, smiling up disarmingly at the little man.

"It's a lie, Judge!" cried Carl Bentley. "Look! She still has the gun in her hand."

The judge looked as requested, and his eyes grew so wide they seemed about ready to explode.

"Are my eyes playing me false?" he asked, in a voice choked with emotion. "Do I see what I see or do I don't, or whatever it is? As God is my judge I can't bring myself to hear the truth." He glared out over the courtroom as if he were trying to decide whether it would not be better to sentence everyone in sight to a life of penal servitude and then call it a day. Then he fastened his gimlet-like eyes on the two state troopers. "You've put me on the spot," he said in a cold, thin voice. "You'll be asking me to go riding next. Don't answer. It is inconceivable to me that you have allowed this woman—the most irresponsible of all God's less agreeable creations—to confront your own judge with a revolver in her hand. It is inconceivable, I say, yet it has come to pass. Do you know what I'd like to do? I'd like to claw off your buttons with these!"

As if to make himself thoroughly understood Judge Clark thrust out two skinny hands and wriggled their fingers horribly in the pallid faces of the two state troopers.

"That's what she did to me," put in Carl Bentley, thinking the moment propitious for attempting to get on the right side of the judge. "She dragged my trousers off with her own bare hands."

"Shut up, you!" mouthed the judge.

"I wouldn't touch that person's trousers with a pair of tongs, Your Honor," Tim declared scornfully.

Judge Clark looked down at the disputant out of a pair of venom-drugged eyes.

"Tongs?" he muttered in a puzzled voice. "How did tongs get into this case?"

"They're not really in it," answered Tim. "This case

is about my honor, Your Honor. I've been saying so all along."

"You haven't a spark of honor," retorted Carl Bentley bitterly. "You never had any honor. You lost it before you'd finished cutting your teeth."

This was too much for Sally. After all, it was really her honor that was being thus publicly assailed. She completely lost her temper.

"Shoot him, Tim!" she cried in a high-pitched voice. "He's insinuating things."

"Insinuating?" laughed Tim madly. "He's damn well making a clean breast of them. I'll load him so full of lead he won't even need a coffin."

As Tim leveled the automatic, Judge Clark and Mr. Bentley emitted piercing screams, but for vastly different reasons, the latter's being one of unadulterated terror while the judge's was merely the cry of an infuriated soul.

"Unarm that woman!" he shrilled passionately above the tumult of the courtroom. "Am I to be forced to sit on this bench and witness a cold-blooded murder?"

"But the thing isn't loaded, Your Honor," one of the troopers shouted.

"What!" cried the judge. "You say it isn't loaded? That settles it. That finishes everything. I'd like to crash you over the head with the butt of it. What do you think my court is, a nursery in which to practise Chicago? Will I be asked to join you in a game of ping-ping next."

"Pong," corrected Sally.

"What's that?" asked the judge suspiciously.

"Pong," repeated Sally.

"Pong what?" inquired the judge.

"Ping-pong," said Sally briskly.

"Are you trying to play games with me?" the judge asked severely.

A peal of high, girlish laughter bursting from the be-whiskered lips of a full-grown male turned the anger of the small jurist to profound alarm. He looked at Sally as if she were some visitant from a remote planet.

"Have my ears gone back on me, too?" he muttered in a tremulous voice. "Surely no male creature can make a noise like that. It s positively uncanny. I shall have to punish this person under the law prohibiting female impersonation."

When Sally had gained control of herself the judge leaned over and spoke to her in a confidential voice.

"How did you ever manage to make a noise like that?" he asked. "It's the most extraordinary thing I've ever heard."

"It's an old family custom, Judge," Sally replied recklessly.

"Must have been a peculiar family," the judge observed thoughtfully. "Most confusing to live in. I daresay it was terrible for the neighbors."

"Nobody ever spoke to us," said Sally.

"Can't say as I blame them," commented Judge Clark. "Where I'm going to put you nobody will ever speak to you either."

"Come, come!" boomed Tim in a deep bass voice. "Let's get on with the case."

Judge Clark spun about in his chair and looked with horror on the fair face of the speaker.

"Something's happened to *her* voice now," he exclaimed. "Are you two prisoners trying to befuddle me? Is this whole ghastly business a deep-laid conspiracy to rob me of my reason, or has that already gone? For God's sake don't tell me it was a custom in your family too."

"As a matter of fact it was," Tim replied easily. "But that's neither here nor there. It's a matter of my honor against his honor, Your Honor."

"That's one of the most baffling utterances I've ever heard," stated the judge.

"How so?" inquired Tim. "I merely said that I was counting on your honor to judge rightly between his honor and my honor, Your Honor."

"Don't go on and on," barked the judge. "What has my honor got to do with it?"

"Not a thing," replied Tim sweetly, returning to Sally's soft accents. "Why, a man of your integrity can't be seduc——"

"Stop!" shrilled the judge, seizing his last lock of hair. "Clear the court! Drive 'em out! Woman, do you realize what you're saying? Look at me. I'm a judge!"

"I wouldn't like to be a judge," said Tim in pitying tones. "But tell me, Your Honor. Can't they even be seduced?"

"Madam, are you trying to debauch me?" demanded the judge. "Do you realize that every word you utter is making the case blacker against you? I can hardly believe this object here attempted to assault you. He wouldn't have found it necessary."

"But he did, Your Honor," said Tim earnestly. "I swear to God he did. The first time he tried to assault me——"

"Am I to understand that he attempted to assault you more than once?" interposed Judge Clark.

"You are, Your Honor," replied Tim. "He was indefatigable about it. Kept it up all morning until finally I lost my patience. 'Sally Willows,' I said to myself, 'if this guy keeps on trying to assault you, you'll never get any housework done.' You know how it is, Your Honor. A woman can't give up her entire day to warding off assaults. And I do like to keep my home looking neat and nice. You can't do that being assaulted, Judge, because as I was saying you don't know anything about assaults—not those sort of assaults, you know. It's simply impossible to try to dust and sweep with one hand and repel assaults with the other. Simply impossible. The broom gets tangled and the dust all spills and—of course you can use one foot, but that's not very ladylike and it might prove disastrous. Have you ever been caught by the foot? Well, it doesn't matter. So after doing everything in my power to make this person get it through his thick head that I was in no mood for assaults, and certainly not at such a time, what with my housework and all, I finally got my husband's gun and drove him out of the house. What else was there for me to do? I ask you that."

"Madam," thundered the judge, "I've let you run on. Experience has convinced me that is the only thing one can do with a woman. Is there one tittle of truth in all the loose things you've been saying? I ask you that."

"Tittle?" repeated Tim as if puzzled. "I don't quite understand."

At this moment Tim's face underwent a sudden alteration in its features. He jumped as if someone had pinched him. Then he stood still as if listening, and an expression of surprise and alarm spread over his face.

"What's the matter with you now?" demanded the judge.

"I don't know," answered Tim faintly. "It's very odd. Very odd indeed. I think I'd better sit down."

"But you must know what's happening to you," protested the judge. "Haven't you the slightest idea?"

Tim merely shook his head and indulged in several small jumps and budges while the judge's eyes grew strained with curiosity.

"Can't you even guess?" he asked.

"I could, Your Honor, but I'm afraid you might get mad," said Tim.

"No, I won't," Judge Clark promised eagerly. "Go on and tell. I won't get mad."

"It's really quite the most bewildering thing I've ever experienced, Your Honor," said Tim, looking the part of a thoroughly bewildered and alarmed young woman. "My appendix seems to be jumping. It's like an assault. That's why I was afraid to tell you. Thought it might make you mad. The fact is, Judge, I've been kicked often enough on the outside, but never before on the in. And that's what's happening to me now. Someone's deliberately kicking me."

"The most extraordinary story I've ever heard," observed the judge. "Can't make head or tail out of it."

"Neither can I, Your Honor," gasped Tim, giving another startled little jump. "I'm scared."

"You're making me extremely nervous," Judge Clark complained. "Can't you stop it?"

Sally had been observing her husband's strange antics with a puzzled expression. Her face now cleared and she actually indulged in a series of girlish giggles. His Honor turned reproving eyes on her.

"My dear sir, I want you to know this is no laughing matter," he snapped.

"It certainly is, Your Honor," came the amazing reply. "He's such an awful fool. Why, it's only Baby stretching. She's going to have a child."

"What?" cried the judge. "Here—now? My word!"

"When I get my hands on that baby I'll give it a piece of my mind," exclaimed Tim. "A nice time it picks out to be rollicking about on its own."

"Come! Come!" spluttered Judge Clark. "Madam, just remember this, you can't have a baby here. It's outrageous. Using my court as a maternity ward. It's an imposition, I tell you. Abandon the idea."

"It's not my idea," Tim shot back. "And who wants to have a baby in your old court, anyway? I'm not going to budge. I want to sit down. There it goes again. The fresh thing."

"You may sit down," said the judge, "but don't lie down. Don't try to have that baby. If you do I'll arrest you for something." He paused and looked distractedly about him. "I'll arrest you for contempt of court. Mr. Willows, please speak to your wife. Prevail on her to desist. Make it clear to her that a courtroom is not the proper place in which to bear a child. Do something. Do anything."

"Your Honor," said Sally respectfully, "when a baby wants to get itself born nothing's going to stop it. It goes right ahead regardless of time and place and all the laws you can pass." Sally turned to Tim, who was sitting miserably in a chair that one of the state troopers had sympathetically provided. "Think you're going to have your baby now?" she asked.

"How should I know?" demanded Tim. "I'm not a shark at this business. I'm merely an amateur—a rank outsider. But I feel as if I'm going to have something—a whole string of babies, perhaps."

"Oh, this is simply terrible," put in the judge. "Really, it is, you know. I'm very much upset. Why didn't you tell me you were that way, madam?"

"Why should you be upset?" demanded Tim. "You're not having this baby. I wish you were." Judge Clark started violently and gazed with injured eyes upon the prospective mother. "Anyway," went on Tim, "I thought all along you knew. If you'd only used your eyes you could have seen I was highly pregnant."

Judge Clark looked at the small object of his anxiety as if it were not only highly pregnant but also highly explosive—a dangerous mine in the path of decency. Tim was growing a little calmer. The baby which by rights his wife should have been bearing had evidently decided to call it a day and had resumed its orderly repose.

"I'm feeling better now," declared Tim. "Sorry to have caused all this disturbance, but I daresay the little monster was getting impatient at having his mother heckled and baited and assaulted and mistreated in general. He isn't old enough to realize that suffering is a woman's lot in life."

"I'm sorry, madam," said the judge, mopping his face with his handkerchief. "I can understand many things now that previously were not quite clear. I can by no means understand all." He considered a slip of paper for a moment, then turned accusingly on Carl Bentley. "According to this paper," rasped the judge, "you intend to prefer charges of attempted murder, defamation of character, and mental anguish against a woman who at any minute now is going to become a mother. Do you wish to withdraw those charges or would you rather hear me sentence you to twenty years of hard and humiliating labor?"

"From the way you put it," said Bentley, still suspecting Sally of some trick, "I think it would be wiser to withdraw the charges."

"Then I'll call the whole thing off," cried Tim. "And after all, Your Honor, some of you men are like that. It's merely their idea of being clubby and entertaining. Then, of course, there are lots of women who feel slighted unless a man tries to assault them at least once each time he calls. But I'm not that way. I'm magnanimous, Judge. I might have my faults like everyone else, but my worst enemy can't say that I'm not magnificent—I mean magnanimous."

"Then you're at liberty to go your separate ways," replied Judge Clark impressively. "And I hope most devoutly they never again cross mine. I'm getting altogether too old for this sort of thing. I'd prefer to spend my closing days dealing peacefully with mere murderers and cutthroats and dope fiends and people I can understand."

"May I have my husband's gun back?" Tim asked one of the troopers. "He'll be awful mad at me."

The chivalrous trooper slipped the gun into Tim's hand. He examined it a moment, then carelessly pressed the trigger. Immediately there was a tremendous explosion and Carl Bentley instinctively resumed his running. From under his desk came the impassioned voice of Judge Clark.

"What damn fool gave her that gun?" he shouted. "She'll murder the lot of us. Overpower her and take that gun away."

"It's all right, Judge," said Tim calmly. "No harm done, but I almost had twins that time."

"My God, so did I," moaned the little jurist, his lock of gray hair appearing like a flag of truce above the top of his desk.

"I just wanted to see if it was loaded," Tim explained sweetly. "I guess it was."

Incoherent noises issued from the lips of the judge. They left him greedily scrutinizing the buttons of the two state troopers. The little man appeared to be counting them.

CHAPTER XVI

An Inspired Advertisement

SINCE THE DISORDERLY INCIDENTS LAST RECORDED, much bulk had been added to the girth which Tim wrathfully protested belonged to his wife. The social standing of the Willowses in the snooty community of Cliffside had utterly collapsed. It was now lying in a condition of supine indifference. Sinning in Cliffside was about as well established a practice as elsewhere— better than in many places. But a public and noisy demonstration against established convention such as the Willowses had staged on more than one occasion was not to be tolerated. Nice people objected strongly to having adultery, which they considered to be about the best-dressed of all the vices, dragged through the streets in rags and made the butt of indelicate observations. People who took their infidelities lightly—who tossed them off, so to speak—were not to be trusted and were little better than communists. And in Cliffside one had to be much better than a communist to attend even a dog fight. Furthermore, the Willowses, like the suspect Claire Meadows, made a practice of allowing other people to mind their own business, callously disregarding the fact that life in a community like Cliffside would be unbearable indeed unless everybody paid strict attention to everybody else's affairs. The people of Cliffside took their windows seriously. They were made not so much for the purpose of light and ventilation as to enable discreetly curtained observers to keep abreast of the current dirt. For example, it was well known that Mr. Willows, when at home, could be seen at virtually any time clad only in a strange and revealing garment, and that for no apparent reason he was given to sudden bursts of high spirits signalized by grotesque

211

and obscene dances which made his single garment even more revealing. He was suspected of being a little mad. Also, it had been duly noted and recorded that for many months past Mrs. Willows had taken up the practice of smoking her husband's cigars and in other disgusting ways emulating his example. So careless of appearances were the Willowses that their joint existence was much more than an open book. It was a public reading in a loud voice. Consequently Tim and Sally Willows were people to be watched, rather than cultivated. They were much better seen at a distance than heard at close range. Fewer and fewer so-called friends dropped in to visit the Willowses. It was a dangerous thing to do. Some scene of violence and unmannerly conduct usually resulted. So Tim and Sally were left very much to themselves, for which they were heartily thankful. And, even handicapped as they were by their reversed positions, they began to understand, better than they had in years, that they were irrevocably bound to each other as much by their mutual hates as by the interests they shared in common, many of which were deplorably low. No married couple in Cliffside could polish off a bottle of bathtub gin with greater conviviality and enterprise. Having literally spent some time in each other's shoes, they had gained a different perspective both of themselves and of each other, and this had been an incalculable help in the maintenance of congenial relations. The situation was still a trying one for Dopey, but then all situations were trying for that craven-spirited animal. Mr. and Mrs. Twill had philosophically reconciled themselves to a life in which the irrational was the only possible standard of normal conduct.

As for Mr. Bentley, that gentleman had rubbed himself completely off the already smudged face of the social horizon. Few young matrons, no matter how viciously disposed, were quite willing to seek romantic diversion with a gentleman who bounded along public highways in a union suit that flapped in the back. This last little detail lost Bentley many a pleasant interlude.

Claire Meadows had become an accepted influence in the lives of Tim and Sally. She instructed Tim in the

rather exacting laws governing the conduct of a prospective mother, and she heartlessly put a stop to his
grog. And strange to relate, Sally experienced no
feeling of jealousy for what had once occurred. She
was much more interested in devising means and ways
for the abduction of Claire's own baby from the brute
of a husband who had carried his resentment beyond
the bounds of human tolerance.

"It wasn't his baby anyway," Claire Meadows had
naïvely explained on one occasion, "although I hardly
recall the name of the little tike's father. It was just
one of those things that happen when it's raining and
you don't feel like reading or going out, and your own
husband hates children and wants you to keep your figure."

The Willowses understood perfectly, especially Tim.

Sally and Claire were now discussing various wild
projects over a couple of highball glasses, while Tim,
casting them envious glances from time to time, was
seated at his desk laboring over what he had come to
regard as Sally's homework. He was too large now to
sit comfortably at the desk, his arms seeming to have
grown shorter or the desk farther removed. He found
himself unable to concentrate on the business in hand.
The advertisement, strangely enough, was about a
union suit, the Never Flap Union Suit to be specific,
and Tim Willows could not think of union suits without
thinking of Carl Bentley, and he was unable to think of
that gentleman without becoming somewhat mercurial.
Finally he abandoned any attempt at a reasoned
presentation of the ineffable charms of Never Flap
Union Suits, and wrote the advertisement he had frequently been tempted to write. This finished to his entire satisfaction, he outlined the illustration to Sally and
instructed her to see that the advertisement was inserted according to schedule in a popular weekly magazine.

"Let none of the powers that be clap eyes on a
proof," he told her. "Fake the damned okays and keep
everything under your hat. I want this to come as a
complete surprise."

"It will," said Sally, when she had read the copy.

"After all, it's your job. I don't mind losing it for you one little bit.

She did.

Some time later she was urgently requested to make one of a party that was even at that moment awaiting her presence in the conference room. As she passed through the general office she was impressed by the unnatural hush that lay over the place. Sally could not shake off the impression that numerous stenographers and clerks were looking at her with an expression usually reserved for the contemplation of corpses and motion pictures of devastated districts.

She opened the door and was confronted by every important member of the Nationwide Advertising Agency, Inc. And at the head of the table was Mr. Gibber himself, although he hardly looked it. The man had become the personification of retribution, beside whom an avenging angel would have looked like the very soul of lax indulgence. Sally noticed that among all the faces turned on them, those of Dolly Meades and Steve Jones alone expressed feelings of friendship and admiration. The others looked too scared to register any other emotion.

"This is going to be flower pots," Sally decided, as she closed the door behind her husband's back. "A nice wide-open break." Then she added aloud, also in her husband's voice, "You wanted to see me, Mr. Gibber?"

"Yes," replied that gentleman. "I do. And for the last time."

After such an inhospitable reception, Sally saw no reason for further disguising her own feelings.

"You almost took the words out of my mouth," she remarked, dropping to a vacant chair. "I have long thought that a world without a Gibber in it would be a far, far better place."

Disregarding this open insult, Mr. Gibber thrust out a trembling hand in which was clutched the current issue of the popular weekly containing among others the Never Flap advertisement. It occupied a full page.

"Willows," thundered the man, "I hold you and you alone directly responsible for this crime against our high calling. You, like a snake in the grass, have fouled your own nest."

"I was always under the impression that snakes were rather nice about such things," replied Sally. "However——"

She did not finish her sentence, but rose and considered the advertisement with a critical eye. Mr. Gibber, as if hypnotized, held it out for her inspection until she had finished reading the copy and had resumed her seat.

"First time I've seen it inserted," she continued easily. "Rather good position, I think. Very arresting illustration, also. I am pleased."

Mr. Gibber shrank back as if in the presence of some loathsome object. His fingers drummed on the long table as he strove to master his indignation. Sally reached out and drew the magazine to her, then, holding it at arm's length, she studied the illustration with her head slightly tilted to one side. It was, as she had said, an arresting illustration. The artist had caught the spirit of the thing splendidly.

In the foregound an aged and enfeebled gentleman was seated on a piano stool. On his meager body hung, in limp, dispirited folds, a garment remotely suggestive of a union suit. In an attempt to relieve the feeling of depression created by this obviously world-weary individual, a top hat had been tilted at a rakish angle over his dim right eye. The other one, unobstructed, looked bleakly out on life. An exceedingly decrepit and revolting-looking woman, presumably his wife or mistress, for her shrunken figure was also draped in an ill-fitting union suit, was standing near him, with one arm raised as if it were beating time to a tirade of vile and abusive language. The old gentleman appeared to be already too low in his mind to pay much attention to what she was saying. Somehow he gave the impression that this sort of thing had been going on for years and years. The progeny of this unlovely couple, three boys and two girls, had been no better endowed by nature than their parents. But this was only to be expected. The observer could not conceive of those two human wrecks begetting a normal child. These children, the

oldest being no older than fourteen, were pale, emaci-
ated, and ill-tempered, and were clad in oversized
union suits. They seemed to be enjoying the worst of
bad health and dispositions. The two girls were coughing lustily while the boys stood about in attitudes of
pain and dejection. They seemed more capable of raising rickets than rackets like most normal boys. Yet one
also gained the impression that very little would be required to precipitate a general row. Taking it all in all,
it was a singularly realistic illustration of contemporary
home life. Sally admired it immensely. She felt that
Tim had struck a new note in advertising.

"I am proud to assume complete responsibility for
this," she remarked. "Of course, I didn't draw the illustration, but I suggested the idea. As you would say,
Mr. Gibber, it's mine, all mine."

Mr. Gibber choked and snatched the offending magazine from Sally's hand.

"Mr. Gibber!" she said reprovingly. "Don't be
rude."

Once more Mr. Gibber choked, then cleared his
throat of the vile words he was craving to utter. Like a
man convalescing after a long and debilitating illness,
he smiled weakly round the table.

"Mr. Willows," he said, "I have no desire to cause
you undue humiliation, but I feel that the least you
deserve is to hear this advertisement read aloud in the
presence of your erstwhile fellow workers."

"Go right ahead," Sally good-naturedly replied. "It
will do them no end of good. That piece of copy, Gibber, together with its illustration will start a new school
of advertising, most likely."

"Most likely," repeated Mr. Gibber bitterly. "A
school of blithering idiots."

Under the stress of his emotions Mr. Gibber was
growing almost human. He cleared his throat, elevated
the magazine, took a deep breath and started to read.
His voice failed and he broke down completely.

"You read it, Mr. Graham," he muttered in a husky
voice. "It's too much for me. This incident has made
me begin to feel my age at last."

Mr. Graham, a serious youth who eschewed all

forms of healthy dissipation in favor of the "Message to Garcia" and "Acres of Diamonds" and other such literature, considered himself highly honored at having been selected to play such a prominent part on this historic occasion. Gratefully he accepted the magazine and began to read in a clear voice and with great determination. Nothing short of death was going to stop him now.

The copy that Tim had prepared for Sally was to this demoralizing effect:

"A MESSAGE TO THE MISSHAPEN
"BE OF GOOD CHEER

"If your physical development is 'way below par take heart, because now your worst defects can be comfortably covered and no one will be the wiser"

"My God," came the whispered voice of Mr. Gibber, "what disreputable things was the man hinting at there?"

"I think I understand, Mr. Gibber," Dolly Meades replied.

"Don't explain," said Mr. Gibber hastily. "Hurry on, Mr. Graham."

Mr. Graham read:

"Men who are far from super and women who are perfect frights, attend. In the past you have been shamefully misled by underwear advertisements. You have been given to understand that in order to conceal your nakedness you must belong to clubs, know how to play games including hoop-jumping, riding innumerable horses at once, and mounting on poles to dizzy, not to say dangerous, heights. Stamp these deceptions under your feet whether they be flat or slew."

"Imagine," murmured Mr. Gibber. "Flat or slew. Could anything be more revolting? But go on, my boy, go on. Finish this sacrilege."

The boy went on:

"In the past you have been deluded into believing that you were cut off from the comforts of underwear unless you maintained at least one maid or a gentleman's gentleman.

"A vile deception!

"As a matter of actual fact you neither have to be nor to possess anything in particular save a modest piece of change to be qualified with the best to drape your unsightliness in

Never Flap
Indomitable Union Suits

"Unprepossessing under the most ideal circumstances, these union suits nevertheless make you look no sillier than those of another make.

"Once in a Never Flap outfit you can be as old and ugly, as broken in mind, body, and estate, as pot-bellied, sunken-chested, bald-headed, evil-minded or short-winded as you jolly well please, and not give a rap.

"You can be a maniac or a master mind, a physical wreck or a perfect specimen, a croucher in dark places or a strutter in the public eye, and still look equally at a disadvantage in these ridiculous yet somewhat necessary garments. They possess the one feature that all mankind in common has long craved—they

Never Flap

"If you must look silly in something why not look silly in these?"

Long before the finish of this example of sheer lunacy young Graham's voice had taken on a hushed and frightened note. At the end it had trailed away to an appalled whisper. The majority of the faces round the table were grave with consternation. Steve Jones's and Dolly Meades's registered profound approval.

"Were you quite yourself when you wrote that?" Mr. Gibber asked at last. "Quite sober?"

"Quite," replied Sally mildly. "Never more so in my life."

"It can't be true," protested Mr. Gibber. "I am still unable to bring myself to believe that all this is not a terrible dream and that soon I shall wake up and find everything as it was before. Why did you not let someone see a proof?"

"I wanted it to come as a surprise," said Sally innocently.

"Oh, my God!" gasped Mr. Gibber. "Imagine that! He wanted to surprise me. Did you hear what he said? Ha, ha! No, a thousand times, no. He wanted to ruin me. To demolish me. That's what he did."

The eyes that he turned on Sally were pained, heavy, and pleading. For the first time she began to feel a little bit sorry for the man. Mr. Gibber was really suffering.

"Why did you do it?" he asked, almost humbly. "Why did you do this thing? We have been good to you here—given you latitude—excused things. Before you go for good tell me what prompted you to do this mad act?"

"Mr. Gibber," replied Sally, quite seriously, "that advertisement is the inevitable reaction of an experienced copy writer against the school of romance, idealism, and optimism that has emasculated the profession for many years. It is the expression of a fundamental craving for the realities of life. Until recently I could not refer even to such a common article as a fork without calling it the glittering servant of cultured lips or some other such balderdash. It was getting unbearable for my friends." Sally paused and took a deep breath. "Then this reaction set in," she continued. "I made no effort to encourage it. The thing was stronger than I was. That's why I still feel the advertisement we have just been privileged to hear is an inspired piece of work. You see, I suddenly realized that things were things, that a chair, for instance, was in reality a chair and not the comfortable companion of one's leisure hours; that a piano was actually a piano and not the inspired creation of singing souls; that a union suit, whether it flaps or remains discreetly closed, is, after everything has been said and done, merely a union suit instead of the ideal garment for men and women who appreciate the artistry of master weavers." Once more Sally paused and looked hopefully at Mr. Gibber. "Then, sir," she continued, "I had a vision. Suddenly I seemed to be seeing the whole world stripped to its union suit. Mr. Gibber, I saw literally millions of mortals clad only in union suits, some of which flapped coyly while others didn't. But that doesn't matter, although I will say that those whose union suits didn't flap looked much nicer—not quite so helpless and unprotected, if you get what I mean. The lame, the halt, and the blind, the physical wreck and the perfect example of manhood and womanhood passed before my eyes. There were kings in that great procession as well as crooks. There were bishops as well as bouncers, athletes as well as scholars. And, my dear, good sir, every mother soul of them was clad simply in a union suit. It was a horrifying vision of democracy, of stupendous and compelling magnitude. Spellbound, I gazed. And what was my delight and surprise, my dear sir, when who should come puffing and panting up well along toward the rear but you yourself, Mr. Gibber. You were an amazing sight, Mr. Gibber—immense! A figure to give one pause. And I am glad to say your union suit did not flap. Let me describe——"

"Enough!" screamed Mr. Gibber. "Enough! Take this madman from my sight and give him two weeks' extra pay. Give him anything he wants so long as he goes away and never comes back again."

Steve Jones and Dolly Meades escaped from the conference room on the pretext of following Mr. Gibber's instructions. Some minutes later Sally kissed the reception clerk for the last time and departed homeward. Tim, now very far gone, sat, as he had once prophesied, like a jovial Madam Falstaff and listened enthralled to his wife's story.

"That's the first job I ever lost," he observed at last, "and I'm glad of it."

"It's the first one I ever had," replied Sally, "and I hope to God it's the last. It was like dwelling in a world of make-believe—a regular fairy-tale world."

"We've pretty well shattered it, anyway," said Tim. "And you know, Sally, I wouldn't be at all surprised if that advertisement pulled big in spite of Mr. Gibber."

Tim was right again. It did.

CHAPTER XVII

Two Letters and a Crisis

IT IS DIFFICULT TO SAY WHETHER OR NOT HIS PAST AS-
sociation with Mr. Ram influenced Richard Willows,
Tim's uncle, to intervene at this critical moment in the
affairs of his terrifically metamorphosed young nephew.
The fact remains that this staunch defender of the unfaithful and protector of women's more intimate rights
did intervene most effectively and in so doing radically
altered the course of the Willowses' misdirected days.
Dopey was also affected by this sudden change no less
than were the Twills themselves, the craven beast's
last hope in the immutable order of things.

The sad truth is that since Sally had been discharged
from Tim's job these two irresponsible young persons
had found themselves in water of an alarmingly rising
temperature. They were very much with child—at least
Tim was—but depressingly without work.

"We have an overabundance of the one and not
nearly enough of the other," remarked Tim, ruefully
surveying his vast proportions in the mirror. "Something tells me on good authority that it won't be long
now."

"Too much baby has made Daddy a big girl," replied Sally, looking up from her sewing. She was making baby things and finding it rough sledding with
Tim's fingers. "A conservative estimate would place it
somewhere in the neighborhood of a quartet."

"Why not make it a glee club and be done with it?"
was Tim's morose response to this.

What money remained to them in the bank did not
overtax their mutual inability to add, or rather, in this
case, to subtract. The answer to their problem was rap-

222

idly approaching zero. For once they found arithmetic too simple for their comfort.

"If I wasn't so confounded large," observed Tim, "I'd try the badger game, but no man would let himself be lured by this figure."

"You might tell your victim you were concealing a jug of wine," suggested Sally, seriously considering the possibilities of working the badger game on the local banker.

While this unholy session was in progress Mr. Ram from his perch on the bookcase sorrowfully regarded Tim and Sally and racked his brain for some solution of their problem. He did not approve of the badger game. Never had. He had always considered it a particularly dirty trick. It had been played on several prominent members of his family in centuries past and had set all Egypt chuckling. Why was it, he wondered, that these two young persons always thought of low devices? There was no pleasure to be had in losing one's moral values if the values themselves were negligible. What Mr. Ram liked was the gradual dissolution of a person's moral structure over a period of years. It should be done artistically so that a few untried vices were left to comfort one's declining years.

The little idol was in a quandary. The situation for which he was responsible had become more complicated than he had anticipated. It had contrived to get itself out of even his fine Egyptian hand. When he had first become aware of Tim's pregnancy he had been highly amused, but as the months passed and Tim gave no indication that he was ever going to stop getting larger Mr. Ram's feeings underwent a gradual change. He began to regard his victim's bulk with a shocked and sympathetic eye. After all, was not he, Mr. Ram, a man at heart? Did he not entertain himself all of man's narrow prejudices against bearing children? Mr. Ram was sincerely sorry for what he had done. Not only had he established a dangerous precedent, but also let Tim in for what at best was a most disconcerting ordeal. However, too many inches had already been added to Tim's girth for Mr. Ram to take any definite action. Therefore, Mr. Ram was no less delighted than were

Tim and Sally when the letter that follows was received from the former's uncle and the little idol's best friend. Sally brought the letter up from the dining room and gave it to Tim. He read it aloud to her to prevent her from leaning too heavily on his shoulder, or rather, on her own shoulder.

"MY DEAR BOY [*the letter began*]:

"According to my last information from you some member of your household was going to have a baby. Whether it was you or Sally or your dog or one of the Twills I was unable to decide. If it is you, all I will say is that I am not a bit surprised. America has been responsible for some remarkable innovations. I have long suspected that this would happen. Once begin to share your rights with a woman and you'll very speedily find yourself left without any rights to share."

"True talk, that," remarked Tim, looking up from the letter. "My uncle is a man of great merit and wisdom."

"True talk, my eye," said Sally, inelegantly. "That uncle of yours is a libidinous old associate of scarlet women."

Tim looked pained and resumed reading.

"As your inordinately nosey wife has probably already noted the postmark [continued the letter] I have at last brought my aged bones and depleted seraglio to rest on the meretricious shores of the Mediterranean, the happy expiring ground of expatriated physical wrecks and moral lepers, to both of which class I now definitely belong.

"It has taken me years of the most exacting debauchery to achieve my present rank of distinction. Yet even while I am being almost literally carried along on my daily walks by two of my most indomitable mistresses, I feel that the sacrifices I have made for women have not been made in vain.

"The trouble is that these two Jezebels detest each other so thoroughly that at times I become a little nervous lest they drop me in order to indulge in violence. Once I attempted a wheel chair. Never again. The two ladies fought so actively for the privilege of pushing me over a cliff that the chair itself was spun like a top and all of the cocktails I had ever taken seemed to wake up and confront my already weakened system.

"It is not nice. I am still filled with awe and wonder whenever I think of Solomon and all the mistresses he had and the honorable years he attained. Compared with his, my life has been a failure. I have merely skimmed the surface. However, I have done my best, than which I am told angels can do no more, although there is no evidence that they ever tried. But then, I know little about angels save that they seem to have spent most of their time singing, attending, and avenging, one of their number having originated the business of professional bouncing.

"But I run on and already I hear the sounds of female voices raised in high discord in the next room. Among these unpleasant voices by all odds the highest and most furious is that of a Russian countess who unfortunately escaped the firing squad of the usually painstaking Bolsheviks, the only fault I have to find with the Soviet regime. Why should it expect me to shoot its confounded countesses?

"I have another mistress whom I suspect not only of having poisoned an English army officer in India, but also of entertaining the most fantastic hopes of being able to play the same low trick on me.

"Both of these ladies fight so violently with each other all day long that at night they are so spent with fury I am forced to put the poor old things to bed. This is no way. They are mistresses in name only.

"There is another lady attached to my establishment who has recently become paralyzed in every limb. So you see, my boy, I am really defeating my own ends. What was once an active and flourishing harem has become an old ladies' home. I often think of chucking the lot of them out and treating myself to a new deal, but somehow I never get round to it. Some of these women have been with me for years. We've become used to each other and we understand our various little likes and dislikes, only with the women it seems to be mostly dislikes. Anyway, I figure it out that it's better to be poisoned by an old and tried mistress than ruined by a new one.

"As a matter of fact I have a feeling that everything would be quite comfortable if they would only give up their eternal battling and quit stealing my grog. There is no logical excuse whatsoever for this last failing. With an abundance of wine and spirits on all sides of them they nevertheless have the puerile idea that mine might be just a little bit better or stronger or something. Perhaps they do it for the malicious joy they take in irritating me, or because they hope to get each other into trouble. I don't know.

"We see a good many tourists here—trippers, I believe they are called by superior persons who have been for a week on the Continent. You may be surprised to learn that I am not at all unfavorably impressed by the American continent. True enough, they manage to get themselves remarkably drunk, but I see no reason to blame them for putting into practice what Europeans defend in theory. Then again, they buy an alarming quantity of useless things quite cheerfully, although no one realizes more keenly than they that they are being thrice cheated as well as despised by their sycophantic, franc-frenzied vendors, who fawn in their faces and sneer behind their backs. And I find American women entirely charming. They have lovely feet and legs as a rule and a refreshing capacity for enjoyment. Which reminds me I should be doing a little something about attaching an American Example to my international collection of female ruins. Perhaps you might bring one over with you when you come. There I go forgetting again. I overlooked telling you that as soon as whoever's going to have that baby has it, I want you to transfer your entire household to this address. Don't forget Mr. Ram. There are some matters I would like to take up with him.

"One of the reasons for this summons is that I'm seriously considering getting out a book—*Miserable Mistresses*, or some such title—and I am depending on you to do the writing. It will be an education in itself. In return for this service I will support both you and yours in relative luxury, and when I die I shall leave you not only lots of money but also all of my mistresses who have not already preceded me to the grave.

"How is that for a generous uncle? On second thought you can burn the residuary mistresses with my body. This, I think, would by far be the wiser thing to do. They are very noisy.

"I am, my dear boy, your expectant uncle, or to make it clearer, your mother's husband's brother,

"RICHARD WILLOWS,"

And in this letter there was wealth—wealth enough to maintain the Willows establishment, including its bootlegger, for a couple of years. This wealth was in the form of a draft, one of the handsomest bits of paper Tim had ever been privileged to behold. Uncle Dick, true to his prodigal nature, had been more than lavish. Tim passed the draft to Sally.

"That," he observed, "is sufficient to take the whole lot of us round the world."

"Without the necessity of drawing a sober breath," replied Sally. "Wish you'd hurry up and do that baby into English."

"Well," said Tim, "this gives me something to work on. It almost reconciles me to my unfortunate position. What's that other letter?"

"Oh, this," answered Sally. "It's nothing. Some old letter from our one-time job."

Tim opened the envelope, looked dumbly at another scrap of paper, unfolded the letter and read:

"MY DEAR WILLOWS:

"I am enclosing your regular salary check for the past few weeks just as if nothing had ever happened to interrupt our mutually pleasant and profitable relations.

"You had hardly left the office before I realized the true significance of your advertisement. However, I kept this knowledge to myself and awaited results.

"True enough, my perspicacity once more justified my patience. Our advertisement, Willows, has proved a huge success. You may think this remarkable, but then, of course, your experience is not nearly so vast as mine. I can say with truth that I suspected what would happen all the time. However, as I have already said, I kept this knowledge to myself.

"I am now prepared to share the honors of success with you. Of course, you were hardly aware of the true value of this advertisement, but you were in a sense responsible for its creation. I wish to be entirely fair. Therefore, I suggest that you report to this office at the earliest possible moment. We shall have a conference then with a view to creating an entire campaign along the same lines. I shall be glad to incorporate your ideas with mine should they prove of any value.

"I am sure we should both of us feel highly gratified at the results of our mutual efforts.

"Sincerely yours,

HORACE GIBBER, *President*.

"P.S. For some reason the staff has gotten the idea that you have asked to be reinstated. To avoid confusion I have made no effort to alter this impression, which in a sense is nearly the correct one. However, it makes no difference.

H. G.

"Well, for heaven's sweet sake," said Tim. "That tears it. I'm going to have a baby. I'm so damn mad I can't think of anything else to do. The old son of a mother who never rejected an improper suggestion. I'm going to have that baby. I'm going to have it almost immediately."

He rushed to a table and, seizing a pen, wrote on a

piece of paper, "To hell with you, Gibber," After this he signed his name and thrust the sheet into an envelope, which he addressed to Horace Gibber at the Nationwide Advertising Agency, Inc.

"Post this as soon as you can," he told Sally, "but not before you have cashed his check. Remember that. Get the money first, then send the letter. Now for that baby. Hurry, Sally. For God's sake, do something. I am brought to bed with child. I am accouching. Take me somewhere. Quick."

"Where do you want to go?" asked Sally, becoming excited herself.

"Where?" repeated Tim indignantly. "In the middle of Times Square, of course, or some other equally appropriate spot. Take me anywhere you feel like. I've got to lie-in."

"Now don't get all flustered," pleaded Sally. "Be calm about this matter. Where would you like to lie-in? We have the money now."

"In the Bide-a-Wee Home, of course," chattered Tim bitterly. "With the rest of the dogs. Be a little more helpful. I daresay you won't actually believe I'm going to have this baby until I hand it to you all tied up in a nice, neat package."

"You run on so," complained Sally. "What makes you think you are going to have this baby, anyway?"

"There are certain things, Sally," said Tim, with great dignity, "that are revealed only to a prospective father. That baby is on the way. Don't ask me why."

Suddenly Sally had a bright idea. She hurried to the telephone and buzzed the operator.

"Where's a good place to go when you want to have a baby?" asked Sally when she had succeeded in attracting that young lady's straying ear.

Tim emitted a groan of disgust.

"I don't want to have a baby," said the operator. "But if I was in your place I'd go into hiding. Shall I give you Information?"

Sally hung up and looked fearfully at Tim.

"The operator doesn't seem to know," she said.

"Then call up a preacher or a druggist," suggested Tim. "Maybe the police station could give us a hint."

"We've had enough to do with the police," said Sally resolutely. "They'd probably lock the both of us up for disorderly conduct. Be calm, Tim. I'm thinking."

"And in the meantime I'm childbearing," her husband shouted. "Do you want me to whelp my young single-handed like a wolf of the fields?"

"God helps those who whelp themselves," Sally observed briskly as she once more hurried to the telephone.

"Think you're funny, don't you?" cried Tim. "I swear to God if you don't do something I'll have this child right here on your hands."

This time Sally called up the nearest hospital and made all the necessary arrangements.

"Why didn't you do that in the first place?" Tim demanded.

"Didn't occur to me," she answered, "but I'll remember it the next time."

"The next time?" cried Tim, grabbing up a handful of cigars and making for the door. "Don't be foolish. The next time I have a baby you can . . ."

The end of this declaration was muffled by the clatter he made on the stairs, but Sally did not need to be told. Motherhood had done little to elevate Tim's choice of expressions.

CHAPTER XVIII

False Alarm

By THE TIME SALLY HAD DRIVEN HER CHATTERING husband to the hospital she herself was a nervous wreck, while he had abandoned words in favor of weird noises. Forgetting utterly the rôle of prospective father she should have been playing on this occasion, she left Tim in the car and rushed through the entrance and addressed the reception clerk. That gentleman was busily engaged in sorting a seemingly endless stack of cards, from which he refused to lift his eyes when Sally spoke to him in the high, flurried tones of a hard-pressed woman.

"My husbands wants to have a baby," she told the clerk.

"If he succeeds I'll give him an apple," the clerk answered, selecting a fresh card and scrutinizing it closely. "It's quite out of the usual. In fact it seems silly. Your husband should be on the receiving end of the line. Now, if it were you, madam, I might be able to do a little something."

"No," protested Sally. "It's urgent. You don't understand."

"It's you who don't understand," put in the clerk. "If your husband is old enough to be married he should certainly know by this time that he can't have a baby. Perhaps you'd like his mind looked into. We have several fine alienists here, but, unfortunately, no paternity ward."

"But he's going to have a baby," said Sally helplessly. "I know it."

"Go back, lady," replied the clerk in a bored voice, "and tell him not to be so stupid. He can't steal your stuff and he should have better sense than to try it.

He'll just be wasting a lot of time and it will all come to nothing."

"But he's having it out there in the automobile," protested Sally.

"Come, come," murmured the clerk. "This is going too far. I'd go away if I were in your place, or somebody'll come along and stick you in the psychopathic ward."

In the face of this possibility Sally remained silent. And all the time Tim was probably having his baby alone in the automobile. She was afraid to go back. Presently the clerk looked up and started slightly.

"Where did that woman get to?" he demanded. "Are you the gentleman who wanted to have a baby?"

"Are you mad, sir?" replied Sally in Tim's voice.

"I'm afraid so," answered the clerk. "What do you want?"

"My wife wants to have a baby," said Sally.

"Well, thank God for that, at any rate," remarked the clerk. "Had a woman in here just now whose husband was insisting on having a baby. Wouldn't take no for an answer. Fancy that. Poor sap doesn't know when he's well off. If men had to have babies there wouldn't be any sex life left."

"Perhaps Mr. Volstead would introduce an amendment for birth prohibition," Sally suggested.

"It would be a damn sight more popular than his other one," remarked the clerk. "But what about this wife of yours? How does she want to have this baby?"

"I didn't know there was a choice," said Sally, a little timidly.

"No, no," replied the clerk impatiently. "You don't seem to understand. I mean, does she want to have it in the ward, in a semi-private room, or do you want a special room for her?"

"Oh, I've already made all arrangements," said Sally. "Just telephoned them in. My name's Willows. Wife's Mrs. Sally Willows. Private room and all."

At this moment Tim came struggling up the stairs.

"Say, Buddy," he called out. "Where's a good place to have a baby around here?" Then he spied Sally. "Oh, there you are," he continued irritably. "I could have had the whole Grand Army of the Republic out there in that damned car for all you cared."

"Is this your wife?" asked the clerk.

"It is," replied Sally, without any show of pride.

"Then ask her to stop smoking that cigar in the hallway, will you. It's against the rules."

Tim disgustedly tossed the cigar stub away and substituted a new one for it.

"Any objections to my chewing on the end of this thing?" he demanded.

The clerk looked slightly dazed. This Willows outfit struck him as being somewhat hardboiled.

"No," he replied politely. "If your husband can stand for it I guess I can."

"He'll damn well have to stand for it," rasped Tim. "Think of what I have to stand for. Bet you wouldn't go through with it. All you have to do is to sit pretty and make a lot of poor women have a lot of poor babies. You're virtually a murderer, you are."

"Calm yourself, madam," said the clerk hastily. "I assure you I'm not responsible for all those babies."

"There you go," snapped Tim. "What did I tell you? You wash your hands of the whole business. You just sit pretty and——"

A woman, howling for "mommer," was dragged by at this moment between two sweating relatives. Tim forgot what he was saying and began to mop his forehead.

"My God!" he gasped. "This is worse than capital punishment. The Last Mile isn't in it with this charnel house."

The reception clerk summoned a nurse and Tim, with Sally in attendance, was led to an elevator and thence to his private room. Sally was told to wait about in the hall until called for. She withdrew somewhat timidly and stood outside Tim's door, studying her strange surroundings. She felt very excited and at the same time low in her mind. Something fundamental in her nature kept telling her that by rights she should be having this baby. In a sort of dim way she seemed to realize that she was better equipped to go through with this thing than was Tim. In addition to this she felt that she really would like to bear Tim a child if only to be able to tell him he didn't know what pain and suffering really meant. She would have gotten a lot of presents and petting if she'd had this baby. And Sally wanted presents and petting. She didn't like being a father. She wanted to be a woman—herself—as nature had intended her to be. Talk about the "Well of Loneliness," she herself was in a bottomless pit. And she felt terribly afraid for Tim. She was actually suffering for him. If she could only change places now with the stupid old thing. It was terrible for him to have a baby. He was much too nervous and fastidious. Her thoughts were interrupted by the sound of Tim's deep voice raised in bitter protest.

"For God's sake," she heard him saying, "you're not going to do a thing like that to me, are you?"

"But I have to," replied the nurse impatiently. "Don't be so stupid, Mrs. Willows."

"Perhaps I am," said Tim, "but if I had even so much as suspected you were going to subject me to this crowning humiliation you'd never have dragged me within a mile of this hospital. Who thought up this little indignity?"

"It has to be done, Mrs. Willows."

"Well, go ahead and do it, but please watch your step. This isn't a bit funny. What are you laughing at?"

"You're the silliest patient I've ever had," came the nurse's voice. "You don't seem to know a thing about this business."

"I know much more than I ever thought I would," replied Tim. "I could write a whole book about it and if I did I would strongly advise all women to leave their husbands at the altar, to have nothing whatever to do with them."

"Don't make me laugh, Mrs. Willows, and do hold still. I'd hate to hurt you."

"I believe I'd die if you did. Do you think I'm going to die? I wouldn't like to die, but I think I am. I think I'm going to die like a dog—like a dirty dog."

"You won't die, Mrs. Willows. They seldom do."

The woman who had entered the hospital calling lustily for "mommer" now began to summon the entire family at the top of her voice. It was a hair-raising sound. Even Sally shivered.

"That poor woman is most certainly dying like a dog," she heard Tim saying. "Don't tell me she can possibly live after making such sounds as those."

"Oh, she's all right," said the nurse reassuringly. "that woman will have her baby like an old veteran. We have her here almost every spring. Yelling like that is a tradition in her family. It's a good sign."

"Do you think I ought to yell a bit?" asked Tim.

"Not unless you feel like it," replied the nurse.

"I want to do what's right, you know," went on Tim. "You see, I shouldn't be having this baby at all."

"No?" said the nurse politely.

"Oh, no," replied Tim. "It's not in my line. I'm really a man."

"What!"

"Yes indeed, nurse. I really am a man all except my body and that belongs to my wife. It's all very confusing."

"You'll feel lots better in a little while, Mrs. Willows. Such ideas will pass away. There. I'm all finished. I'll have you ready in a couple of shakes."

Doctors, internes, and nurses. Nurses of various types and classes. Scared faces waiting on the dictates of inexorable nature. Adventure, expectancy, and stark primitive anguish. Triumph and safety. Shattered hopes and muffled hearts. Life and Death impatiently brushed elbows along the corridor of that ward. And men, like poor dumb beasts, waited guiltily wherever they were put, and vowed to themselves that if their wives only came safely through, they'd be much better husbands and try to understand the talkies. Then a quick change. With mother and child doing well, off go those poor dumb beasts to receive grog and congratulations. Many a fearful hangover has been the result of a successful birth. Sally began to feel that every nurse that passed her was looking at her with scornfully accusing eyes. It wasn't fair. Women wanted to have babies just as much as men. As a matter of fact no end of women looked upon a baby as the ball to the chain—an anchor to keep the irresponsible old hulk from drifting into forbiden ports. And who could blame them? mused Sally. Men and women were merely animals that put their fur coats in storage or pawn instead of shedding them all over laps and landscapes.

Tim was being wheeled out on a table. A half-smoked cigar was clenched between his teeth. When he saw Sally he held out a hand and took hers.

"Just like an hors-d'œuvres wagon," he observed. "Only I'm more like a high tea. This is Baby's first ride."

"Pretty soft," said Sally, stooping down to kiss him.

"Yes?" drawled Tim, looking at his wife vindictively. "I'm glad you think so. You and Mr. Ram have gotten me in a nice fix. A pretty pair, the both of you. Like hell. And don't be too set up. How do you know you're the father of this child? Did you ever see our ice man? He has the loveliest mustache. Like the horns of a dilemma. One end points to heaven, the other goes to hell. I chose the Low road and I hope you're satisfied. Tell my chauffeur to shove off for the delivery department or I'll begin to bawl for mommer."

Sally kissed the loquacious man again, but said nothing. As if fascinated she followed the table down the long hall. Tim kept telling anyone who would listen that these damn doctors and nurses were putting him on the spot as well as taking him for a ride. "Don't ever get with child," he warned a venerable gentleman with a flowing beard. "They'd cut Niagara Falls off as quick as a wink." The old gentleman shuddered and repeated a few lines from the Talmud.

At the doors of the operating room Tim rose on one elbow and looked spitefully back at Sally.

"Don't think I'm reconciled to this, my fine lady," he sang out. "Don't think I bear child willingly. No, I tell you. A thousand times, no. Never will I be satisfied until I see you on one of these damn things. Shove off, nurse. California, here I come."

The doors closed on the still vociferating Tim, and Sally, feeling a trifle embarrased, stood as close to them as possible.

"Hello, boys," she heard him saying to the doctors. "Stand and deliver! Snap to it."

There were a murmur of voices and the sound of swiftly moving feet, then Tim was speaking again.

"Look out there!" she heard him exclaim. "Quit mawling and hauling me about or I'll call this whole business off. What on earth are you doing with my feet? Leave those feet alone. You don't bear child with your feet. And I don't want to go bicycle riding, anyway. I suppose you'll be putting me on an electric horse next. Ouch! What you doing now? Well, of all the damn things. Have a heart, Doc."

"Would you be satisfied with two very small babies or would you rather have one fairly large one?" Tim demanded.

"Madam," replied the doctor, exasperated beyond measure, "I don't care if you have a yak so long as you have something."

"What!" Sally heard Tim shout. "A yak? What a queer mind you have, doctor. Fancy having a yak. Is there any possibility of that? By God, there is. That devil, Ram, is capable of anything. Get me out of here, nurse. Quick. I don't feel at all like having a yak today."

"Calm down, Mrs. Willows," came the doctor's voice. "I was merely fooling."

"Sure," replied Tim. "I know you guys. You've got a swell sense of humor. You keep on asking me to do something down all the time. First it's bear down and then it's calm down. Next thing I know you'll be asking me to jump down. I'm not going to have that yak, that's all there is to it. Another day, perhaps. Might as well take me back now. Just what is a yak? I don't feel in the mood, anyway. I've changed my mind. That's a woman's privilege. Shove off, nurse. Are there any books in this dump?"

"Well, Mrs. Willows," said the doctor, "I can't very well make you have a baby."

"I'm afraid not, Doc," replied Tim.

"Madam," came the voice of the doctor, "you're the hardest case that has ever come into my hands. Nurse, you should never have brought her in here in the first place. She isn't ready yet. Take her out and don't bring her back until you can get some sense into her head."

"Come on, nurse," said Tim. "Let's get ourselves out of his hands. I don't like the looks of this place. This obstetrician might get obstreperous. Try that when you're stewed, Doc."

Tim was wheeled back to his room and it was a matter of three days before he had his child. Those three days will never be forgotten by the staff of the maternity ward. Tim almost succeeded in disrupting the entire hospital. When Sally called on the morning of the third day she was met by the head nurse. Tim was not in his room.

"Where's the patient?" Sally demanded.

"Search me," the head nurse replied with a helpless toss of her hands. We can't keep track of her, Mr. Willows. She might be anywhere in the hospital, for all we know. Last time I saw her she was playing pinochle with a couple of interns and smoking a big black cigar. She's a strange woman, your wife, Mr. Willows. We can't make her out. Seems to have absolutely no feminine instincts. Can't understand how she ever came to be having a baby. You'll have to say something to her. Indeed you will, sir. She's upsetting our hospital. We have to keep an eye on her all the time to see that she doesn't go lugging somebody else's baby off to her own room. Says she's practising up. Yesterday she had three of them at once. For a moment it looked as if she were trying to juggle them. And last night she stole some whiskey from one of the laboratories and kept singing about someone who had made her what she was and who she hoped was satisfied. It's too bad, Mr. Willows, the way she goes on. Really it is."

Sally left the head nurse still talking and went in search of Tim. She found him at last, seated in a pantry-like arrangement, arguing passionately with two internes. In his hand were clutched some bills.

"What?" he snapped, glancing up from the table. "You back again?"

At the sight of Sally both of the internes rose.

"Mr. Willows," one of them began excitedly, "your wife is deliberately cheating us. She's gotten all our money and now she wants to play for our pants. When we tell her she's cheating she flies into a rage and tells us we're retarding her pregnancy. It's not fair. Look at all the money she has."

"It is fair," cried Tim. "You're not having a baby. I got to get something out of it, don't I?"

"We didn't ask you to have a baby, did we?" the interne shot back.

"Ask me to have a baby?" Tim laughed scornfully. "You'd have to chase me over seven counties to have a baby."

"And she keeps on changing her voice so rapidly that we don't know how many players are sitting in on the game," the other interne complained. "She gets us all rattled, Mr. Willows. Make her play fair."

Sally smiled in spite of herself and promised to make Tim behave. The upshot of it was that Tim grudgingly gave back to the internes a small percentage of his winnings and Sally got permission to take him out for a little walk.

"Take her for a long walk," urged the doctor. "In fact, Mr. Willows, we don't care how far you take her. If she wasn't your wife I'd suggest taking her down to the river and pushing her in. The other night she came barging into the operating room when a woman was having twins, and asked me if I had a nail file. Can you imagine that? And when I told her I hadn't she said I was a hell of a doctor. Last night she got one of our finest surgeons up at four o'clock in the morning just to find out whether she had a corn or an ingrowing toenail. A woman about to be a mother not knowing a simple thing like that . . ."

Sally also left this person still talking and took the cause of dissension for a walk. The cause insisted on being taken to a movie and then complained loudly and bitterly because there was not sufficient room between the rows of seats.

"Don't they expect maternity cases ever to go to the movies?" Tim demanded. "There ought to be a law."

The picture was one of those charming underworld idyls in which everyone stood on the wrong spot and went riding in the wrong car. It was tastefully decorated with machine guns and dead bodies. In the midst of a particularly optimistic fusillade Tim emitted a gasp.

"That does it," he said. "Here comes baby. Oh, dear, what shall I do? Get me out of here quick. Will you pardon me, mister? I'm going to have a baby. No. No. You'll have to do better than that. Get clean out into the aisle or I'll be having this baby in your lap. Hurry up, you lug."

It was like a bad dream for Sally. All Tim could do was to take frightened little hops and declare to the audience that he was going to have a baby. Somehow she managed to get him out of the place and into the automobile.

"A typical American birth," groaned Tim. "Bearing a baby to the music of machine guns. I suppose it will sleep on a sandbox and cut its teeth on a gat."

"Yes," agreed Sally, "and no doubt its favorite candy will be a nice box of bomb-bombs."

"Put your foot on it," pleaded Tim.

Ten minutes later they were back in the hospital and twenty minutes after that, to the relief of the entire organization, Tim was delivered of his child and became by virtue of the achievement the first male mother on record.

CHAPTER XIX

The Mystery of the Maternity Ward

THE NURSE DECIDED IT WAS HIGH TIME FOR THE pseudo-Mrs. Willows to favor her baby with its first nursing. The baby, from the noises it was making, was evidently of the same opinion. Together they entered Tim's room. It was still quite early in the morning. Tim was sound asleep.

With the baby in her arms the nurse approached the bed and looked down. Then every vestige of color and intelligence left her face. Even the baby stopped his bawling and looked a little shocked as well as disappointed. The nurse drew a scandalized breath and passed a hand across her forehead.

"Am I mad?" she asked herself. "Have I qualified as a full-fledged nurse after years of grim, grubby effort only to be deprived of my reason? I had better sit down on something quite safe and solid and pull myself compactly together."

She quietly left the bed, carefully sat down in a comfortable chair, and went into a huddle with the baby. This thing had to be thought out, and perhaps in this crisis two heads would be better than one. With fingers that trembled slightly she undid the infant's swaddling clothes and examined every inch of its body. Feeling somewhat reassured she proceeded to redress the baby. She had made no mistake regarding the child's sex. She was still capable of differentiating between the two. This was something. This was a lot. The nurse felt encouraged, but in no sense optimistic. She was still quite mad so far as the parentage of this child was concerned.

What the nurse had seen when she had looked down on that bed had been more than enough to make an

entire hospital staff doubt its sanity. To state it baldly,
what the nurse had seen was a man, a gross, self-satisfied man badly in need of a shave, sleeping luxuriously
in a bed in which a wife and mother should have been.
In fact, where a wife and mother must still be or else
the entire universe was terribly, terribly wrong, and
there was hope in neither science nor religion, and this
baby was probably not a baby at all but a snake in the
grass or the man in the moon or a couple of other
guys. The nurse began to giggle nervously, bouncing
the baby the while with increasing vigor. Why
shouldn't she sing and dance and make a morning of
it? Perhaps it would be amusing to find the head nurse
and tear off all her clothes. It might be still funnier,
though, to set fire to all the beds and squirt the extin-
guisher in the house doctor's eyes. The nurse was not
sure. She was convinced, though, that she was getting
worse, getting madder and madder by the minute. With
a violent mental effort she pulled herself together and
tried to fix her mind on the problem. To her eternal
undoing the problem was sitting up in bed. Tim, wild-
eyed and incredulous, was frantically examining his
person.

"My God!" he cried, with a delighted smile. "I'm a
man again. Fancy that, nurse."

"I don't care what you are," the nurse replied aggressively, "this baby's got to be nursed."

"I hope you don't think I'm going to nurse it?"

"You certainly are," replied the nurse. "You bore
this child and now you're going to nurse it."

"With what?" asked Tim triumphantly.

The nurse paid no attention. She had lost her belief
in everything. She clung tenaciously to one fact: this
object in that bed, whether it was fish, flesh or foul, had
given birth to a baby, and she, the nurse, was going to
see that it suckled its baby or died in the attempt.
Resolutely she approached the bed and thrust out the
baby at Tim.

"Suckle this young," she said fiercely, "and make it
snappy."

"What do you mean, suckle this young?" demanded
Tim. "Have some sense, nurse."

"No," said the nurse, "I won't. I once had a little sense and this is what happened. It's much nicer being mad."

"Couldn't you get one of these mothers round here to lend the little chap some breakfast?" asked Tim. "Why not nurse it yourself?"

The nurse laughed sarcastically at this irregular suggestion.

"You must be a man," she replied. "You're so dull about such matters. Even if I could nurse that baby I wouldn't."

"Why not?" inquired Tim, shocked by the woman's bitterness. "I take that as very unfriendly, nurse."

"How do I know the thing is a baby?" she demanded. "It might be a lion or a tiger. It might suddenly turn into you."

"You embarrass me," replied Tim. "Let's change the subject."

"The subject doesn't need changing," said the nurse, beginning to laugh wildly. "I just changed the subject. See!" And she thrust the baby into Tim's face.

"Nurse, you're getting positively common," asserted Tim in a reproving voice. "What are we going to do about all this?"

"Want to know what I'm going to do?" demanded the nurse. "I'm going to take this child and chuck it out the window."

"My God! Don't do that!" cried Tim, springing from the bed.

He presented an appalling figure in his short hospital nightgown. The nurse took one look at him and then blinked rapidly as if trying to clear her eyes of some painful object that had lodged there.

"Why shouldn't I throw the child out of the window?" she asked. "You're not its mother."

"I know," retorted Tim, "but if you went about chucking through windows every child I didn't bear, the world would be littered with babies."

"Why should you care?" asked the nurse.

"I don't want to be a party to a murder," protested Tim.

"What you've done to me this morning," said the

nurse, "is a whole lot worse than murder. Once I was a sane woman and an efficient nurse. Now I'm a gibbering idiot. I wish you could take a look at yourself. A regular scarecrow you are—a scarecrow with long, skinny toes."

Even at that tense moment Tim could not help wondering why his toes should always be singled out for criticism.

"What's the matter with the toes?" he demanded, turning them up for inspection.

"Everything," replied the nurse. "They should have been fingers. They look like withered asparagus."

"God!" gasped Tim. "How revolting. Try to be a little nicer."

She thrust the child into Tim's arms and left the room. While she was gone Sally came rushing in. She was every inch a woman. She took one long look at her husband, then snatched the baby from him.

"You certainly look a sight," was all she said. "Those toes."

"A hell of a lot of gratitude you show me for bearing your baby for you," he retorted.

"Ram is responsible for all," replied Sally, busily preparing to nurse the baby. "He's changed us back."

Tim disappeared behind the screen as the nurse entered the room. She was carrying a suitcase.

"Your wife must have sent this over," she began, then took one long look at Sally. A piercing shriek followed.

"Oh, God, how did you get that way?" she shouted. "He's switched on me again."

She ran out of the room and fled screaming down the hall. Within a very few minutes the head nurse and the house surgeon arrived. Sally ducked behind the screen and pushed Tim into view.

"How did you manage it?" asked the surgeon.

"What?" asked the startled Tim.

"How did you manage to sneak into this hospital?" continued the surgeon, keeping a strong grip on himself.

"I didn't," replied Tim. "I've been here all the time."

"Then you must be a woman," said the surgeon.

"I am not," said Tim.

"You are so," snapped the surgeon. "Didn't you bear a child?"

"I did, replied Tim. "But I've just recently had a change of sex."

"I'll have to look into this," asserted the surgeon.

"You'll do nothing of the sort," snapped Tim.

"But you must be examined."

"I think you can trust me in this matter," replied Tim, with some show of dignity.

"But I'd like to see for myself." The surgeon's voice sounded somewhat wistful.

"Sir," replied Tim, "you don't know what you're asking. I'm afraid your interest is more personal than professional."

The surgeon left the room.

"This will all have to be hushed up," said the head nurse. "If you wanted to go gallivanting about I can't understand why you picked out a maternity ward. There's more here than meets the eye, I'm afraid."

"Lots," replied Tim. "And if you don't hurry up and leave this room you'll see it all. I'm going to get dressed."

The head nurse left the room and Sally reappeared. She put the baby down on the bed and took Tim into her arms. His own arms went round her.

"It's good to get you back," Sally murmured. "You horrid old thing."

"I've been through a lot," said Tim.

"I know you have," replied Sally, "but I'll make it up to you. I'll bear you a set of twins."

CHAPTER XX

Dopey All at Sea

DOPEY THRUST AN INQUIRING NOSE FROM HIS BOX AND sniffed delicately at the small bundle. The small bundle made noises and endeavored to snatch at the nose. The nose, as if insulted, promptly withdrew. Presently it emerged again. Two eyes studied the bundle with growing alarm. The thing was actually alive. It might even be capable of inflicting pain. Down went the nose while the body attached to it shivered nervously. The bundle failed to attack. Dopey opened his lids and tried to look up without lifting his head. If he remained quite still, perhaps the bundle might mistake him for a chair or a table or, at least, a dead dog. The bundle was looking at him steadily and intently, but not hostilely. For a few moments the bundle and the dog took stock of each other, then Dopey transferred his attention to Tim and Sally. They seemed to be all right. The bundle had not molested them. In fact, it was allowing itself to be carried in Tim's arms. That suggested helplessness. Helplessness suggested safety. Dopey raised his head, boldly sniffed the bundle, and allowed his nose to be handled. It was rather pleasant. Such small paws could not be dangerous. Then Dopey did a remarkable thing. He crawled out of his box, seated himself beside it, then glanced significantly first at Tim, then at the bundle, and finally into the box. Although it made him look rather ridiculous the great dog repeated this eyerolling operation several times.

"Why, the sweet old thing is actually offering his box to the infant," exclaimed Sally.

She found a clean towel and placed it on the floor of the box. Tim carefully laid the baby on the towel. Dopey settled himself grimly by the box and prepared to guard its contents. There was a proud light in his eyes, although his sensitive spirit was slightly dashed by the reflection cast on his person by the placing of the towel. They might have spared him that. A little delicacy would have been more fitting in the presence of a stranger.

Leaving the baby with Dopey, the parents withdrew to the front room.

"He's so maternal," observed Sally, he might try to crawl in with the baby."

"Dopey has the instincts of a gentleman," said Tim.

"That's more than his master has," replied his wife.

In the front room Claire Meadows was waiting for them. At their appearance she threw several pillows off the divan and disclosed a large baby. This infant was possessed of teeth. It was two years old—almost a hag.

"Listen," began Claire hurriedly. "This baby is mine. I've just succeeded in stealing her back. I've got a splendid idea. You're to pretend it's your baby. Everyone knows you've had one. If anyone wants to look at her, squdge her up a lot and say she's yours."

"Rather tough on the baby," observed Tim.

"It's only for a short time," replied Claire.

"That's good," said Tim. "The baby might not last."

"But, Claire," protested Sally, "we can't very well show a baby with a full set of teeth."

"Show the other end," said Claire. "That's easy."

"You seem to have an answer for everything," remarked Tim.

"I suppose changing our child's sex is also a simple matter?" inquired Sally.

"It seemed to be for you," retorted Mrs. Meadows.

"But, Claire dear," protested Sally, "we're sailing in a few days."

"Then I'll sail with you," cried the resourceful Claire Meadows.

"That's a good idea, too," put in Tim.

"I'm not so sure about that," replied Sally. "Do you contemplate establishing a sort of *ménage à trois?*"

"Why not?" asked Tim lightly. "I feel like sowing some almost frantic oats."

"Is that so?" replied his wife. "Then I'll look round and see if I can't dig me up a serviceable old *quatre*."

"Two's company, three's a crowd, and four make a vice ring," remarked her husband. "That will be swell."

"Oh, I can dig up the *quatre*," cried Claire Meadows brightly. "I remembered the name of this baby's father and called him up. He was very sweet about it. He's willing to do anything. We'll take him along."

"That's better," declared Sally. "And if he leaves you stranded, there's always Uncle Dick. He's looking for an American representative."

"Then it's all settled," said Claire. "I'm terribly relieved."

"We're so glad you are," smiled Sally, "but I foresee unseemly if diverting complications."

The sun gleamed down on the boat deck. In a secluded corner three dogs, three high-bred dogs sat before their respective dog houses. One glance at those dogs was enough to show that this was not their first crossing. By no means. Those dogs were bored. There was a fourth house, but no dog sat in front of it. Presently a nose appeared, then two timid eyes. They looked fearfully at the high-bred dogs, then turned away. Those dogs looked sinister to the eyes. Have nothing to do with them. Then the eyes rested on the broad Atlantic and watched with great anxiety the approach of a fat wave. This would be the end.

"Oh, my God," breathed Dopey, "is all that water there yet?"

But God did not answer.

The dog scrabbled round in his house and exposed his gnarled rump not only to all who might care to behold, but also to the tumbling reaches of that disconcerting ocean.

Once there had been a certain box on a floor that did not heave . . . ah, well . . . a dog's life was like that.

Dopey sighed and slept, shivering slightly in his sleep as he dreamed of an endless ocean alive with a drove of waves.